PINNACLE EVENT

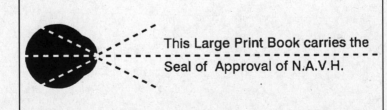
This Large Print Book carries the
Seal of Approval of N.A.V.H.

PINNACLE EVENT

RICHARD A. CLARKE

THORNDIKE PRESS

A part of Gale, Cengage Learning

 GALE
CENGAGE Learning·

Farmington Hills, Mich • San Francisco • New York • Waterville, Maine
Meriden, Conn • Mason, Ohio • Chicago

GALE
CENGAGE Learning

LIBRARY OF CONGRESS CATALOGING-IN-PUBLICATION DATA

Clarke, Richard A. (Richard Alan), 1951–
    Pinnacle event / by Richard A. Clarke. — Large print edition.
    pages cm. — (Thorndike Press large print thriller)
    ISBN 978-1-4104-8287-7 (hardcover) — ISBN 1-4104-8287-1 (hardcover)
    1. Large type books. 2. Political fiction. I. Title.
PS3603.L377P56 2015b
813'.6—dc23   2015019411

Published in 2015 by arrangement with St. Martin's Press, LLC

Printed in Mexico
1 2 3 4 5 6 7 19 18 17 16 15

*To those many government employees
who keep us safe, secure, and
free to exercise our liberties*

PROLOGUE

TUESDAY, AUGUST 9
INDIAN OCEAN

Alone in the water, below the gray rain clouds, *Octavius* crept forward at barely five knots. Had the captain still stood on her deck, scanning the horizons, he would have seen nothing but the waters of the Indian Ocean stretching away, empty under the low sky. Abandoned by her crew the night before, the ghost ship moved in a broad circular path, her death spiral. There was no one to hear the engine thumping below, the computer humming in the deckhouse, the flag of the Comoros snapping from the stern in the stiff breeze. Silently a stream of data moved up from the computer to the satellite dish and then into space. Images from the cameras, the readings from the engine room, automated pilot data, all shot the thirty-three thousand kilometers to the Thuraya satellite in encrypted packets that

7

took a quarter second to travel that distance.

Data packets came down, as well. Automatically decrypted on arrival in the laptop in the deckhouse, the final message was brief. It was routed down a fiber optic cable to the device in the hold. The 512-bit code caused the device to activate the detonation sequence, beginning with an electrical charge to the high-intensity conventional explosive. That explosion caused a bright flash and sent a large, bullet-shaped package of highly enriched uranium shooting down a tube into a hole in the uranium mass.

The presence of the added uranium in the mass caused it to reach criticality.

The intense light and heat were instant and immeasurable.

The iron and steel that was MV *Octavius* vaporized first, as X-rays, gamma rays, and neutrons rushed out. Oranges, yellows, purples, greens, and a bright white leaped, twisted, churned, and fled the nuclei of the uranium like a mob let loose from imprisonment.

In less than a second, the surface water for a half a mile around underwent molecular transformation and some of it was ejected eight miles up as steam. The waters beyond the blast zone were sucked up and then thrown down, sending a small tsunami out in all directions. At the center of the eruption, a giant toadstool stood roiling, poisonous as the fungi it resembled. The sound waves traveled slower, for hundreds of kilometers, simultaneously deep, sharp, and growling.

In the complete silence of space, twelve hundred kilometers from the Thuraya satellite, another communications satellite was at work. The AEHF-2 rested in a geosynchronous orbit. The Advanced Extremely High Frequency satellite of the U.S. Space Command's 4th Space Operations Squadron picked up signals from American forces throughout the Indian Ocean area and nearby, from Bahrain, Bagram, and Brisbane. It converted their electronic packets into laser beams and shot them to its sister the AEHF-1, which then sent them down to Arizona.

The AEHF-2 was just a big router in the sky for the world's largest Internet provider, the Defense Information Systems Agency, but on the bottom of the American satellite sat a small dome, covering a series of specialized sensors. In the 1960s similar sensors had been so large that they had filled a satellite, which had been code named Vela. Although the sensors had officially been known by an ever-changing series of Pentagon acronyms, unofficially the original name Vela had stuck.

Any report related to a nuclear weapon being detonated, lost, or stolen moved across the Defense Department communications network with the highest precedence, knocking all other message traffic back in the cue. Such messages were tagged on the subject line: PINNACLE EVENT. When a message with that caption arrived at a command post, audio alarms sounded.

While the cloud was still rushing skyward from where the MV Octavius had been, the Vela sensors on the bottom of the AEHF-2 sent a series of data packets from space on a circuitous path to the Pentagon's National Military Command Center and seven other command centers. At one of them, on Patrick Air Force Base in Florida, the message packets caused a red light to begin spinning in the Operations Room of the Air Force Technical Applications Center. As the duty officers at AFTAC looked up, they heard a prerecorded female voice speaking slowly, calmly, as though she were informing them that the airport shuttle train doors were about to close.

"Attention, attention. There has been a

Pinnacle Event. Repeat, Pinnacle." The red light spun its beam across the room. "An atmospheric nuclear detonation has been detected. Repeat, nuclear detonation."

1

MONDAY, AUGUST 15
GRINZING
VIENNA, AUSTRIA

Herman Strodmann rang the bell as he drove the first trolley of the day out of the little, end-of-the-line station at 0600. He loved driving the number 38 route because he could walk to work from his cottage, at the edge of the Vienna Woods, on the hill above the village of Grinzing. He walked by the house where Beethoven had written the Second Symphony. He thought of the 38 tram as a time machine, taking him in half an hour from the quaint, traditional wine *stubels* and *heurigers* of eighteenth-century Grinzing to the hectic modernity of downtown Vienna. He especially liked the first kilometer of the route, when the tram had its own railbed to the right of the road. On that stretch he did not have to share the street with cars.

13

There he could get the two-car trolley up to a decent speed. As he was doing just that, he noticed a blue BMW in his rear mirror.

The car was accelerating quickly up the Grinzinger Alle behind the tram. It was going to overtake him quickly, Strodmann thought. What was the rush so early in the morning? As the tram approached the corner of Hungerbergstrasse, the exclusive railbed ended and Strodmann guided the trolley on to the street. As he did, for a second he lost sight of the BMW. Then, suddenly, it was veering right in front of the tram, aiming into the Daringergasse. Herman Strodmann hit the brakes just as the trolley smashed into the BMW and rode up over it, crushing the passenger compartment.

In seconds, the BMW 525 erupted into an orange ball of flame shooting twenty-five feet in the air. The flame scorched the windows around the trolley driver's seat and leaped in the small, open side window, giving Herman Strodmann second-degree burns on his left arm. He quickly threw open all the doors for the few passengers to get out and then he leaped from the crippled tram. He could see that the flames instantly incinerated the man driving the BMW.

Karl Potgeiter had known when he bought

the car that it was a younger man's vehicle. Although he was seventy-two, partially retired, and now working as a consultant to the UN's Vienna-based, International Atomic Energy Agency (IAEA), he was fit and looked much younger than his years. A nuclear physicist, he was a South African citizen, but had lived in Austria for twenty-two years. Every weekday morning, he drove himself into Vienna for an early *Frühstück,* breakfast, at his favorite haunt, the Café Lantman next to the Burgtheater on the Ringstrasse.

That morning, his usual waitress, Maria, wondered where he was. She learned about the crash a few hours later. Word spread quickly as to why the 38 tram route was closed. Later, Maria would read that poor Dr. Potgeiter's body was burned beyond all recognition and was only identified by dental records. It did not help her calm down to see the picture of the flaming car dominating the front page of *Kronen Zeitung* the next day. Maria knew he had been such a nice man, such a good tipper. She also knew that it was such bad luck. There were so few fatal accidents with the trolleys.

HERZLIYA, ISRAEL
Dawid Steyn and his wife, Rachel, enjoyed

living in Herzliya Pituah, near the beach. It was an expensive neighborhood, but the house was big enough for her mother to live with them and take care of the girls. It was also close to Israel's Silicon Valley. Rachel could drive to work at Google in ten minutes, including the time it took to drop Dawid off at the train station. For Dawid, the train ride into Tel Aviv gave him just enough time to scan *The Jerusalem Post.* He usually tried to get a seat on the upper level of the double-decker train that ran from Binyamina through Tel Aviv to Ashkelon. On the 0708 train, that was usually not a problem. If he waited for a later departure, the upper deck filled up before the train got to Herzliya, but Rachel was an early riser and Dawid had adjusted to her ways long ago, so making the early train was easy.

His eighteen-minute commute, from Herzliya, a town named after the father of Zionism to a train station named for the original Israeli military, the Haganah, reminded him every day of the origins of his adopted country. He and his father had moved to Israel after his mother died, when Dawid was ten. His mother had been Jewish, so Dawid gained Israeli citizenship automatically through the Right of Return. Now, with his father dead, Dawid Steyn carried on the family's international investment business from a small office in Tel Aviv. No one could tell from the Steyn office suite's modest size that the firm managed over two billion dollars in assets, and as of this week it was two and a half billion.

He looked up as the train stopped at Tel Aviv University, watching the students disembarking. They looked so young, but he reminded himself that it was almost fifteen years ago that he had graduated from that school. In less than a decade, his own girls could be riding this train to University, if Rachel's mother could ever let go of them.

At 0726 the big, red, double-decker train from Binyamina pulled into track three at Tel Aviv Haganah Station, from which Dawid would normally catch the line 16 Dan bus to his office near the beach promenade. He was among the last to get off the train, at the rear of the crowd making its way up the platform to the escalator, his head still in the *Post* as he walked. There was a push, then a shove. Startled, Dawid looked up as the man hit against him hard, sending him off the platform and on to Track 4 just as the express from Nahariya pulled into the station.

Dawid Steyn, thirty-five, was the first

person to die on the tracks at the Haganah Station. It was almost 0830 when the Tel Aviv Police reached Rachel at her desk at Google. Her first emotion was guilt, that she had been wrong to mock Dawid's paranoia, his theory that people were following him.

THE ADDRESS HOTEL, MALL OF THE EMIRATES
DUBAI, UNITED ARAB EMIRATES

"Room service," he heard from outside his door. Marius Plessis thought room service was the best part of his condo-apartment in the hotel, that and the fact that he could walk to all the restaurants and stores in the Mall. It was also a five-minute taxi ride to his office and a fifteen-minute drive to the marina where he kept his boat.

He threw on his robe, tying it closed as he made his way to the door. He had set the time for breakfast delivery at 0900. Was it nine already? He had gotten in late from the airport the night before. His flight from Zürich had not landed until after midnight. Rubbing his eyes, he opened the door. "Please, set it up on the balcony," he said to the waiter. Half the year, the weather in Dubai was delightful and he enjoyed being outside as much as possible. The other half it was so hot that, if he had to be in Dubai then, he tried never to leave the air-conditioned environments.

Marius stepped into the bathroom as the waiter pushed the food dolly cart to the balcony. When he emerged, the polite, young Indian stood waiting for him on the balcony, holding the morning papers. "The *Khaleej Times*, sir, and your *Financial Times*, as usual," the waiter said. Marius added a tip and signed for the breakfast.

He regretted that they did not serve "real" bacon. It was one of the few things that he missed, living in Dubai. As he devoured the scrambled eggs, Marius Plessis folded the salmon-colored *Financial Times* so he could read the story on the rise in the price of natural gas. He wondered if it was too late to invest in the new Australian shale fields. He would have to find somewhere new to invest soon, now that the money had hit the accounts he managed. His advisors at the Dubai International Financial Center had been at the office for hours already, strad-dling the Asian and European markets. He thought he should call them after breakfast, or maybe he would just go over there after lunch at La Petite Maison. It was a better restaurant, he thought, than the London original, behind Claridge's.

Finishing breakfast, he rose and stretched, looking north toward Iran. It may be a troubled neighborhood, he thought, but there could be few better places to live than in Dubai. You could get anything here, anything, and nowhere was the standard of living higher. With a modern, high-rise, luxury condominium here and another in Vancouver for the summer months, what more could he ask for in life? He never missed the land of his birth, let them have it. They were destroying it, as he knew they would. His two daughters were happily married and living in Toronto and San Diego. He saw them and their babies just enough. They would never approve of the female friends he had here, some of them younger than his daughters, but what was money for if you did not get enjoyment from it. At seventy-one, he was still in great shape, with a little assistance from the pills.

Perhaps, he thought, he would visit the gym after going over to the DIFC. His trainer would be there today, at the hotel's marvelous spa. He heard the waiter entering the suite to collect the food cart. Marius looked down at the dancing fountains, forty-six floors below, and smiled, contented with his life now, after all of the earlier strife. Then he felt his legs being grabbed at the

20

ankles, his head was over the railing and he was in the air, off the building, falling toward the fountains.

The *Khaleej Times* would not carry the story of Marius Plessis's death. Suicides, like his, did not fit in with the themes that the Ruler wanted reported in his papers and, in reality, there were hardly any suicides in the emirate except among the guest workers on the construction projects. White men like Plessis almost never killed themselves in Dubai.

CLARKE QUAY
SINGAPORE

"I don't think you need me anymore, Dr. Coetzee," the attractive Asian woman said, dabbing her mouth with her napkin. "Your Chinese is almost flawless, but I do enjoy our lunches and tutorials, so I will not complain if you wish to continue." The couple sat at an outside restaurant on the water, enjoying a late and long lunch, in a modern complex of bars, restaurants, and shops where once the old freighters had docked. Now the ships were so large that only the giant cranes could handle their container cargo, at the computerized terminals across the harbor. The current cargo piers were like conveyor belts for the containers, with hundreds of ships lined up just beyond the harbor, waiting their turns to offload and load up.

"Weemin, my Chinese is only fair. When my associates drop the English and start talking rapidly in Chinese, I only pick up about half of what they are saying to each other."

"That may be, sir, because they do not want you to know what they are saying. They may suspect that you have been taking Chinese lessons for years now. After all, they are all spies at the Security and Intelligence Division, the SID, they must know about me," she said, smiling at the older man.

Cornelius Coetzee looked slightly embarrassed. "I may have led them to believe that our relationship is less than platonic. I don't think they know I speak and read Chinese. There is never a Chinese language document in the office. English is the government language, the business language. Chinese is only spoken at home, and, as you say, when they want to keep things from me."

"How do you know, Dr. Coetzee, that I do not work for your colleagues at the SID? I may report everything to them," Weemin said, laughing.

"Because you work for my employers' archrival, the internal security boys, ISD. My dear, I have known that for years and I must say that your reports to them about me must be very boring indeed."

"Cornelius, how can you think that?" she protested, mildly. "And if I did work for ISD, why after all these years of having nothing to report about you would they keep sending me out to meet you?"

Coetzee chuckled. "Because they hate the SID so much that any chance they could learn some inside tidbit is worth it to them, however silly that is."

"I think there is another reason that you want to improve your Chinese," she suggested.

The check came and Cornelius Coetzee produced a credit card. "Oh, really. And what, please tell, might that be, my little spook?"

"You advise the SID only one day a week now, not because they do not want you to spend more time with them, but because your investments take more and more of your time." She was dropping all pretense now of being only a Chinese tutor. "You have been investing heavily in China and doing very well where others have not. And just this week you received a great deal more money to invest. They may ask you where that money came from?"

Coetzee, too, had ceased to play the part of the doddering, old, retired spy. "Who might ask me, Weemin?"

"The Internal Security Division, or even your friends at the SID. They must know, too," she said.

He signed the credit card bill and punched his PIN into the handheld machine the waiter brought to the table. When the waiter was gone, Dr. Cornelius Cotzee looked Weemin Zhu in the eyes and said, very softly, "You know, Weemin, I think you are right. My Chinese has gotten to the point where I don't need you anymore. May you live a long and happy life." He rose from the table and walked toward the street, leaving her sitting, somewhat stunned, by the waterside.

He strode quickly toward River Valley Road, past the modern, chain stores and bars, ignoring the sign that read THE PARTY NEVER STOPS AT CLARKE QUAY. The anger was rising up inside him. He had worked for this little city-state country for more than two decades, helping their fledgling foreign intelligence service in tradecraft, talent spotting, and agent handling, everything he had done so well in his own country. His advice had helped them penetrate the U.S. Navy, the Australian Army, the Indonesian President's office, and the Malaysian police. And what gratitude do they show? When the money entrusted to him by his old colleagues suddenly increases, they think he's been paid off for spying on Singapore? He had been completely loyal to his new home. Furthermore, who would pay him half a billion dollars U.S. for spying on Singapore? He would have to sell their giant casino complex, that ugly monstrosity, to get paid that kind of money.

He knew that getting mad like this was not good for his blood pressure, so he exhaled and tried to calm down. He reached the road and thrust up his arm to hail one of the ubiquitous blue taxis. As he did, a 9mm bullet pierced his forehead just above his nose. Cornelius Coetzee leaned backward and then folded like a Macy's parade balloon, falling to his knees and then forward, his head hitting the sidewalk and covering it with a quickly expanding pool of bright red blood.

Hearing the shot, Weemin Zhu ran toward him, pulling a handgun from her purse, but there was no one to shoot at, no indication of the shot's origin. She looked down at Coetzee and knew that the single bullet had been fatal. She replaced the gun in her handbag and removed her mobile. She called the Watch Command at the Internal Security Division and identified herself. "I need a response unit immediately at Clarke Quay. There has been a murder of my subject. The police will be here soon. Do you want me to tell them that this is my case?"

They did want her to. The Internal Security Division thought the police would never be able to figure it out and, besides, maybe Coetzee's murder would reflect badly on their rival, his employer, the SID. After all, they said to Weemin, a murder in Singapore had to be an espionage-related event. There was no street crime in the city.

THE ROCKS, SYDNEY
NEW SOUTH WALES, AUSTRALIA

"I'm taking the rest of the day off. Got some chums in town, going to go do the Manly thing with them," Willem Merwe announced to his staff as he bounded out of the office of Merwe-Wyk-Roux in the restored brick building in the old part of town. "See you all in the morning."

His small team was used to him disappearing for rugby, or volleyball on Bondi Beach. It was clear to them that the younger

26

Mr. Merwe was nothing like his late father, who had spent long hours poring over investments and accounts. They should have known that he would be different as soon as he moved them from the downtown office tower to the funky town house in the Rocks district. "Roux in the Rocks," Willy had jokingly proclaimed, his only attempt at a rationale to the staff for moving. The real reason, his staff knew, was that he wanted to abandon the staid old image and become more hip. He never wore a tie and he biked to work. Despite his youth, his investment strategies which included Chinese computer components, media and real estate had paid off. One of them must have just hit big, the staff assumed, because he had told them that morning that there was a substantial amount more to invest and he wanted "transformational" ideas.

At twenty-nine, Willy Merwe looked like the All Australian Male — tall, blond, broad shouldered, with the muscled legs of a champion bicyclist. No one on Bondi would have guessed he was an immigrant and, if they had, no one would have cared. He was cool and Australia was a nation of immigrants.

Merwe locked his bike on the rack at Circular Quay Ferry Terminal and ran for the 0315 boat from Pier 3 to Manly Beach, across Sydney Harbor. He made his way upstairs to the bar, got a KB Lager and then climbed higher up to the top deck, which was open to the sky and the breeze.

He looked back at the Sydney skyline and smiled. It was a view that always made him happy, the Opera House, the Bridge, the skyscrapers. He never understood why so few people came up to the top deck, like now, when he was the only one there. Why also did people live in these crowded financial centers like New York, Tokyo, or London, he wondered, when you could bloody well do the same bit of business in a city that was livable and liked to have fun?

He knew his team at the office thought he was going over to Manly Beach for a good time. He did not want to disabuse them of that idea, because it was actually to meet up with some people from his father's organization who had showed up in town without notice and suggested a get-together where they might all look like old buddies doing the tourist thing. His dad's old organization was now his, he supposed. The role was something that he inherited, something he had been trained to do because he had been designated as his father's successor. There was always a designated successor. Even he had one now, a guy about his age in New Zealand, Paul Wyk.

Willy Merwe, however, planned to do the job for the next twenty years. He would manage the funds, hidden in various safe havens, grow the principal, pay the families on a regular basis, and make emergency disbursements when he thought that one of the families had a legitimate need for more. If any family did not like his decision, they could appeal to the four others, but no one ever did. He was fair and he was generous. He was also more successful with his Discretionary Investment Fund than any of the other four had been in the last two years. Now that they had made the Deacquisition Decision, as he and Karl Potgeiter had advocated, there was a real opportunity to put some big money to work. Willy Merwe never forgot what he had learned in his finance class at Wharton: there are opportunities only open to big money, opportunities to get IRRs in the forties. "It takes big money to make big money," Professor Meitzinger had said. Now, Willy thought, I am going to do just that.

Instead, he felt a sharp, overwhelming pain in the back of his skull, so dominating his consciousness that he never felt the fall until he hit the water. His brain was so jarred by the impact of the strike to his head that it was unable to send messages to his arms and legs. His body was swept up in the spinning water of the ferry's propeller wash. No one would be too surprised that another drunken passenger had fallen off a Sydney ferry and drowned. Unfortunately, it happened a lot.

2

SCIFs, Sensitive Compartmented Information Facilities, weren't supposed to have windows, but his did. Dugout loved to stare out at the Potomac and the jumble of trees on Roosevelt Island. Usually there were rowers on the water on Sunday afternoons, but not today.

Sunday afternoons were a great time to work. No one else was in the building, except maybe the guys in the little room that passed as an operations center and they were probably watching football. It was even more pleasant for Dugout to work when Sunday was like today, rainy. It was not a cold or windy rain, just steady, and it darkened the sky. A good day to be inside, with hot Earl Grey tea in a mug, sweetened by honey he had bought at the farmers' market.

Dugout blamed the dark sky for his sleeping in, but it may also have had something to do with the fact that he had played the last set before closing at Twins on U Street. Hadn't gotten home until after three. The jazz kept him sane, he told himself, playing the tenor sax oiled his neural pathways. He wondered how Mrs. Wrenfrow's neural pathways had been doing since he had left her yesterday.

Mrs. Wrenfrow was what Douglas Carter III, Dugout to his friends, called the kludged-together cluster of servers that ran his modified Minerva software. He had named it after the ever-helpful woman at the Belmont Public Library who had assisted him in finding Curious George books when he was in kindergarten and obscure volumes and articles on mathematics when he was in high school. Minerva, the software package that ran on the computer cluster, was a big data analytics package he had gotten his old boss to buy him from a Silicon Valley start-up. Dug had modified it significantly, made it a kick-ass machine learning program, able to plow through the exabytes and zettabytes of data he could access, legally and otherwise.

Saturday afternoon he had set Minerva looking through the last two years of international interbank transfers for any unusual patterns involving noninstitutional players, individuals. NSA had gladly given him access to the data. His goal was to find pseudonyms of people who were actually Mexican government officials with overseas accounts, which had been the recipients of large deposits from suspect senders. Winston Burrell, the National Security Advisor, had in mind giving a list of miscreants to the new Mexican President who was going to visit the White House in two weeks.

Dugout, with his long hair, looked a little like the typical image of Jesus, but with glasses. He had been recruited to PEG from DARPA, the Pentagon's creative, geek hive. Raymond Bowman, PEG's first Director, had promised Dugout all the toys he wanted, the chance to work on "things that matter," and most importantly, a work schedule of his own making. Dugout hated the nine-to-five mentality and seldom showed up before ten in the morning or left work prior to midnight.

For almost five years now, it had been a perfect home for Dugout, an eclectic band of geniuses with an all-access pass to the treasure trove of data gathered by U.S. intelligence and a sub-rosa virtual pathway for their analyses to get to the West Wing. Then, last year, Ray Bowman had left, gone on indefinite leave of absence. As PEG Director, Ray was supposed to be a desk jockey, but Winston Burrell had asked him to save the U.S. drone program from its critics, foreign and domestic. In the process, Bowman had been forced to go operational, become a field guy, and stop a major terrorist attack in the United States. In the end, he had stopped the attacks, but also had dealt up close with a lot of deaths, including some people very dear to him. After that, Bowman had checked out, disappeared, and left Dugout to catch some of the balls the National Security Advisor had sent bouncing off the left field wall.

Dugout tapped his keyboard to uncover the results of his search. He was surprised at how many people around the world had gotten several deposits into their personal accounts, each of ten million dollars or more. He then asked the program to list those who in one month got sums totaling one hundred million dollars, and then in one hundred million dollar increments up to one billion dollars. Then he asked the software to sort the people into groups with similarities of some sort. What popped up first was not what he was expecting, but with Minerva the unexpected was getting to be the norm.

What was at the top of the list was a group of five men who had each received deposits over a one-month period totaling five hundred million dollars each. What they had in common was that they were all South Africans living abroad. Dugout paused a moment to try to guess what else this group of men had in common that made them suddenly so rich. Nothing came to mind.

He entered their names into a master database of current intelligence and media reports. The current intelligence files had nothing, which meant that nobody in the seventeen U.S. intelligence agencies cared about them. The media files, however, had a few small stories about each of the men. The stories were about how they had died, mostly in bizarre accidents. They were all, now, dead men.

Well, that was something else they had in common, he thought. Then he saw the dates of the stories.

He tapped on the links and pulled up the media accounts of their deaths. All five men had died on the same day, August 15, indeed at almost the same time, in five different countries. When he taught intelligence analysis classes, he always pointed out that coincidences do actually happen. This, however, was more than a co-incidence. He doubted very much these were accidental deaths, although the media stories indicated that, except in Singapore, the police thought they were.

"All right, Minerva, let's see what you can do with this one," he said aloud to the empty room. "Time to turn on the Way Back machine." He began searching the intelligence archives. Some of the dead South African men had been in their seventies and eighties, so he tapped into files going back to the 1970s, files which had been digitized in recent years. While the search was underway, he made another mug of Earl Grey and tried to recall if South Africa had organized crime. It must, he thought. Everywhere does.

Crime, however, was not the correlation that Minerva made, not unless you think that making nuclear weapons is a crime. These men, or their parents, had all done just that in the 1980s and '90s in South Africa. Their names showed up many times in reports on the Apartheid regime's weapons activities.

It came as news to Dugout that South Africa had ever made nuclear weapons. He tapped into the databases for a quick tutorial, entering the terms "South Africa" and "nuclear weapon."

Minerva answered that request with a long list of references, in chronological order. The most recent report was not, however, from the 1990s. It was from earlier this year. He pulled up that file. The highlighted sentence read: "Although it is unlikely, South Africa must be considered one suspect for the recent nuclear detonation in the Indian Ocean. South Africa is one of two nations suspected of a similar shipborne nuclear test in 1979."

The recent nuclear detonation in the Indian Ocean? That, too, was news to Dugout. His next query hit a roadblock. In answer to his input "nuclear test, Indian Ocean, 2014," he got the following: "An intelligence report matching your query parameters is restricted. Contact your supervisor to determine if you can be made eligible to access the file. Reference TS/Q/G/20160909/A751." From the file designator, Dug realized that the report had been written in August. His five dead men had all expired in August.

With his clearances, it was not often that Dugout hit roadblocks in his data searches. As he stared out the window, wondering what to do next, he realized that one of the few cars in the parking lot below belonged to his nominal supervisor, Grace Scanlon, the new Director of the Policy Evaluation Group. Well, if she were in the office on a Sunday afternoon, at least he probably would not need an appointment. He printed a few files and wandered upstairs. So much for a relaxing, rainy Sunday afternoon alone with his computers, he thought, as he strode up the stairs two at a time.

Grace Scanlon had been the Vice President of a Pentagon-funded think tank in California. A year ago when the previous Director of the Policy Evaluation Group had placed himself on indefinite leave, National Security Advisor Winston Burrell had tapped her to take over what he thought of as his personal intelligence analysis unit. She had proved a good analyst and a natural manager, but she remained largely clueless about the ways of Washington. Dugout was not surprised to see her in on a Sunday afternoon. She had impressed everyone at PEG as being a hard worker and, the rumor was, she had left her boyfriend behind in Santa Monica.

"God, I thought I looked scruffy today," Grace Scanlon said, looking up to see Dugout standing in her doorway. "What the hell happened to you? A gang of homeless men stole your clothes and left you theirs? And the hair. Have you been electrocuted?"

He was still getting to know the new Director. People had said she was blunt, had a "New York City street sensibility about her." Now he knew what they meant. "Sorry to interrupt, but I just hit on something I think you should see."

A few minutes of story telling later and Dr. Scanlon was pulling up the restricted report on her desktop monitor. She scanned it and summarized for Dugout. "Nuclear detection satellite saw the double-flash indicative of a nuclear explosion on nine August in the middle of nowhere in the Indian Ocean. No corroborating intelligence from SIGINT or HUMINT helps to explain who might have done the detonation. Analysts speculate about various countries, but they have no evidence to support their guesses. Case remains open."

"So there was a detonation on nine August," Dugout said scanning his notes, "and on twelve August each of five South Africans formerly associated with their nuclear bomb program gets a half billion dollars deposited into their accounts. Three days later they are all dead."

Grace Scanlon stood up from her desk. In

her old gray tracksuit, Dug thought she was no one to criticize him for looking scruffy. "And you are the first one to make the connection?" she asked. "And you just made it a half hour ago?"

"As far as I know, yeah, I am the only one who has seen all three pieces. The bomb blast, the money, and the murders. From what I can tell the local authorities in four of these cases classified the deaths as accidents. Only the guy who got shot in Singapore was classified as a murder."

"Hard to avoid the conclusion that the cause of death was the bullet between his eyes?" she asked. "You know, Douglas, for the first time since I began working here at PEG I actually think I know a secret that nobody outside of this little outfit knows. We have a little secret. Or should I say a big one?"

"So have you come to the same conclusion I have?" Dug asked.

"My conclusion is we don't have all the pieces of this jigsaw puzzle, but the ones we do have could be arranged into a very scary picture." She walked close to him and spoke softly. "We're going to have to see Winston Burrell tomorrow on this. I'll get the meeting. In the meantime, you tell no one, but do see if you can find a few more pieces to the puzzle. Hopefully, they won't look like a mushroom cloud to Winston when you're done putting them together."

"I'm afraid they may look like a whole mushroom garden," Dug said.

"He's going to fucking love this," Dug heard her say as he walked out the door. "Potential loose nukes in the middle of a presidential election campaign."

3

MONDAY, OCTOBER 17
ST. JOHN, U.S. VIRGIN ISLANDS

The rear wheels spun, trying to gain purchase on the gravel. He knew if he took his foot off the accelerator, the Cherokee would quickly slip backward and go over the side to crash on the rocks by the sea.

Then suddenly the Jeep lurched forward and he pressed down harder on the pedal. As happened when he was nervous, Dugout began narrating his life in real time to himself, his mind racing. He thought of the story that would have run in his hometown paper: "Douglas Carter III, known to his friends as Dugout, was killed in a Caribbean car crash." If that happened, his mother would be surprised and upset when she learned he was to be cremated. He had never shown her his will.

Then the road shifted left at almost 90 degrees and the grade shot up farther. And he was on the left-hand side of the road. Why the shit, he wondered, did they drive on the wrong side when this was part of America? We had bought it or stolen it years ago, from the Danes or the Brits or Spanish or somebody, probably before there even were cars.

Surely there were rules, he thought, regulations, about how ridiculous a hairpin turn could be. Sweet Jesus. And then the road switched right and climbed some more, just as one of those absurd Jeepney things came crashing down hill. Stretched, open-air buslike Jeeps, he had only ever seen them before in the Philippines and some places in Central America. But America was not supposed to be a third world country. Right now was the exception. This Jeepney looked like it had been painted in Haight-Ashbury in the 1960s by Peter Max. *"Ayyyah,"* a passenger cried as the thing missed him by inches and went on cascading down the road.

What was this road like when it rained, which the guy at the car rental place had told him it does every day? What if you had popped a few before driving? He made a mental note to find out the fatality figures.

Then, finally, the road, if you could call it that, began to descend gradually and flatten out. He felt himself exhaling, loosening his grip on the wheel. It will be just as bad going back, his interior voice said to him in that maddening way it had of providing a running commentary on his life.

Now, there was civilization up ahead. Or, at least, there were buildings, small colorful houses, and a little town. He passed a concrete schoolhouse, painted in pastels, on the left. On the right was a tiny firehouse, too tiny for what sat outside it. What looked like a Book-Mobile truck, but with lots of antennae, was on the side of the road, its Day-Glo yellowy green paint job shining in the sun. USVI MOBILE COMMAND POST were the words painted in large letters on its side. It proved his theory that everyone but him had been given a mobile command post by the Department of Homeland Security. And he was probably one of the few people who would know what to do with one.

This mobile command post could never make it on those roads. It must have arrived by barge to sit here until discovered by archaeologists in some future era. Whatever would they think of it, he wondered. Then he spotted what he assumed was his destination.

The parking lot had a half dozen or more

cars scattered in it, indicating, no doubt, that this shack was the bar, Skinny Legs. The online guide had said it was "seedy but charming." The first descriptor was self-evidently true. A chicken walked in front of him through the dusty lot and he found himself wondering what they served here for lunch. He realized that it was after eleven in the morning and all he had eaten so far was a donut he had grabbed in Red Hook on St. Thomas before getting on the water taxi.

The low ceiling in the shack would have been oppressive if there had been walls, but Skinny Legs was a kind of open-air sports bar. Red Sox, Bruins, Celtics, and Patriots banners and memorabilia hung from the ceiling and covered the walls. Boston in the tropics.

He sat on a barstool and waved at the woman behind the bar. "What'll yah have, hun?" she asked in a voice that indicated to him either Dorchester or Southie.

"Margarita." Then he had to ask. "Dorchester or Southie?"

"Dot. You?"

"Belmont."

She screwed up her face. "Rich kid, huh? Belmont Day School or BBN?"

"Belmont High, actually," he said and

smiled in the way that usually worked, that made him seem sweet and innocent, or so he had been repeatedly told by now ex-boyfriends.

"That was before he went to MIT, Joannie," Ray Bowman's voice said from behind Dugout. "I'll serve this one. We don't actually do margaritas here, 'cuz we don't have a blender. So how 'bout a Painkilla?" Bowman moved behind the bar.

Bowman looked smaller, Dug thought. Maybe it was the flip-flops. Or maybe it was the Hawaiian shirt. And there was a surprising amount of gray speckling his three-day beard.

"As long as it's not too sweet," Dug replied.

"I knew it would be you. No one else could have found the trail," Ray said, handing him the plastic-covered menu. "Want food?"

"You know what Vela is?" Dug asked.

"Some sort of cheese you squirt? Don't have any. Get the fish tacos."

"What kind of fish is it?"

Ray smiled, "No one knows. It's white. Not bony. Probably cod, but, no one knows really."

"Okay, but hold the fries. Is there a fruit cup instead?"

"You serious?" Ray laughed. "You bring me any Havanas as an inducement?"

"I did," Dug said reaching into his backpack. "Inducement to do what?"

"Whatever stupid shit task they sent you here to get me to take on for them," Ray said reaching for the Cohiba.

"So, once again, did you ever hear of Vela?"

Ray lit the cigar and took a drag, letting a large cloud of smoke flow over the bar. "Coits?" he said, walking out from behind the counter.

"As in interruptus?" Dug asked.

"No, that's coitus," Ray said, pushing Dug off the bar stool. "Let's go outside. Come on." Dug looked at him oddly, but followed Ray out into a sandy backyard and the noonday sun.

Ray Bowman grabbed four heavy, iron horseshoes and handed two to Dugout. "Best three outa five. Let's start at the end under the tree."

"Whoooah. This can't be regulation length. It's like a mile to that little post," Dug said.

"It's regulation, all right. I'll give you a break, though, I'll go first." Ray's first toss landed eight inches to the right of the post. Dug had been watching Ray's style of motion and imitated it perfectly, landing his

47

iron standing up, two inches to the right of the target. Then, it slowly fell backward, leaning against the post. "Leaner," he announced.

Ray Bowman scowled and then stepped into his toss with determination, his horseshoe knocking the leaner off and then bouncing and landing three feet behind.

"Mutually assured defeat, huh?" Dug asked as he stood in. He paused, stared at the target, moved his arm back, stepped forward, and launched. "Ringer," he said as the *cling* rang out from the horseshoe hitting the post. He pushed his Maui Jim's up on his head and said. "Vela was a constellation of satellites launched in the 1970s. Simple birds with one purpose, to detect nuclear explosions aboveground."

"Okay," Ray said as he relit the Cohiba.

"In September 1979, Vela detected an explosion off South Africa," Dug continued.

"So?"

"South Africa later admitted having made nuclear weapons," Dug explained.

"Didn't know that."

"And, before ending apartheid and handing control over to Nelson Mandela, the white government reported to the UN that it destroyed six nuclear weapons. End of inventory," Dug said.

"Ancient history then," Ray said and waved at the waitress inside Skinny Legs. "Two Red Stripes, please Joannie."

Dug looked Bowman in the eyes. "We have reason to believe that white South Africans just sold nuclear weapons."

"To who?"

"To whom," Dug corrected. "That's what they want you to find out."

"Christ, I'd forgotten how pedantic you could be," Ray Bowman said as he took the two beers from Joannie. "Come on, Dugster. Let's walk down to the water."

They passed a dozen or more boats that had been brought up on the land, apparently a while ago, their paint faded, tropical vines gradually covering them. The beached boats gave the little harbor town a sense of insouciance, of the pressure to "do something" having lifted and drifted off. "Up there," Ray said pointing to one of the steep, verdant hills behind the town. "That's where my cottage is. But then you know that, I assume."

Dug took a swig of the Red Stripe. "Let's just say I haven't been looking in every sleazy bar in the Caribbean."

The two men walked up on to a brightly painted, little restaurant on the water's edge. They helped themselves to an outside table under the sign SERAFINI'S CARIBBEAN-ITALIAN. A grandmotherly woman quickly appeared from inside.

"Hi, Robbie. Need a menu?" Mrs. Serafini asked.

"Robbie?" Dug asked when she'd left them.

"Well, I did take some measures to cover my tracks, but, since you're here, obviously not sufficient ones."

Dug buried his face in the menu. "I always knew where you were. Never lost track. Don't ask how."

"Well, I guess in a way that's comforting," Ray replied, scanning the boats on the water. "Although it was nice to pretend to myself that I was free."

"You are free. They can't make you come back. It's just that they're stumped. And scared. When Dr. Burrell tells the President he has his best people on it, he knows it isn't true. His best guy is bartending on St. John."

"And painting. Watercolors initially, but I'm experimenting now with oils and acrylics."

"Who are you, George W. Bush? Nuclear bombs could ruin the country in a way that we could not ever fully recover from," Dug said putting down the menu.

Mrs. Serafini reappeared and interrupted. "Here's a pitcher of the sangria you love, Robbie. The special today is the grilled grouper." They both ordered the special.

"The special every day is the grouper, but she does change the sauces. Tell Winston Burrell to cool his jets. Bombs made over thirty years ago are not going to work," Ray insisted.

"These ones will."

"How do you know that, Einstein?"

Dug leaned forward across the table. "They tested one of them in the middle of nowhere, in the southern Indian Ocean. The replacement for Vela, a package on the new Milstar, picked it up, the telltale double flash of a nuke going off. Radiation detectors on Diego Garcia confirmed. Later, Australia did, too."

Ray put down his glass of sangria. He pulled on his stubbled chin with his right hand, a mannerism Dugout knew well. It meant Raymond Bowman was pausing, processing.

"We think the explosion was required by the buyers before they paid up for the rest of the lot. Proof that what they were buying worked."

" 'We'?" Ray asked.

"PEG still exists. It didn't go away just

51

because you quit. Grace Scanlon is running it. The Policy Evaluation Group still sits up on Navy Hill and still answers the National Security Advisor's questions, does his special tasks."

"And what's this special task?" he asked.

Before Ray's question could be answered, Mrs. Serafini brought out two plates of fish. "Careful, boys, the plates are hot."

"Simple," Dugout replied. "Find out who bought the nukes. Find the bombs before they get them into the U.S. Grab the bombs. Oh, and, make sure there aren't any other bombs left over somewhere else."

"That all?"

"Easy for you to do. You'll be back bartending at Skinny Legs for their New Year's party. I hear it's a hoot," Dug said with his mouth full of grouper.

"It's better than the scene at Jost Van Dyke's," Ray said.

"Who's he?" Dugout asked.

"Eat your fish. Then we'll go somewhere private and talk. You need to tell me a lot more."

"So you'll help?"

"No, I didn't say that," Bowman replied. "You came all the way down here. You might as well tell me your whole story. I like to hear stories." He refilled their glasses with the fruity red wine.

After lunch, having consumed two beers each and a pitcher of sangria between them in two hours, Ray led Dugout down the road and through some high grass to a small cove. On the little beach in a boat cradle, sat what appeared to be a wreck, a twenty-four-foot wooden sailboat, paint peeling, sections of the hull missing.

Ray pointed to the boat, proudly. "She's mine."

"What happened to it, a hurricane sometime in the last century?"

"It's only been out of the water two years," Ray replied. "It's a project. Everyone needs a project. Besides, when I am here, I am alone. Nobody ever comes down here."

"Did you ever stop to wonder why?"

"When did this supposed nuclear explosion take place?" Ray began, as he lowered himself to the sand under a palm tree on the shore of the cove.

"Nine weeks ago."

"Well, then, it probably wasn't what you think it was, because by now any terrorist group worth its salt would have turned some city somewhere to radioactive ash," Ray said.

Dugout has assumed a yoga position on the sand. "Maybe, but the bomb experts at

Oak Ridge and Los Alamos are pretty certain that the double flash was a nuke going off. The air samples they got later were a ninety-six percent positive match. And besides, then there were the murders."

"Ah, murders. This gets better. Do tell."

"Six days after the double flash, several expat, white South Africans either murdered or died in suspicious circumstances. Tel Aviv, Vienna, Dubai, Singapore, Sydney. Turns out they all had connections back to the South African bomb program, either themselves or their fathers."

"Who killed them?" Bowman asked.

"Dunno, but just before they died they each got about a half billion U.S. dollars deposited into accounts they controlled. Thousands of money transfers, from a rat's nest of *hawalas,* Bitcoins, anonymous offshore accounts, stolen credit cards, stock sales, you name it."

"So, you of all people ought to be able to trace through that and find out the origin," Bowman said.

"Tried. Still trying. No joy. It was very well done. Dead ends everywhere."

Bowman squinted and shook his head. "Doesn't make sense to pay a guy and then kill him. Why pay him? How'd you get on to all this anyway?"

"Minerva, the big data analytics package you bought me, was running a scan looking for interesting money laundering and found the thread. When I pulled on it, I found almost two and a half billion bucks had run around the world and then ended up in these accounts." Dugout was getting excited telling the story, his words coming increasingly faster. "Checked the owners and found dead guys, all of whom had died within hours of each other, spread out all over the world. Asked what did they have in common and, bingo, they all go back to the Apartheid nuke program. And when I check the database on that program, I find that there is an open investigation about a double flash in the Indian Ocean just days before these guys got popped."

"The flash Velveeta detected?" Bowman asked.

"Vela, but yeah. So I tell Winston Burrell over at the White House and he goes all sorts of ballistic and says it's an al Qaeda plot to blow up American cities just before the presidential election and he thinks these guys are slowly smuggling the bombs in and getting them in place."

"What guys?"

Dugout came out of the cross-legged lotus position and stood up. "That's just it. I have no clue. Al Qaeda, Muslim Brotherhood, ISIS, North Korea? I struck out. So did everybody else. So Burrell sends me here, to get you on a secure video link with him."

Bowman got up off the sand so he could look Dugout in the eye. "No way. There is no secure video at Skinny Legs or anywhere else on this rock and I am not going off island to talk to Winston."

Dugout smiled back at him, then bent over and unzipped his backpack. He removed what looked like an iPad. Then he extended a black tube that looked like a Pringles can. Ray guessed it was a satellite antenna. Dugout plugged it into the iPad and tapped at an on-screen keyboard. Quickly a face appeared on screen.

"Situation Room. How can I help you, Dr. Carter?"

"Dr. Carter?" Bowman repeated, laughing.

"I need to speak to the National Security Advisor. He's expecting my call," Dugout said to the screen.

"Yes, sir, let me patch you through to Dr. Burrell," the man on the screen said.

"He's expecting your call, is he?" Bowman frowned at Dugout. "You working directly for Winston these days?"

"Grace doesn't mind. Grace, the person

who took your job when you disappeared? Anyways, Winston gives me special projects. I usually meet him at the Cosmos Club, in a private room, for dinner," Dugout admitted.

"How nice for you."

Dugout then plugged red Beats earphones into the iPad.

The image that then appeared on the screen looked like it came from a camera behind Winston Burrell's desk on the first floor of the West Wing. The National Security Advisor could be seen sitting down and adjusting the lens, zooming in on his own face. Dugout passed the modified iPad to Bowman, who put on the earphones and sat back down on the sand, looking at the screen.

"I would have thought the beard and hair would be longer," Burrell began.

"And a happy Monday to you, too, Winston," Bowman shot back.

"Long time no talk and all that. Look, Ray, what Dug Carter has told you is all true and then some. The Agency has been on to the government in Pretoria and they know these dead guys as the Trustees, the heads of an expat network of South Africans who all had connections to the Apartheid government's defense industry and their nukes.

"The Intel Community is all agreed that these South Africans must have kept some bombs, tested one to prove to a buyer that they worked, then sold the buyer the others. Problem is that the Intel Community has no idea who bought the bombs or where they were, let alone where they are now. My assumption is al Qaeda and that some of them are already here, probably got one a few blocks from the White House."

Bowman frowned, skeptically, at Dugout. Winston Burrell continued unabated. "You may not have noticed down there in the Caribbean, but we are in the end stages of a presidential election. Imagine if they blow up a city and then make a demand of the two candidates to pull all our forces out of the Middle East or they will blow up another two cities. Both candidates will agree to pull out, do whatever they demand. Hell, I don't even know if we could go ahead with an election after even one city had been nuked," Burrell concluded. "It would be a constitutional crisis."

"So, what do all the nice departments and agencies suggest you do, Winston?" Ray asked.

"Homeland Security wants to launch a

search with radiation detectors. Trucks and helicopters running around in DC and New York with scanners. They want to stop any cargo from entering the U.S. unless it's been searched first overseas."

Bowman scowled at the screen. "You can't do that, Winston. There would be a general panic. Everyone would flee the cities."

"I know. Self-evacuation is what the FBI calls it. Sounds like a laxative. But seriously, if we do that everyone will leave town and no one would vote. The economy would tank," Burrell said. "But if we do nothing and a city blows up? Then it turns out we knew about the threat and didn't warn the public?"

Burrell looked more agitated than Bowman had ever seen him, the usual confidence bordering on arrogance was gone. Burrell continued to pour out his concerns, "My fear, as I said, is they blow up one city and then make demands and say they will blow up more cities unless we meet their demands. The election would be a few days off and there would be huge pressure on the President and the two candidates to give in to their demands. But at this point we don't even know who *they* are."

"What have you told the President?"

Bowman asked.

"It's more like what he's told me. He wants to seal the borders and start searching for the bombs. Of course, then the bombers would know we were on to them and probably blow up their first nuke. Besides, we can't survive as an economy if we stop and search everything. We only look at about one or two percent of containers entering this country now. If we looked at all of them, the country would grind to a halt. Everybody is on 'Just In Time Delivery' from China or wherever."

Bowman could see where this conversation was going and he felt his back muscles tightening. "Well, Winston I will give it some thought here with Dugout and send him back to you with some ideas."

"The fuck you will. The election is November eighth. I got POTUS to agree to give you two weeks to find out who these bombers are and snatch them, grab their nukes. After two weeks, if you can't find them, we institute Operation Rock Wall, close the borders, and search for the nukes. Then everything will go to hell in a hand-basket," Burrell told him.

"Excuse me," Ray Bowman replied. "I am a private citizen. This is not my job. I tend bar."

"I told POTUS last night that I would ask you, on his behalf. He remembered how you stopped the attacks on the subways and the drones. He agreed to the two-week delay only if you were running an operation in parallel to the Intel Community. He said they'll never crack this, but you might. You could name your terms. Dugout could get you started and he will give you top cover from cyberspace. You know everybody around the world who you would need to work with. Look, think about it overnight and then say yes in the morning. Don't make the President call you himself."

The screen went to black. Raymond Bowman sat on the sand in an old bathing suit, stained Skinny Legs T-shirt, and faded Red Sox cap. He knew that the world he had built for himself was fragile, maybe artificial, but he had wanted it to go on longer. He wasn't healed yet from all the killing on the last job and he certainly wasn't ready to do it all over again.

"Top cover from cyberspace?" Bowman repeated. He turned and looked out at the turquoise water. "What have you been feeding him?"

"I suppose you could say no." Dugout was standing behind him.

"And I will, tomorrow morning," Ray

61

insisted, "and I won't take any calls from the Oval. Thank you so much for visiting, by the way. You have really made my day."

"Right. So where do I spend the night? I was planning on going back today."

"I can hook you up at Gallows," Ray replied as they headed back up to the Jeep.

"Hook me up to the gallows, hang me just because I did my job and found you?"

"Don't be a literalist tool, Duggie. It's a nice resort on the harbor side in Cruz Bay. The only hanging done there is at the bar. Come on, get a move on, I have to get some Champagne before the store closes at six. This is not Manhattan."

"Coulda fooled me."

On his way back from Gallows Point, Ray Bowman took a right up a steep driveway to a gated villa. He knew the camera in the stone wall holding the gate would let the people inside see who he was. It took about two minutes and then the gate swung wide. A tin-sounding voice came from a little speaker under the camera, "Come on in, Ray. Just in time for cocktails."

The cocktails were mojitos. They were always mojitos, which Ray didn't mind because Dr. Sidney Rosenthal made such good ones, with fresh mint from his own herb garden. Rosenthal said his retirement job was as an herbatologist.

They sat looking across at Tortola and the scattering of small islands that dotted the Sir Francis Drake Channel. Sailboats and ferries were making their way back to ports and the sun was moving toward the horizon in the sky right in front of them. In another hour it would be gone below the waves and would color the few clouds that special Caribbean pink orange.

"How are you sleeping these days, Ray?" Dr. Rosenthal asked.

"Like a rock, except when Cody jumps up on the bed in the middle of the night." He paused. "Cody is our dog."

"I know."

"Well, he's more Emma and Linda's dog than mine, but he sleeps in my cabin."

"What's up? You're nervous today."

"Rosy, you have been really helpful and I think it's all behind me. I haven't had the dream in weeks. I am enjoying bartending. I love my ladies. Emma's having our kid in the spring. The watercolors are getting better. This may be what contentment looks like."

Rosenthal looked at Bowman and then out at the sea below them. "What's happened, Raymond?"

"They want me back. Just for a short time,

just for a special job."

Rosenthal shook his head. "It would ruin everything you have achieved, no matter how short the job. The PTSD will return. You might not be able to get that contented state back and, if you do, it will take a long time."

"I can't tell you what it is, the job, but it is very important, not just important for The Man, but for all of us."

"Raymond, you have PTSD for god's sake."

"We could all end up with PTSD if somebody doesn't do this job and do it right," Bowman shot back. "And quickly."

"And you're the only man who could, huh?"

Ray Bowman exhaled and looked at his old canvas boat shoes. "Seems unlikely, I know."

"I didn't mean it that way, Ray, I'm sorry. If The Man is who I think he is and he has confidence that only you can do it, well, I accept that." Sid Rosenthal emptied his mojito.

"If I go, will you help me when I get back?"

"I'll double my rates," Rosenthal insisted.

"My math was never great, Rosy, but I think doubling zero is still nothing."

"I'll make you bartend at all my parties."

"I do that anyway." Ray stood up to leave. "I'll let you know what I decide."

"Sounds like you already have."

Ray laughed. "Let's see how tonight goes."

The sun did disappear below the waves as Ray drove back to Coral Bay and then up the winding, rock-studded road to the hillside complex of brightly colored little buildings and shacks he had made his home.

He walked in carrying two bottles of Perrier-Jouët that he had persuaded his friend Tommy, the bartender at Gallows Point, to add to the bill for Dr. Carter's suite. On an island as small as St. John, there was a conspiracy of bartenders.

"Oh, shit, something's happened," Emily Sullivan exclaimed when she looked up from her canvas. "Or gonna happen? But it's something you have to apologize for, Ray, isn't it? No other reason you'd be comin' home with the bubbly on a Monday."

"Em, Em, it could be just because I want us to celebrate your finishing your latest masterpiece," he responded.

"It ain't anywheres near finished and you know it, arsehole," Emily countered as she hugged him. "Besides, you oughta know I can't drink that stuff now."

"Did someone say we have the bubbly tonight?" Linda Fazio asked, emerging with her arms covered in clay. "Emy's painting is not done, but I have just thrown a magnificent little vase and we can damn sure celebrate that. Pop one open there, bow man.

"Bring the bottles to the pool," Linda said and threw her red sports bra across the patio.

Ray and Linda managed to empty both bottles of Champagne and even persuaded Emily to have a little taste. And somewhere along the line before they all went into Emily and Linda's bed, it had come out that Ray had to go away for a few weeks to help out an old friend who was in trouble. "Less than a month, really, not even that long."

TUESDAY, OCTOBER 18

It read 0317 on his watch, as Ray stood alone and naked on the little brick patio of his yellow and purple cottage, which had originally been the garage and toolshed of Emily and Linda's hillside house. Cody had followed him home and curled up inside the cottage, as he always did. "The girls have the house, the boys have the doghouse," Linda was fond of telling the

66

few visitors they allowed to join them for feasts on the lush hill, usually after long hikes in the National Park that backed up to their property.

He looked down on the handful of lights still on below in Coral Bay and felt once again that warmth and satisfaction of being home, being grounded, settled, centered. It was a new feeling for him, one that he had not really known before in his adult life. This was where he belonged, in a little compound, half overgrown with jungle, hanging on the side of a hill, on an island without an airport, half off the grid. Whatever he did on this new job for Winston, he had to keep foremost in his mind that he had to limit his risks, he had to get back here. He heard something and turned to see Emily holding a Sig Sauer P290RS in her hand.

"I thought you'd need the gun you gave us." To attract women to guns, Sig had made a version of the P290 with a pink stock. It looked like a toy or some sort of ice cream treat. Ray had bought it for "his women" as a joke, but they had loved having it. Seeing it now in the hand of a beautiful, naked woman, made him laugh aloud.

"No, you guys keep it. I'm clumsy, but I'm not the Pink Panther, not Inspector

Clouseau." He put his arm around her. "Come on and help me pack. I haven't done that in a while." They wandered together into Ray's little cabin, essentially one room dominated by a bed.

"Are you running away, now of all times?" Emily asked, as he threw a suitcase on the bed. "I thought you were finally calming down, that you had found your place in the universe and it was here."

Ray walked around the bed and embraced her, feeling her bulging belly against his flat abs. "Emy, I'm not running away. I just have a job to do, just one more job, and then I'm back here, back here for good."

"Bowman, we don't just want you in our lives, Lin and I need you in our lives. We're better together as three and we'll be even better together as four."

Ray sat on the edge of the bed and, tugging lightly on her arm, he pulled Emily down to sit next to him. "I feel like I have a stake in the future now, Em, our future, together. That little one we created," he said, caressing her belly, "I need to do this for her. It's part of my role, making sure she's safe."

"It could be a him, you know," Emily said.

"Either way, there may be something about to happen that would set us all back, collapse the global economy, create chaos. It could even affect us here. If I can help in some small way to stop it, as my last job in that business, I need to do it," Bowman said, softly, and then lightly kissed Emily's stomach. "And I promise I won't put myself at risk. And I will be back in plenty of time to be here for the fun part when she starts kicking."

Linda stood in the doorway. "You'd better be back soon, asshole, because I am not building the nursery addition all by myself. I need a carpenter's assistant and that would be you."

Soon after sunrise, Ray found Emily's mobile phone, called Gallows Point and was put through to Dugout's room. "I want you to meet me in half an hour. There's a little beach."

Bowman drove down the hill and got back on "The Road," as the locals called the loop around the island. He passed Cinnamon beach and Trunk Bay, Peace Hill and Hawksnest Beach. They were all still empty. It was early and the tourist season did not really start until Thanksgiving. He abruptly pulled off the road into a parking area big enough for two, maybe three, Jeeps. Dugout was already parked there.

Bowman jumped out of his open-top Jeep

and walked through a small iron gate into what seemed like a tunnel through a rain forest. The descending path was covered by a canopy of trees and vines. Dugout followed, stumbling over tree roots and rocks, balancing his backpack. In a few minutes the verdant tunnel opened onto a small, white sand beach and a turquoise cove. No one else was there.

"My private beach," Ray said, "most of the time." There was a boarded-up cinder block house, but none of the picnic tables and showers with which the National Park Service had dotted the other beaches on the island.

Bowman stood and faced him. "You know what they call this beach?"

"Ray's Hideout?"

"It's named after a guy who bought it in the fifties, built that little shack over there. He was trying to get away from his past, from the killing he had been involved in. Kinda like me. But he was also haunted by images of a future in which cities went up in flames from nuclear bombs." Bowman walked away from the beach, toward the shack.

"In the end, it didn't work for him. Being here. He went back to the mainland, back to work," Bowman said, looking at Dug.

"He was the man who built the H bomb."

"Who the hell lived here?" Dugout asked.

"Oppenheimer. This is called Oppy's Beach."

Dugout wasn't sure what Ray Bowman was telling him.

"So you're in?"

"You've ruined it for me. You and Burrell. I can't sit down here in paradise thinking about cities being nuked, not any more than Oppy could. But if I'm doing this thing, so are you."

"Sure, but remember we only got two weeks. Then it's Rock Wall," Dugout replied. "They close the ports, the borders, they start looking everywhere with Geiger counters."

"And if Winston's right, when he starts Operation Rock Wall, the bad guys will respond by nuking the first city. And even if they don't, the country will tear itself apart in panic." Ray Bowman began walking toward the path to the road. "How were you planning on leaving the island?"

"If I am leaving with you in tow, I can call in a Coast Guard helo from Puerto Rico. It can be here in two hours. In the meantime, I can teach you how to use the iPad."

"However much of a Luddite I may be compared to you, I do know how to use an

71

iPad," Ray said taking the device. "My three-year-old niece knows how."

"You've never seen one like this. I designed it myself."

"Oh, good. I kinda liked the one Steve Jobs designed," Ray shot back.

"This one is secure, encrypted, has a telephone and video phone function and connects to an Air Force communications satellite."

"That's nice, Duggie, but I'm going to need identities, passports, credit cards, cash. And I'll need Winston's office to phone ahead and open the doors I can't open by myself. Occasionally, I may need help from the Fort, the Bureau, or the Agency."

"All of whom, as I recall, were great friends of yours."

"Don't be a wise ass. It's unbecoming," Ray replied. "Look. I'll always let you know where I am and what I am up to."

Dugout had a wide grin. "Don't worry. I'll know."

4

WEDNESDAY, OCTOBER 19
CAFÉ GRIENSTEIDL
VIENNA, AUSTRIA

"Ein grosse schwartze, bitte," Bowman said to the elderly waiter.

"Mit strudel?" the old man asked.

Charmed that some things never changed, he replied, "Okay, *warum nicht?*" He had taken a seat by the window, with a view across the narrow street and the Michaelerplatz to the Palace and the Spanish Riding School. Like most of the people in the cavernous, old café, he paged through a newspaper. Unlike most of them, he also scanned the room to see if his guest had arrived, or if anyone else of interest was present.

"Raymond, you chose this café for the Lipinzaners? You like horses now?" Jonas Moe must have come through a back door. He was at the table before Bowman knew he was in the room, an unpleasant reminder to the American that certain of his skills had atrophied while he tended bar in paradise.

"No, Jonas, I chose it because it's a short walk from my hotel and a long way from UN City. No need for your fellow international civil servants to see us together."

"Ein Americano, bitte, und ein Sakertort mit slag," the Norwegian told the passing waiter, who looked at him as if requesting service was rude or impertinent. Jonas Moe had been in Vienna long enough to know that unless he grabbed a passing waiter, it might otherwise be a very long time before he was served. He had been in the old city for twenty-six years, as a senior staff member of the International Atomic Energy Agency, a UN nuclear inspector. Moe had also been one of Bowman's personal sources on the Iranian nuclear program, passing on the full results of the Agency's inspections and sometimes carrying some extra equipment with him to Iran.

"Any chance to get off that UN island in the Danube. I hate that late twentieth-century architecture, so cold, impersonal. Give me an old Viennese café any day. And any chance to see my good friend Raymond, who the drum signals had said was gone from government, out of the spook world. But here I see it is not so? The drums have told false tales again?"

"Let's just say that I am doing some research. Perhaps I am writing a book?" Ray responded.

"With respect, Raymond, you could no more have the patience to write a book than you could train the dancing white horses across the Platz. But I will play along. What would this book be about, Iran and its nuclear weapons program?"

The elderly waiter brought the coffee and cake. "I will have you know that I was an accomplished horseman one summer in Montana, admittedly many years ago," Moe asserted. The waiter departed.

"No, not Iran again. Ancient history. South Africa."

Moe's eyes darted quickly up from his chocolate cake and his expression became more serious. "The double flash in August that I am not supposed to know about, that your government failed to mention to the IAEA. Finally you are taking it seriously?"

"I don't know anything about a double flash."

"Of course you do."

"I am concerned with more ancient history," Bowman replied. "Nineteen ninety-one. The destruction of the six South African nuclear bombs. IAEA went in after they were disassembled and had a look. The records say you were on that mission."

Jonas Moe withdrew a pack of Marlboros and lit a cigarette. They were not in the larger smoking room of the café, but this room was almost empty and the waiter would not object unless some tourist complained. "You have been snooping in the records of a UN Agency again? You Americans are worse than the Chinese, hacking into everything." He flicked an ash into his saucer. "My first field mission with the Agency. Two months in South Africa. Very pretty country and great wine, so tragic their race hatred."

"The IAEA report said the bombs probably were destroyed. The enriched uranium from the bombs was placed under safeguard, under seal, and monitored with cameras," Ray recalled.

"Highly enriched uranium was declared by their government. We placed it under seal. We audited their production records. It seemed that we had all the HEU they had made. This is all in public documents, reports."

Although Ray loved cigars, the cigarette

smoke was already affecting his sinuses. "But you thought the records were doctored, that they had produced much more HEU?"

"You have hacked into my brain, too? Accessed my old cerebral files?" Jonas Moe asked.

"You thought that some warheads were never destroyed, that there was extra HEU they used to make more warheads, which they kept, somewhere," Ray asserted, bluffing.

"When you are Russia with forty thousand nuclear weapons, half of them unsafe, you can disassemble the old ones and harvest the uranium for other uses. You Americans have also cut your own inventory in half over the last twenty years. But when you have only a few, they are very special to you. And in 1991 when the world was in flux, the Cold War ending, the Communist bloc disintegrating, Apartheid finally being abolished, and Nelson Mandela about to be freed and to take over . . . in this sort of world do you give up all your crown jewels? No, you doctor your books."

Bowman noticed that the café was beginning to fill up as the morning wore on. He was relieved that his one-time source had snubbed out the cigarette. "So, Jonas, did they do a good job doctoring the books?"

"They tried to, but that's all they needed to do really. Botha was meeting with Mandela. It was all about to end, peacefully. The UN was not going to call them liars about the nukes."

Bowman knew Jonas Moe's concern over nuclear weapons proliferation was a driving passion, his life's work. He found it hard to believe that a younger, even more idealistic Moe had turned a blind eye to nuclear weapons going missing. "But you wanted to make sure that the bombs did not get into the wrong hands," Ray suggested. "How did you do that?"

"My Team Chief, an Argentine, would have whitewashed it, but I told my South African counterpart that I would not. I was young and brash. The South African, good fellow he was, was a physicist with their Atomic Energy Commission. He was pissed at ARMSCOR, the defense industry because they had taken over the program. He told me to take a good look at the HEU production numbers from the Y Plant. He hinted that they were faked."

Moe looked up and right into Bowman's eyes. "I couldn't prove it, but unless they were terribly inefficient, they probably made almost half again as much HEU as what they reported. My official submission was that there were 'apparent inconsistencies.' "

"But your bosses here in Vienna wanted the story to go away," Ray guessed aloud, "and so upon further analysis the inconsistencies became plausible numbers, within the statistically acceptable band."

Moe nodded. He looked off into the distance, remembering those days. "But, Raymond, they knew I knew. The South Africans were fully aware that I was not fooled. So months later when I was back there again, my South African counterpart had me over to his house for dinner. After the feast with the family, he took me down to his *lager,* his private workspace under the house.

"He showed me a video, like a secret documentary they made, of how they had made some missile warheads and then shipped them secretly to Israel in 1994, not that the Israelis needed them, but it was a way of saying thanks for the Israeli help with the Jericho missiles that would have carried the South African weapons. And in the end, the South African team that had made the warheads just could not stand to see them destroyed. So they gave them to Israel."

This was the part of the interview that Bowman had the most trouble planning. He did not want it to seem to Jonas Moe that this entire discussion was about him, or his possible failure a quarter century earlier. "It was credible, this video?" Bowman asked.

"My South African counterpart was. He joined IAEA and became a colleague. He worked on the Pakistan and India problems for years. Later, when he retired, he still consulted with the Agency. He was a good friend of ours, my wife and me, for many years, poor man. We miss him. We used to go hiking together in the Wienerwald."

"I take it he has passed on?" Ray asked.

"This summer. Awful, really. A tram hit him out by Grinzing, smashed into his car, split the fuel tank, horrific explosion and fire. I just hope he died quickly and did not feel the flames."

"Well, if you believed him and the documentary that the bombs went back to Israel, what do you think caused the new Indian Ocean flash," Ray asked, "assuming there was one, of course."

Jonas Moe moved the last bit of Saker-torte around on his plate with his fork. He did not look at Bowman. "That's what I have been wondering. Mainly in the wee hours of the morning, when I should be asleep. It seemed so much like the 1979 test on a ship in the middle of nowhere. But it can't be the South Africans. Everyone who was involved in that program is either old or dead, and none of them are even living in South Africa anymore. And besides, their warheads all went to Israel or were dismantled." Moe looked at the man who had paid him for information for years. "Maybe it was North Korea. They do odd things."

Ray smiled at his old source. "Yes, they do." He signaled for their check. It was always hard to get them to give you a bill in Vienna. "Jonas, tell me one more thing if you will. The Israelis. Did you or anyone in the IAEA ever ask them whether they were given the warheads or what they did with them?"

Jonas Moe stood to leave. As they shook hands, he spoke in a low voice, his mouth near Ray's ear. "The Israelis would not talk to us. They never did, until they started giving us information about Iran lately." He picked up his pack of Marlboros and moved quickly to a side door in the back of the room, a door Ray had missed when he first entered the café.

He had chosen the café so that he would be close to his next meeting, but it took Ray Bowman another fifteen minutes to get the check and leave the café. He had to hurry through the rain to his appointment two blocks down the narrow Herrengasse in the Palais Modena, the two-hundred-year-old headquarters of the Bundesministerium für Inneres, the BM.I, Austria's secret police.

5

WEDNESDAY, OCTOBER 19
PALAIS MODENA
VIENNA, AUSTRIA

After showing a passport to the guard at the front door, he was escorted upstairs to the office of Gunter Rosch, Deputy Director of the BVT, the Bundesamt für Verfassungsschutz und Terrorismusbekämpfung, the Office for the Protection of the Constitution and Counterterrorism. Apparently the Austrians thought those were two distinct missions, but close enough for one agency to handle.

Rosch's office had been a salon when the Modenese Duke lived in the Palais. The ceiling was twenty-two feet high and decorated in a rococo style. The computer terminal on the Deputy Director's desk seemed incongruous, like a visitor from the twenty-first-century future appearing in the middle of a nineteenth-century present.

"Great to see you, Ray. Welcome back to Vienna" Rosch boomed as he crossed the large expanse of his office. "I am told you are here as a tourist and I should not tell your embassy on Boltzmanngasse that you are in town. Special project or something?"

"I didn't tell the U.S. Embassy that I was coming," Ray said, shaking the firm hand of the tall, broad Austrian. "It's kind of an off the books project." Herr Rosch guided him to two oversized wingback chairs by a working fireplace. "That warmth feels good on a wet autumn day," Ray continued. "I am afraid Gunter that I can't tell you a lot about why I am asking the questions I have, except to say that they could be related to saving a lot of lives."

"Raymond, I trust you. Our relationship has been tested. With all of the investigation of the U.S. drone strike on the terrorists here in Vienna, it never came out that we had tipped you to their presence," Rosch recalled. "And it never came out that we suggested that you might want to act unilaterally, since our laws did not permit us to do anything."

"It was a bit messy," Ray admitted, "but I do still believe that we prevented bombings on your subway and on U-Bahns in Germany." A white-coated young man entered the room with two small silver trays, each with a glass of water and a cup of the thick sludge that the Viennese think of as coffee. Ray paused in his conversation.

"Don't mind Konrad. He is a sworn officer, indeed an armed officer, whose real job is to provide protection to my office suite and the Director's," Rosch explained. "In the unlikely event that the Ottomans or the Mogul come back and get through our first three lines of defense."

Bowman sipped briefly at the sludge and quickly returned the cup to the silver tray. "Karl Potgeiter, a retired IAEA inspector, still consulting with them, died in a car crash in Grinzing last August. He was originally from South Africa. I wonder if you had a file on him, and if the crash was investigated as possibly more than an accident."

Rosch turned to the armed waiter who was about to leave the office. "Konrad, please go to my computer and pull up the file on this Potgeiter for us." Rosch clearly trusted the young waiter and aide-de-camp. "While we are waiting, Ray, I must tell you that I was impressed at who arranged this meeting for you. Not every Caribbean beach bum has the White House as his concierge."

"Here it is Herr Rosch," Konrad called out from the other side of the room. "Shall I summarize?"

"Bitte, Konrad, *ja."*

"South African nuclear physicist, worked for the IAEA. Suspected of prior involvement in the Apartheid regime and its nuclear bomb program. Lived in Grinzing. Wife deceased in 2013. Son lived nearby. No suspicious reports or inquiries about either man," Konrad read out.

"And his death?" Ray asked.

"Traffic fatality. Erratic driving. Collided with a tram. Tram driver cleared of any wrongdoing."

"You think there is more?" Rosch asked, looking over his glasses at Bowman.

"We think he was involved in a South African expat organization called the Trustees that controlled large sums of money," Bowman replied. "I am also slightly suspicious of the reason for the erratic driving. It would not be the first BMW to have been hacked. Could I perhaps see the accident investigation report. And maybe talk with the son?"

"Well, I could ask the Wien Polizei for their traffic investigation. That may take a day to get here." Rosch rose from the armchair and went to read the computer screen that his aide had called up. "Meanwhile, perhaps Konrad could help you find the son." As he neared his desk, one of the telephones on it rang. Rosch listened to the caller for a minute, thanked him, and hung up.

"Well Raymond, you may not have wanted the American Embassy to know that you are here, but you seemed to have failed in that regard."

"How is that?" Bowman asked, stepping away from the warmth of the fire.

"Seems you were followed here by a team of three young men from Boltzmanngasse. Perhaps it's just a training exercise for your CIA friends."

Ray laughed aloud. "Gunter, the only way you would know that is if your guys were doing countersurveillance on me."

Rosch spread his arms out, the palms of his big hands showing. "Raymond, naturally we are giving you the services we afford our friends. Would not want some al Qaeda fellow pushing you in front of one of our trams." He turned the computer screen so that the American could see what he had been scanning. Bowman's German was insufficient for the electronic file to have much significance to him. "I notice, Raymond, you did not ask me to help you get access to his bank accounts with these vast sums of money. I trust you have already accessed them in some way, without, of course, violating the Austrian Bank Secrecy Law."

Ray Bowman smiled at his colleague. "I would not want to burden you with too many requests, Gunter."

"Well then, Konrad, this is a chance for you to get back on the street. Take a car and go find the son, this Johann Potgeiter. Be polite about it, but get him to talk."

6

"The crash was just there," Konrad Voltke pointed. "Potgeiter was coming down the street into the city, as was the trolley. He sped up to pass the trolley and turned right in front of it, attempting to get into Daring-ergasse, but he was not far enough in front of the number 38 and it hit him when he turned. The tram driver did not have time to stop. The car exploded and burned poor Herr Potgeiter beyond all recognition. The file says they did the identification with dental records."

They were sitting in one of BM.I's many, blue BMWs, a five series. "Why would Pot-geiter want to turn into that street? Where does it go? Where was he going?" Bowman asked his young driver.

"It's a residential street, nothing special,"

Konrad replied. "Herr Potgeiter was driving into the Innenstadt for his morning coffee and newspaper read, as was his custom, at least that's what the accident investigation report says. I called a friend in the Polizei and he read it to me. The actual file will show up tomorrow morning."

"So, why veer right into Daringergasse?"

"Why indeed? You think he was drugged, perhaps, Herr Bowman?"

"No, Herr Voltke, I think he was hacked, or rather, his car was."

As they drove up the Grinzinger Alle into the little town, Bowman scanned the BM.I police file on the dead man's son, Johann. From what he could discern from the German language report, the son of the late South African physicist was forty-two and had become an Austrian citizen. He worked as a financial analyst and investor in the private equity arm of an old Viennese bank. Speaks English. Married to an Austrian woman, he has three daughters. Since his father's death, they had moved a few streets over into the father's larger house, the house Johann had grown up in. There was nothing suspicious about him. Nonetheless, the BM.I had a file on him. Some habits die hard, Bowman thought as they entered the square.

The Potgeiter house looked modern, white, with a lot of glass. A man who could be Johann was taking grocery bags from the back of a Volvo station wagon in the garage, as the BVT car pulled up. "Herr Potgeiter?" Konrad called out as he and Bowman walked up the short driveway. "Konrad Voltke, Federal Interior Ministry."

"Oh, no, not about the taxes again?" Potgeiter replied.

"No, we are here about a request from the American government. Herr Thomas here is with their Treasury Department. We would like to talk with you about some funds that transferred through American banks."

"It's a routine money laundering investigation, but you are not the target or under suspicion," Ray Bowman said, showing his identification as Harold Thomas. "We just need your help." Johann Potgeiter showed them into the house.

The three men settled around a table in the informal dining area off the kitchen. The picture window looked up at the vineyards on the hill behind the house. In a city of small apartments, this was a spacious home. California style, Johann called it. He spoke in German-accented English.

"When my father died, I took over managing many of the accounts he ran as a favor to his friends from the old days. Many of South African expats trusted him to manage their money and he did very well for them, I must say," Johann said. "Naturally, I didn't ask them where their money came from. I assume they liquidated their land and such in the old country in time, before the land values crashed after the takeover. Such crime there now, nobody wants to own things there."

"Except gold and diamonds, of course," Ray added.

"Yes, stocks in the mines are still doing well, but the rest? Such destruction of value there has been in the country of my birth. They were not prepared to govern and they have driven so many of the good people overseas. Like my father, like me."

"So you don't know where the funds came from, except that they were from friends of your dad's?" Ray asked. "Just before he died, your father received a series of deposits totaling five hundred million dollars in a few days' time. Do you know about that?"

Johann Potgeiter shook his head. He seemed a typical upper-middle-class Viennese, but he was being unusually cooperative with two men who had just appeared on his driveway. "To tell the truth, while he picked good investments, he kept bad records. I don't really know too well what happened before he died."

Konrad Voltke looked at Ray Bowman in a way that suggested that there was not too much point in pressing the issue with Johann, at least not now. Bowman nodded his head, indicating that Konrad should pick up the questioning.

"About his death, I'm sorry to bring you back to that day, but did you talk with him that morning," Konrad asked in perfect English.

"No, unfortunately. Usually we would speak in the evenings. I had talked to him the night before and he was in good spirits. Naturally, I have been over all of this with the Polizei."

"And do you know why he was turning into the street, the Daringergasse?" Konrad inquired.

Johann Potgeiter stared out and up at the vineyards. "I have wondered that so many times. So many times because I have to drive that way so often, past the spot." He turned back to Konrad Voltke. "My conclusion is that he forgot something at home and was going to turn around. He could be so focused in thought sometimes that he would not notice the world around him.

That's why we never had him babysit with our girls. They are hard enough for us to handle."

Bowman wondered to what degree Johann Potgeiter's answers were rehearsed, or at least thought out, not spontaneous. Had the son of the late nuclear bomb maker been waiting for a visit like this from the authorities? Bowman knew he needed to change the tempo of the discussion.

"Your father was a member of the Trustees, a cabal of the leaders of the former South African defense industrial complex. So, have you replaced him in that role? Are you coordinating your investment decisions with those of the other Trustees who also each got a half billion dollars days before your father died?"

Potgeiter did not blink. "I am not a Trustee of anything, Herr Thomas. And no one tells me how to invest." His demeanor did not change. "And, as I said, I don't really know about funds that moved around before my father died."

Bowman tried again. "Johann, if you knew that your father was murdered, that the controls for his car were hacked and he was driven into the oncoming tram, that he did not drive himself into it, would you want to find out who did that to him?"

Johann Potgeiter was silent for a moment, a blank look on his face. He turned to the Austrian security man. "Is that what happened, Herr Voltke?" There was still no emotion.

Konrad Voltke was caught off guard, first by Bowman's line of attack and then by Potgeiter's question to him. "The Polizei's official conclusion is that it was a traffic accident, but we, ah, we wondered if you accepted that?"

"I have no reason not to accept what the Polizei told me. Unless there is some new information. Is there, Herr Thomas? Does the U.S. Treasury Department know something that the Polizei missed?" He pronounced the words U.S. Treasury Department in a tone that almost implied he thought his houseguest was perhaps from some other part of the American government.

"We are always suspicious when billions of dollars slosh around in strange channels and then people die, Herr Potgeiter," Bowman said rising from the table. "If you should be contacted by the Trustees, please do let us know. Thank you for your time."

Back in the BMW, Konrad Voltke looked at a text message on his mobile. "The boss wants to see us at his home. It's not far, it's here in the Eighteenth District."

"What did you think of Johann?" Bowman asked as they drove down the hill.

"Practiced liar."

"What part?"

"I couldn't tell, perhaps all of it," Konrad replied.

The Deputy Director of the BVT lived in a house that looked too small for the tall iron gate and fence around it. Indeed, it had been an out building, a carriage house, for the larger villa next door. The fencing had been part of the original estate. Now it was a small home in a neighborhood of large homes, many of which had been divided up into multiple units. Konrad had an electronic gate opener that worked at his boss's house. He was obviously a regular visitor. "I often drive him to work," he explained as they parked.

Inside, the former carriage house seemed spacious and warm. A wing addition provided a large, open plan dining room and kitchen. Bowman heard music coming from the second floor. "My sons," Gunter Rosch said, pointing upstairs. "They say they cannot study without their music. I think it is why their mother volunteers at the hospital in the late afternoon."

At home, the Deputy Director of the

Austrian domestic intelligence service looked more like a farmer: unfashionable blue jeans, a plaid short-sleeved shirt, and a tall beer in one hand. "So you had a successful meeting with Potgeiter?"

"No we didn't, I'm afraid," Bowman said, taking a proffered glass of the local brew. "He was uninformative."

Konrad Voltke joined them. "I've been out at the car, using the radio to chat with my boys down at the Polizei. The charred wreck of the late Potgeiter's car was crushed after the investigation. We will not be able to examine its computers."

"*Ach,* so," Rosch smiled. "Well, if Johann was not informative, his neighborhood was very interesting. My countersurveillance team on you detected two, amazing, two distinct sets of people looking at the house while you were in it. You are quite a magnet, Raymond."

"The U.S. Embassy boys and who else?" Ray asked.

"That's what is so fascinating. Neither one of them were the Americans from this morning. We waved them off at the Palais Modena and they stayed away after that."

Rosch was smiling, hardly able to contain his enthusiasm that his team had stumbled into something fascinating. "My countersurveillance unit on you was not big enough to handle such a surprising situation, but they got enough information that we should be able to track down your tails and identify them. It was a good drill for my boys. They had never caught a double surveillance before."

The enthusiasm was contagious. "Well, maybe we are flushing the birds we wanted to find. Maybe I should stay a few more days before I go to Israel," Ray thought aloud.

"May I suggest you do consider altering your travel plans, Ray? I talked to a friend today, after you left my office, my counterpart in South Africa," Rosch said. "They knew all about the Trustees and they, too, are suspicious about their deaths. In fact, the investigation is apparently their number one priority. They would very much like to compare notes with you as soon as possible, in Cape Town."

"Never been to Cape Town," Ray replied. "Well, I can delay the trip to Israel a couple of days if the South Africans have been investigating all this and think they have something to share. Tell him I accept his invitation."

Gunter Rosch emitted a good belly laugh. "You are booked in First on the Qatar flight tomorrow morning out of Schwechat to Doha and then on to Cape Town, courtesy of my friend Mbali, but, Raymond, make no mistake, Mbali Hlanganani is definitely not a him."

7

THURSDAY, OCTOBER 20
ABOARD QATAR AIR FLIGHT #808
DOHA TO CAPE TOWN

The din was gone. Cocooned by the J. S. Bach from the Bose headphones, mesmerized by the clouds catching the sunset's rays below, he felt a clarity as he moved south toward Africa. His mind had been blank for almost an hour. Rarely was he ever fully in a moment, but at thirty-eight thousand feet, sipping the Dom, staring out the overly large window of the Dreamliner, he had let his prefrontal processor idle. He knew what would happen.

When it started again, whatever his internal analytics would bring up first would be the most salient, the thing they had been chewing on while the part of his brain of which he was most fully aware had been thinking about the annoying rituals of the airports in Vienna and Doha.

When they began to surface now for consideration, the thoughts came softly, as though he had always known that they were there, waiting in the queue to be fully recognized.

Why, part of him asked, why did it have to be him, again?

He had found the strength to run away and try a different life after all the deaths, on both sides, in the drone program. For a long time after Sandra's death he woke in the middle of the night in a sweat, thinking that drone was going to fly into his window. That dream had stopped happening, thanks to Dr. Rosenthal and thanks to his new life.

And that new life was pleasant. It was good for his body and good for his mind. He realized slowly what normal was like, realized how on edge his prior life had been. Sure, he was not contributing to anything, except perhaps raising the level of bar service at Skinny Legs, but why did you have to contribute to something? Most people just lived their lives, without any sense of obligation to do anything more than to be good to their family, their friends.

Where had he gotten this crazy internal imperative that he had to contribute on a higher plain, make things better, or at least stop them from getting worse? Why did he think that he had to give purpose to his life when we were, after all, just a speck in a multiverse that no human had ever fully understood?

He had been hiding in paradise, hiding from himself, from dealing with choices he did not want to confront openly. The central choice came down to this: Should he continue to do the work at which he was very good, in a business that was very bad, at least for its participants? It was work that had to be done, but it ate away at those who did it and left them unfulfilled, left some a hollowed-out shell, left others dead. And with some of the now dead, he had let himself develop a bond in life. He had decided that doing nothing, or close to it, was better. The sunsets and the sands, the beer and the books, the wine and the women could fill his day and most of the night.

Yet he had taken the mission. Because it was an excuse to go back to it all? Because this was a mission, which, if it failed, would have consequences that would make life so much worse for so many? Because he believed, despite suppressing his arrogance, that he might really be the only one who could figure it out? But he was an analyst, that was his strength, and now he was once again in the field, alone and at a disadvantage in almost everything he did. Maybe Jefferson and Locke were more profound than he had given them credit for, arguing that the pursuit of happiness was a goal. Well, he had found some degree of happiness on the hill overlooking that sleepy Caribbean harbor, with Emily and Linda. He wondered if he could ever get that back.

The sunset on the clouds was fading, even at altitude. It was night in Zanzibar, below, or was that just the name of a track from Thelonious Monk? The Dom was gone and now a new Bach Passion began to play.

8

THURSDAY, OCTOBER 20
THE BAY HOTEL, CAMPS BAY
CAPE TOWN, SOUTH AFRICA

"My name is Cammil," the bartender began. "You look like you have had a long day." The small Traders bar was empty, but a welcoming fire was lit in the fireplace, despite the fact that the air conditioning was on.

Having been until recently a bartender himself, Raymond Bowman felt suddenly at home with Cammil's greeting, even though he had never been to South Africa before. "Yeah, long flight. Just checked in to the hotel. Very nice place." He had not known what to expect, but the clean, modern airport, the quick ride to this beach resort, the sleek hotel, all made him feel more like he was in Malibu than in South Africa. "What local beer do you recommend?"

"Well, most people will have Windhoek,

maybe their Tafel, but if you be asking me what I would drink on expense account, I would go micro," Cammil explained as he reached for a beer mug. "Best microbrewery now be Robson's East Coast. You like a pale ale, try theirs."

"Well, that's what I'll be having then."

Cammil poured it perfectly, almost to the point of overflowing, but not quite. Then he excused himself. "I be right back, if anyone else show up, you tell them, I be right back."

Ray liked the idea of being alone in a bar again, as he was when he closed up at Skinny Legs. He looked out at the ocean, dark as night beyond the beach. He thought a nice run on the sand and a dip in the waves would be a good way to start the day in the morning, before he got a taxi into downtown Cape Town to meet his hosts, the local security service.

"Is the bartender here?" It was a woman who was seated behind him in a wingback chair by the fire. He hadn't noticed her before.

"No," Ray said, turning and smiling. "He'll be right back."

"That's what the termite asked," she said.

"I beg your pardon?" Ray said, shaking his head at the striking, tall woman in the chair. As he walked toward her, he realized he was staring at her long legs. "I didn't get that."

"Most people don't. Termite walks into a bar and asks, 'Is the bartender here?' " she said. "Here, have a seat with me by the fire, Mr. Bowman."

The jet lag, the strangeness of the last few days, the incongruity of him being in Cape Town, and now a beautiful woman who knew who he was. "My name is Brad Radford," he said, sitting in the chair opposite her.

"No, that is the name on your passport, but you are Raymond J. Bowman" she said in an accent he could not place, a formal, precise, lilting, slightly pinched English. "And you like Cohibas. So there is one here for you. After all, Traders is the best cigar bar in Cape Town. That is why I booked you into the hotel here. That and the fact that it is a little bit out of town."

He shook his head in surprise, then laughed. "You are my host?" Ray asked, sniffing the Cohiba.

"Mbali Hlanganani, at your service, sir." She reached a long bare arm across the drinks table. "Forgive my rudeness. I wanted to meet you at the airport, but the day went long so I thought I would come out and share a drink with you."

106

Cammil had returned and was standing by their seats.

"Mbali, sorry for the delay. I had to go downstairs to find your Pinotage. Here you go. The L'Avenir '99 from Stellenbosch."

"Thank you, Cammil, and thank you for closing the bar tonight for us." She sloshed the purple liquid in the glass and then delicately sniffed the air above it. "Perfect."

"Mondays are slow," the barkeep admitted.

"We'll still pay the usual for closing the bar," she smiled back at him.

"You're a regular?" Ray asked.

"I live nearby. Small place near the beach my father bought for me. I could never afford it on a civil servant's salary, but he has done very well for himself in Durban, part owner of a food store chain with some Indian gentlemen. Durban has always been a place where the races got along, not like Joburg and Pretoria."

"So you're from Durban?"

"Yes, well, KwaZulu. We were Inkatha up there," she said after sipping the wine. "So my family was not ANC."

"And yet you are the Director of the Special Security Services Office. A Zulu? How did that happen?" he asked.

"I did my graduate work on the AWB, the

Afrikaner Resistance Movement. You know, the guys with the Nazi flag imitation? My professor introduced me to Thabo Mbeke and he hired me as a young security advisor. Then, when he became President after Madiba stepped down, Tabo created the SSSO, Special Security Services Office, and put me there. Then after him Zuma liked the work I did tracing some of the state assets that disappeared just before Madiba became President. President Zuma is a Zulu. He wanted a fellow Zulu running the shop. So, like a tree vine in the forest, I kept getting higher because I happened to be attached to the right tree."

Bowman suddenly had the impression he was sitting across from one very accomplished individual, one who had probably overcome a lot of obstacles of race, gender, ethnicity, bureaucracy. "So, where was this very well-connected professor? Where did you go to university?"

"Oxford. They needed a black girl so they didn't feel like racists," she smiled.

"Sounds like you are an expert on racists, the AWB and all that," Bowman observed.

"They are not the real threat, Mr. Bowman."

"Call me Ray, please, or Brad, or . . ." he said. "Who is the real threat?"

"The AWB are farmers, like the Boeremag group were. Big, tall men, overfed, but dumb as oxen. The real white power structures, Afrikaner and English, laugh at those guys and their little Hitler clubs," she said in a softer, but deeper, more serious tone. "The power men ran the banks, the mines, the defense industry, the labs. They had the money and the real arms. They had the Special Forces in the Army and the intelligence units."

"I thought the whites still do run the banks and industry?" Ray asked.

"They do, but we took control of the Army, even Special Forces. We took over the intelligence services and the elite police units right away in the mid-nineties. They still run what's left of the defense industry, but it's nothing like what ARMSCOR was in the eighties. And we no longer have WMD programs in the labs. That I can assure you."

Ray was beginning to think that he might like working with this woman. She was a no-nonsense professional. "So, again, who is the threat?"

"The people I worry about are the expats. When they left they took billions in gold and diamonds, their own and the state's, plus what they could steal from the corporations. That kind of money is power, even if they haven't used it yet. And they do have an organization, still."

"The Trustees?" Ray asked.

"I've known about them for twenty years now. I gather Washington just figured out they exist," she laughed.

"Well, let's say Washington's recent attention to them was occasioned by their all acquiring a lot of money and then, their simultaneously dying by walking into bullets and falling off boats and balconies, and being hit by trolleys and trains," Ray replied.

"Washington does not share enough with us. We are not one of the Five Eyes. The Five Eyes are not just all English-speaking nations, they are all white majority nations." Mbali sat back in her chair. "You all shared with each other, the Brits, the Canadians, Australians, even New Zealand, but not with English-speaking nations run by brown people, not with India, not with Barbados, not with us. So, yes, we do not normally share much with Washington. We believe in two-way streets here, even if we do drive on the left."

"So when Washington asked about the five dead South African expats, you told them about the Trustees," Ray added.

"Yes, and only then did Washington tell us

110

about the flash. Eight weeks earlier it had been. Eight weeks and you did not tell us." She looked like steam might soon come from her ears.

"So you also think the events are related?" Ray asked.

"You know they are. That is why you are here, Mr. Bowman," she said, sounding more South African than British now.

"It's one theory we have, but it's odd that no nuclear bombs have shown up in the months since the flash. No rumors of bombs, at least not that wc have heard," he said, half asking if they had heard any and not told Washington.

"Last week, when our embassy in Washington reported to us that your government's theory is that South African expats may have had nuclear bombs for the last twenty-five years and now they sold some of them, Mr. Bowman, that caused a very great panic here at a very high level, the highest. My boss wanted to know how I could be following the Trustees so closely and miss that they had nuclears in storage all these years. It is now our only priority to find those bombs, before they go off in Soweto, and Joburg, and here on Table Mountain."

Ray squinted in the darkened room,

puzzled. "You think that they would detonate them here? Why would anybody want to do that? The folks back home think they will be detonated in Washington and New York just before our presidential election."

"Tell that to my President, who has been having us do a secret search of all sorts of places — ships, airplanes with Geiger counters. He thinks if the expats had nukes, they had them to cripple black-run South Africa, to create some white breakaway nation, some white Bantustan. He is obsessed with the possibility of these bombs going off here. And if he's not calmed down, it will leak out and there will be a huge panic."

Now Ray sat back in his wingback chair. "Well, it would seem that our two Presidents have at least that much in common."

"So, if you, the ex-bartender, are Washington's answer to how we find the bombs, then I will be like the termite. I will stick with you until you find these bombs and the people who stole them or bought them." She put down her wineglass and stood up. "So, we begin in the morning. Get some sleep. You look like you need it. I will send Marcus and the truck for you at nine. Call my Ops Room if you need anything before then. Here's the number." She dropped a card on the table and for the second time, she was extending her hand.

"Sala kahle, ukuthula," she said.

"I'm sorry, my Zulu is rusty," Ray replied.

"*Sala kahle* means good-bye and *ukuthula,* peace," she said.

Ray stood. "*Ukuthula.* I will see you tomorrow." He shook her hand and she promptly moved to the door.

"Cammil, next time we try the Delheim '99. It aged longer in the wood." She was gone.

Then the penny dropped and Raymond Bowman laughed aloud. Termite walks into a bar. Is the bartender here? Wow, this was going to be a ride.

9

FRIDAY, OCTOBER 21
CAMPS BAY
CAPE TOWN, SOUTH AFRICA

He woke early and ran on the beach, barefoot, then dove into the waves to cool down. It was summer in South Africa and he was reminded again of Malibu. As he showered, it occurred to him that if the South African media ever reported that the security services here were searching containers with Geiger counters, it would be less than forty-eight hours before the story broke in Washington that Homeland Security wanted to do the same thing in the United States, but the White House had delayed them. The Great Panic would then occur. It could happen at any time, just as the bombs could detonate at any time, and yet he had gotten nowhere in figuring out who had the bombs. He didn't really even know yet if there actually were loose nuclear bombs.

As he dressed in his gray summer weight suit, he realized that he was feeling excited, anticipating what it would be like to spend the day with Mbali. She was a professional of the type he enjoyed working with. He had a feeling that the day wouldn't be boring. As the doors of the elevator opened on to the lobby, he spotted a man in a black suit with a sign reading BRAD RADFORD. Nice, they were using the cover name he had for the visit to South Africa.

"Good morning, sir. I'm Lesedi from Mbali's office. Hope you had a good night. We have your car in the underground parking. Right this way," the driver said, leading him to a different elevator bank. "We'll have you downtown in no time."

In the basement, the driver had pulled the Mercedes S-Class up as close to the elevator bank as he could get it. A driver and an escort, Bowman noted.

"Hi, I'm Brad Radford," Bowman said to the driver as he sat down in the backseat. "What's your name?"

The driver hesitated, "Thaba. Thaba my name, sir." Lesedi got in next to Bowman and the car pulled toward the ticket gate. The doors locked.

"Where's Marcus this morning?" Ray asked.

Lesedi smiled, "He'll be meeting you at the office." The gate at the ticket booth rose. Thaba gunned the car up the ramp. Then he hit the brakes. Ray lurched forward. A truck had just pulled across the ramp entrance. There was a deafening noise, another, more, and bits were flying through the air inside the car. Then, just as quickly, it was over, but there was a heavy smell and smoke in the car, a painful noise ringing in his ears. Ray was covered in shattered glass. Blood had spattered in the passenger compartment, Thaba's blood and Lesedi's. Ray could see that Thaba had an entry wound in his forehead.

Before Bowman could react, there were men at each of the car's four doors. One was reaching in the shattered window on the driver's door, hitting the door lock control. Ray's door was opened and a white man with a gun in his hand was saying, "Special Services, Mr. Bowman. You're safe now. Please step out of the car."

Ray dusted the glass off himself and got out. He didn't see any blood on him, but there were stains of something. "Marcus Stroh," the man said, holstering the Sig Sauer. "We need to get you out of here before the police and the press show up. The truck is this way." Ray walked up the ramp toward a white Mercedes Sprinter step van, wondering whether the dead men or their killers were really there to protect him. Something about the man who called himself Marcus Stroh said he was to be trusted. Two black men in suits stood by the van door, holding automatic weapons. Inside, the van was rigged up with a VIP interior that looked like it had been ripped from a private jet. "I'm sorry, sir, we should have spotted their team before they got you. I also should have met you at your room. This is my fault."

As Ray sat in his leather chair in the truck and strapped in, he exhaled. His pulse was still racing. The truck began moving as Marcus closed the side door. "Thank you," Ray managed to get out. His mouth was as dry as it had ever been. He suppressed the urge to vomit. "It's not your fault. I shouldn't have fallen for it. Who were they?"

"Don't know. We weren't advised that there was a threat to you or we would have been set up a lot differently," Stroh replied. "We'll find out though. Now that we have the bodies, the car, the guns. We'll figure it out quickly. If I may ask, sir, who do you think they were?"

"Well, they didn't look like al Qaeda," Ray said, "but then, you never know, do you?"

Stroh nodded. "I'll have my boys collect your kit from the hotel and check you out. We'll put you up at the Service's guesthouse. It's at our training camp. Very nice. And secure." They were moving quickly through traffic, but in the windowless compartment, Ray had no idea where they were. After what Ray guessed was about half an hour, the truck pulled up to a security gate and then down into the basement of a building. As the side door of the truck opened, Mbali Hlanganani appeared in a gray business pantsuit. "Mr. Bowman, my abject apology. Really, Cape Town is not typically like this. Are you all right?"

Bowman stepped out of the Mercedes Sprinter. "I seem to be, thanks to Marcus and his team. Sorry, I'm not a field guy, not used to people being shot to death three feet from me."

"You never get used to that," she said.

"I would like to know who sent them."

"So would I, Raymond, so would I," she said. "But we shall, soon enough. Come, let's go up to my office and get you cleaned up and maybe a little something to calm you down a bit."

Fifteen minutes later he joined Mbali in

her wood-paneled conference room. "Good as new," he proclaimed. He had declined the sedative the doctor had offered. He had taken the vodka shot. "Shall we get to work?"

One wall of the conference room had a flat screen and a whiteboard and Mbali looked something like a professor standing between them. "Truly, Raymond, I am so sorry," she began. "But, yes, to work. Here on the screen are photos of the Trustees, all of whom were killed. Karl Potgeiter was hit by the trolley in Vienna at 0503 Greenwich Mean Time that day, or as you Americans say, Zulu time." She smiled for the first time since meeting Bowman at the truck. "I like calling it Zulu time, for obvious reasons."

Bowman chuckled, forgetting for the moment what had happened an hour before.

Mbali continued, "Potgeiter had been the Director of Weapon Design at Pelindaba."

"Pelindaba?" Bowman asked.

"Where they built the nuclear bombs. After Madiba's election, President Mandela's election, Potgeiter moved to Vienna and landed a job with the IAEA. Partially retired from there a few years back, but worked every day on the Trustee's fund he managed. His son, Johann has replaced him, but then you met him, didn't you?

Viennese police didn't think there was any chance of murder, until you showed up. Now they have reopened the case."

Click. A face appeared on the screen, Dawid Steyn.

"Dawid was the successor as a Trustee to his father, who had directed the nuclear delivery program at ARMSCOR in the eighties and early nineties. It was really a version of the Israeli Jericho missile, with a lot of help from Tel Aviv. He is succeeded as a Trustee by his wife, Rachel. Dawid fell under a train at 0528 Zulu that day. Tel Aviv police have video of a man pushing Steyn off the platform, but they have made no progress figuring out who the man was."

Click. "Marius Plessis," Mbali said as the next face appeared. "Fell from a high balcony in Dubai at 0620 Zulu, an hour after the previous death in Tel Aviv. He had been the Treasurer, what we would now call the Chief Financial Officer, at ARMSCOR until 1993. Dubai police also have a video, showing an unknown man in a waiter's uniform entering the room. No leads. Plessis's daughter who lives in Toronto has started to manage his accounts. She has an MBA from MIT. I am told that is quite an accomplishment?"

"Sure is," Ray responded. "Big quant

program. Math, numbers. Digit heads."

Click. "Cornelius Coetzee took a bullet in Singapore at 0540 Zulu, a rare occurrence there," Mbali said consulting a file. "Singapore Police and also their Internal Security have turned the city upside down, but so far nothing. He had been the Deputy Director for Foreign Operations in the Apartheid Security Service. Was also close to Mossad and to the Taiwanese service. His brother Robert in Hong Kong now has the keys to the kingdom. Robert's a bit younger, manages a hotel chain they own. He had been in the Special Forces in the eighties and early nineties."

"I wonder if he wants to avenge his brother's death?" Ray asked.

Mbali shrugged and continued on with the next victim.

Click. "Willem Merwe fell off a ferry boat in Sydney Harbour at 0525 Zulu. He had become a Trustee after his father died. Dad had been a young Admiral in the Apartheid Navy, last job was as Director of Plans for the South African Defence Ministry. New South Wales Police had no reason to believe foul play. We have asked them to reopen the case and they have agreed to. Willem has been replaced by a Paul Wyk, who is an investment banker in Wellington, New

121

Zealand. Wyk's father had been an Army General in charge of weapons development." She clicked the projector off and the lights rose.

"So, with the exception of the guy in Dubai, whoever did this pulled off four murders in four cities within twenty minutes, making most of them look like accidents," Ray observed.

"Dubai guy slept in," Mbali added. "Otherwise it would have been five in less than half an hour. This is not the work of some group of schoolboys."

"It would be very difficult for any American intelligence or military unit to do that, especially without getting caught. Could your service do that, not that you did?" he asked.

"I would like to say we did, but alas no one would let me and, of course, we are not that good." She poured herself coffee and sat down opposite Bowman. "It took extensive planning, area knowledge, coordination, communications. We would have used teams of twenty or more per target, watchers, comms guys, drivers, safe house landlords, documents men. I don't have one hundred people to deploy overseas. I might be able to field one team like that, but not five. Who could?"

"If the U.S. used the Agency's Clandestine Service and military Special Ops, I suppose we could in a pinch. Otherwise? Russia, maybe Israel. Nobody else," Bowman thought out loud.

"Our conclusion as well. We ruled you out for lack of motive and because the only people you seem to be allowed to kill are al Qaeda and ISIS," she said, pouring him a coffee. "We haven't been able to imagine a motive that would get the SVR out doing this sort of thing. What would be in it for Russia?"

"Which leaves Israel?" Bowman asked.

"Maybe, they could be cleaning up loose ends. Didn't want the story coming out that old South African nuclear weapons in their control had suddenly disappeared?" Mbali offered.

Ray shook his head, no. "First, we don't really know that the Israelis had old South African nukes or, if they did, that anybody took them from them. All I really have is the guy at the IAEA who was told over twenty years ago that the weapons went to Israel. So, we think the bombs were not destroyed. We think one of them went off in August in the Indian Ocean, just like the test South Africa or Israel did in 1979. We think that the Trustees may have had the

123

bombs and sold them and that, whoever bought the bombs, then killed the sellers."

Mbali folded her arms across her chest and looked at Ray Bowman. "You say it like it's just a theory, but it has both your President and mine convinced and both of them are about to go to battle stations looking for these loose nukes. So, for what it's worth, I am buying the theory. I like my job."

Ray nodded. "It's plausible. And, therefore, we have to operate as if we knew with a certainty that it were true. Because, if it is true and we don't do everything we can to get these before the nukes go off somewhere or the new owners threaten to set them off . . ." He let the thought hang in the air.

She stood and looked Ray in the eye. "If they exist, Mr. Bowman, I am going to find those bombs, and soon. That is what I told my President and I intend to fulfill that promise."

"Right, so back to the possibilities then," he said and turned to face the whiteboard. "If the Israelis did get the bombs back then, in the nineties, there is no way that they would have preserved them. They don't need them and they wouldn't want old designs like that anyway. They would have harvested the enriched uranium.

"Besides, no one is getting a nuclear weapon out of Israel and no Israeli agency is going to throw one of their own citizens under a train in Tel Aviv. No, I don't buy it."

Mbali leaned back in her leather chair. "Well, you know the Israelis better than we do. We've never really reestablished close ties. So, if not America, South Africa, Russia, or Israel, who?"

Ray moved to the whiteboard and listed those four nations with a blue marker. "We question our assumptions. Even though it makes no sense, maybe it was one of those four. Or, it was the fifth alternative."

"Martians?" she asked.

"Nonstate actor," he said and wrote it on the board. "Terrorist group? The White House thinks it must be al Qaeda. Narco-criminal cartel? Mega corporation?"

"You mean like Google?" Mbali laughed.

"They don't do evil, just ask them, but there are lots of big companies that have their own little intelligence services and security teams, with ex–Special Forces, ex-spooks," he suggested. "Chinese companies, Russian, Korean, even Saudi, Mexican, and Brazilian."

"Like Carlos Slim, the Mexican phone billionaire. What's he going to do with a nuclear weapon?" she asked. "I think it's far more likely that it was a coup within the Afrikaner world, some offshoot of the Trustees, some parallel group we didn't know about. My President is not entirely nuts to think that there may be some group of weird white folk who want to re-create their old South Africa somehow. Maybe they take over Namibia and threaten to blow us up if there is resistance or if South Africa threatens to invade."

Bowman looked at his new South African colleague for a minute, as he stood in front of the whiteboard and she spun about in her chair. "If there were some coup within the Afrikaner expat world, you would know. It's your expertise, your raison d'être to know what the crazier whites are up to. You don't believe that scenario for a minute, do you?"

"No, not really. We'd have heard something," she agreed. "But there is a guy who might know what's going on. He's one of them, could have become one of the Trustees, but didn't. He stayed here. Instead he and his two boys opened a winery. He's never really helped us very much, but he's agreed to see you. Still loves America."

The telephone rang and Mbali answered,

"Hlanganani." She listened for a second, "Send him in." Marcus Stroh joined them. "Who were they? Who were Mr. Bowman's attempted kidnappers?" she asked without preliminaries.

"We got prints off both of them, Director," Stroh reported. "Both were on record, living in Sea Point. They're with Black Eagle."

"What's that?" Ray asked.

"Nigerian drug group, with Italian Mafia connections. They've set up shop in Joburg and down here in Sea Point. We've let in tens of thousands of Nigerians and they're nothing but trouble," she explained. "But these guys were South Africans?"

"Yes, Director, but working for Nigerian Black Eagle," Stroh answered.

"Find out where their Big Man is. When we have him fixed, I'll call the Chief of Special Branch and set up a raid to pick him up and bring him in," she directed.

"Yes, ma'am, but that could be a big fire fight."

"Not if we do it right, Marcus. They'll never see it coming. First, find him." She looked over at Ray. "You know, Raymond, when a Zulu chief moves about his country, he is accompanied by men skilled with arrows. Today, you are going to be my bow man. We are going on a little helicopter ride to Stellenbosch."

10

The Augusta 129 lifted off from the Special Services compound and took a tourist ride over Table Mountain for Ray Bowman's benefit. The long, flat-topped mountain stood at the edge of the city like a theater prop placed to provide a setting. Cape Town was a city like none other he had ever seen, a gem by the sea. Mbali asked the pilot to swoop over Robben Island, where Nelson Mandela had spent two decades in a cold cell. Once the aircraft set a westerly course for the wine country, they were there in less than fifteen minutes.

The pilot circled the winery, confirming the landing area on radio to an advance team that had checked out the winery. He then gently placed the aircraft down in the cleared space, kicking up walls of dust and dirt. They sat in the cabin with the doors closed, while the engine spun down and the dust storm settled. The copilot then exited the aircraft and pulled open the cabin door from the outside. Hendrik and Pieter Roosmeer were waiting for them, still brushing off the dust. The brothers looked to be in their forties, dressed alike in green polo shirts bearing the logo of the winery and jeans. They courteously introduced themselves, shaking hands first with Mbali and then Ray.

"Our father is waiting inside the winery, in the Library Reserve Room. He's anxious to meet you. Please, follow me," Hendrik Roosmeer said.

Bowman looked out across the rolling hills, covered in vines. Whitewashed stucco buildings were scattered across the valley. Another mountain sat in the near distance, almost as perfectly placed as Table Mountain was to Cape Town. Aside from the mountain, it reminded him of Sonoma, but maybe the way it might have been fifty years ago. The sun was casting a yellow light across the scene. After the beauty of Cape Town from the air and now this magnificent valley, Bowman had to remind himself that the day had begun with men who had kidnapped him and then been shot to death a few feet from him.

Inside, the man at the head of the heavy, wooden table was clearly the laird of the manor. Slightly stooped, but still tall and thin, he had a regal mane of thick white hair. Looking at him, Ray thought this is what Hendrik and Pieter would look like in three decades. The older man was pouring from a crystal decanter into one of the dozen or more wineglasses before him. The afternoon sun was slanting through one of the narrow strips of stained glass that topped off the wood-paneled walls. It seemed like another incongruity to Bowman. This appeared to be a setting for a sommeliers' retreat, not for an interrogation about nuclear bombs.

"Johann Roosmeer, the winemakers' assistant," the old man said, offering his hand to Mbali. "They are the winemakers, the new wave," he said, pointing at his sons. "How familiar are you with our wines?"

Mbali set herself on one of the stools around the tasting table. "I like to think I know something about Pinotage, but I have to admit that I have not had the pleasure of tasting yours, and certainly not the Library Reserve."

"That's because there hasn't been any of our Pinotage. It's been off the market for seven years while we grew new vines, clones, on the hillside, much better terroir for that grape than down in the valley. Here, try." He handed her a tall stemmed glass. "It's the 2014. Very young, a barrel tasting. We have not yet bottled it. The older vintages here in the Library are awful."

She went to taste and then stopped, held her head back and sniffed, rolling the red-purple liquid in the glass. "It has bouquet," she sounded surprised. "Normally the better Pinotage have none. The regular Pinotage can smell like paint or rubbing alcohol. This smells like berries."

Johann Roosmeer smiled in appreciation. "You do know Pinotage. Yes, the good ones have no bouquet and that is because they vent it to get rid of the acetone odor. This clone has no acetone odor and I mix it with twenty-five percent Shiraz and Cab Sav, as is allowed under South African law."

Mbali finished sniffing and tasted, with her head back and her eyes closed. "Wonderful," she said, "truly marvelous. When will it be bottled?"

"Hendrik, can we fill a bottle for our guest? It will be the first bottle of the vintage."

The two brothers took that as their cue to leave their guests in the hands of their father. When they left, he poured three glasses of Shiraz from another decanter. "Hendrik went to the University of California at Davis. So did his sister, but she stayed there. Married an American. So, you see, I have three American grandchildren. But then you know that, don't you? Pieter studied here at Stellenbosch's OVRI. As I said, Hendrik and Pieter are the winemakers. I just assist."

"OVRI?" Ray asked, feeling left out of the discussion to this point.

"Sorry. You are the American, of course you would not know. Our Institute of Oeneological and Vintacultural Research. It's modeled on your UC Davis, bringing us into the twenty-first century of global winemaking."

Mbali tasted the Shiraz. "This has the Boekenhoutskloof beat hands down. This will get the medal this year."

"You flatter an old man," Roosmeer beamed, sitting himself down on a stool. "You butter me up so I will talk? Pieter said you wanted to bring an important American here to talk about the old days. Can't we let them die, the old days? We had the Truth Commission to put all of this behind us."

Mbali put down her glass. "Some things from the old days have come back. The Trustees have all been killed. You were once one of them. Your life may be in danger."

Johann Roosmeer nodded, while looking at his shoes. "I heard about the deaths. Something is obviously going on, but you are wrong about one thing, I was never, what did you call them, a Trustee? They wanted me to go with them, but I could not leave this country. This is home. My people have been here for centuries."

Ray moved around Mbali and sat on the stool closest to the old man. "We have to dig up the past. Because what they worked on here before they left, they may have later worked on abroad. That may be why they were killed. That's why I have come from Washington. We need your help, sir."

Roosmeer took a mouthful of the Shiraz. After a moment, he opened up, as he had apparently always intended to do. "We all saw it coming. Apartheid was a huge mistake. It had to end. The blacks, the coloreds, the Indians all would get the vote in the end, peacefully or violently. We would be the minority.

"In a way, we were like the KGB. They saw the end of Communism, of the Soviet Union, coming at about the same time. Odd

134

coincidence really. The KGB mid-level leadership stashed gold abroad. They got ready to be the new wealthy Russians. Putin was part of that group, I'm told."

Ray nodded his agreement.

Roosmeer continued. "My colleagues planned for years. We sold arms technology abroad, secretly, despite the UN embargo, to Israel, Singapore, Taiwan, Chile, Korea. ARMSCOR was very good in those days, we made the best field artillery in the world, good antitank missiles, antiship missiles, all sorts of things. We did not repatriate the money, the hard currencies, couldn't really. So we grew into having these huge offshore accounts.

"Then the men you call the Trustees hit up the mining interests for diamonds and gold from the reserves, smuggled them out of the country for the future when the blacks would take over. It was worth billions of U.S. dollars, the cash, the stones, the gold. No one wanted just to hand that over to Mandela and his lot."

Ray knew all of that, but he kept the conversation going.

"And the purpose of the money was to rearm and come back, grab a piece of South Africa for a new, smaller white lager?"

"No, no, that was just the talk," Roosmeer

said. "The money was to set us all up abroad in nice new homes, new companies, new lives. It was capital for the diaspora to start new businesses, to buy land so our children could still inherit some great plots from us when we die. Money for emergencies, maybe to get the rest of us out of the country if the race war started. It didn't start, of course."

"And you didn't go," Mbali said. "You were the Deputy Director of the ballistic missile program, just as high up as the others."

"They gave me some money to buy the winery, in case you had not guessed that part. They thought I was crazy to stay. They were wrong," Roosmeer replied.

Ray pressed on. "As a head of the ballistic missile program, you worked closely with the nuclear weapons team. Did you know that they lied to the UN, to the IAEA?"

"I could see that. They told the UN people that the only weapons we had were the six devices, not made at Pelindaba as people thought but a little ways away at an ARMSCOR place called the Circle Building. Each of them weighed a metric ton. They were 1.8 meters long. They were the devices we planned for the testing program. You could not really deliver a weapon like

136

that, although they pretended they would put them in the old Buccaneer bomber. Those bombs we admitted to the UN, they were devices designed to go off in the test shafts, to scare the Cubans and the Communists, to prevent them from invading from their bases in Angola and Mozambique."

Ray filled in the blanks in the story. "So the test weapons from the Circle Building were dismantled and the HEU went back from ARMSCOR to the Atomic Energy Commission at Pelindaba. That was the highly enriched uranium, the weapons-grade stuff, they showed the IAEA. Then they told the UN that was all that they had ever made, when in fact they had more."

Roosmeer poured more of the Shiraz for himself and Mbali. "So you know the story? Why do you need me?"

"What did they do with the rest of the HEU?" Ray asked.

The older man chuckled. "Pretty obvious, no? They made missile warheads for the Jericho-II rockets that I was building from the Israeli designs. Smaller warheads, less HEU than the test devices, about half as much, but higher yields because they were boosted with tritium gas in little bottles. Instead of the eighteen-kiloton explosions of the test devices, they would have a yield of fifty kilotons."

Mbali looked at Bowman. "Sounds like a much bigger bomb?"

"Three times bigger than Hiroshima," Roosmeer answered before Ray could. "We had six of them finished when it all ended in '91. They fit perfectly on my missiles."

"And they were not dismantled?" Ray asked.

Roosmeer rose and went to another decanter. "This one is a blend of Cab Sav, Petit Verdot, and Cab Franc. Like what the Americans call meritage."

Ray stood and walked toward Roosmeer and accepted the glass of the red blend. "One of them went off in the Indian Ocean in August, Mr. Roosmeer. Where are the others?"

"If you know that one went off, I don't. Where did they go from here? Israel, that's what I was told, but I don't know. That was not my job. I made the missiles. Then an American came, young hotshot from the State Department, and got de Klerk to close my missile program, too. We could have used my missiles to send up satellites, but no, they were destroyed, the rocket engines, the missiles, everything I had built." His tone had changed. "That is why I hated de

138

Klerk, Mr. Radford. You want to know where the missile warheads went. Ask the Israelis. Don't you Americans pay for them to have their own country, surrounded by the Arabs? You haven't decided yet that their apartheid is bad, too, have you?"

Mbali moved to cut the tension between the two men.

"Mr. Roosmeer, if those missile warheads are on the loose now as we think they might be, if that is why the Trustees were killed, if that is why something went off in the Indian Ocean last year, we are all at risk. The Pinotage won't be drinkable with strontium-ninety in it."

Johann Roosmeer took off his glasses and rubbed his eyes.

"Avraham Reuven is still alive in Israel. He worked with me and with Potgeiter and Steyn. He was from their Defense Ministry. He might know what happened to the warheads. He lives outside of Tel Aviv, up in the hills." Roosmeer poured the rest of the wine in his glass into the sink. "But be careful. They killed one of the Trustees outside of Tel Aviv, whoever they may be."

As Mbali and Ray walked out of the old winery building, they heard and then saw the Augusta taking off, without them. "Did you only pay them to wait for an hour?"

139

Ray asked over the noise of the helicopter and smiling at his host.

"No, Mr. Bowman, I pay them sometimes to be a diversion, especially when someone is trying to kill my guest. We are driving back to Cape Town."

Two Range Rovers sat at the end of the path, doors open, guarded by men who looked like they had once been on a rugby team. But while rugby teams in South Africa were still largely whites only, Mbali's security team was multiracial. Ray wondered how often she had used white agents when blacks would stand out too much. He tried to guess how many white agents she had, men like Marcus Stroh, the man who had saved his life.

"You said this morning that you knew I had met with Johann Potgeiter in Vienna," Ray noted as they got seated in the Range Rover. "However did you know that?"

"I am not without my ways, Raymond," she smiled as she read a text message. "Now we can take you back to the safety of the guesthouse at our training facility." She paused, buckling herself into the seat. "Or we can go watch Special Branch pick up the Nigerian who runs Black Eagle. See why he wanted to kidnap you. Which will it be?"

11

They saw the blinking blue-and-red lights before they turned the corner. When they stopped briefly at the police roadblock to show their identification, Ray rolled down his window and looked out. He saw the big white house at the end of the block, illuminated by spotlights, thick black smoke pouring out of its upper windows.

"Looks like we might be a little late to watch the action," he suggested to Mbali.

"Coppers, they are always too keen to get on with the shooting," she replied in disgust. "If they killed the Big Man, I will flay them alive. I need to interrogate that son of a bitch."

The driver maneuvered the Range Rover through the scattered police cars and fire trucks, toward the smoking house. When

141

they pulled up to a cluster of police commanders in white shirts, they stopped and Mbali jumped out. She almost charged the police brass. "Where is he, where is the Big Man? Have you killed another one that you were supposed to take into custody, Henry?"

"Here you arrive after all the shooting is over and start yelling," the senior officer responded. "He's in the van, but getting him for you cost me three men wounded." As Mbali changed direction for a large police truck, he yelled after her. "Your debt to Special Branch just got bigger."

Ray Bowman tried to keep up with his South Africa host as she made a beeline for the vehicle holding her prey. Inside the police wagon, a very large man lay on a metal bench in the middle of the compartment, with an officer on either side and a paramedic hovering above him, adjusting an intravenous feed. Mbali and then Ray jumped up into the van.

The Nigerian was wearing a tracksuit, ripped and bloodied in several places where the paramedic had bandaged him. "Let me at him," Mbali said, pushing the paramedic aside.

"I've sedated him, but he's stable," the young woman said to Mbali, stepping back.

"You think you can kidnap my guest, do

142

you, Cletus? We shot your two boys dead this morning for that. What do you think we should do with you? Maybe you bleed out in this truck." She squeezed one of his wounds and the big man let out a scream.

"We didn't hurt anyone, Mbali," he whispered.

"Only because we got there before you could," she spat back. "Now, you listen. You tell me who paid for this job or you die on the way to hospital and we send your rotten corpse to Lagos."

Ray was wondering if she meant it and, if she did, whether it would be better for him to take a walk outside the van. Mbali ripped a bandage from the man's leg. He screamed again. "Talk!" she yelled at him.

"Kranstov, his name is Kranstov. He comes to the meetings we have in Sicily with the others. He show up here yesterday. Said he just wanted a few hours with the American, paid two million U.S."

"How do you communicate with him?" she pushed.

"I don't," Cletus struggled to speak. "He calls me. Burner numbers. He called this afternoon. Wanted his money back."

Mdali stood. She was done with him. She jumped back down to the street. "Should we take him to hospital, ma'am?" the policeman in the van asked after her.

"I don't care what you do with him, but something tells me he won't be alive too long, so don't waste a lot of medicine on him," she answered.

Mbali strode back to her Range Rover, as Ray Bowman caught up with her. "We'll get the phone records. But I am sure Cletus is right. This Mr. K probably used burner phones to call him, but we may be able to see where they were bought and who bought them. Might give us a lead. We'll also check with Border Control to see who landed in the last few days who might be interesting. Did he say 'Knarsoff'? Sounds Russian."

"Sounds like an alias," Bowman suggested. "It will lead nowhere."

"What do you think we should do now?" she asked as they got back in the Rover.

"I'm due in Israel," Ray answered.

"Think they'll let me in?" she asked.

"Who said you were invited?"

"I told you, bartender, I am your termite. Until we find these nukes, where you go, I go."

12

FRIDAY, OCTOBER 21
POLICY EVALUATION GROUP
NAVY HILL, FOGGY BOTTOM
WASHINGTON, DC

The iPad buzzed. Dugout knew it was Ray Bowman calling. No one else could connect to that device. He had designed the two specially converted iPads as a paired set. Each had the necessary encryption key to communicate to the other, but those keys existed nowhere else. Inside the fat iPad 2, there were chips that created what Dugout called a "sandbox," a separate hard drive that could only be accessed after a four-factor authentication.

When Bowman had clicked on the Games folder and then the Hearts card game app, two windows had appeared. He had placed his thumb over the first window for a fingerprint read and looked into the second window for an iris scan. Then a number pad appeared and he had typed in an eight-digit pin he had memorized. Finally, a phrase appeared on screen and he had read it aloud for voice recognition. The entire process took almost two minutes. It was not like hitting 911 on a phone, not particularly good when seconds counted.

"I'm in South Africa," Ray began.

"I know. The iPad has GPS. Besides, I've been following reports about you in the Austrian and South African security services chatter," Dugout replied, setting the iPad up against his desk lamp.

"So you know, half the spooks in Vienna were following me around town. It was like *The Third Man.* Then some Nigerian fucking drug gang tried to kidnap me here yesterday and I end up with brain splatter on me. Find out who hired them. The Nigerian is claiming it's some guy name Kranstov, first name unknown. Check it out."

"Will do," Dugout said, tapping the name in to his search list.

"I thought you were supposed to be giving me some sort of top cover through cyberspace. Where were the warnings Duggie, huh?"

"I didn't hear about those problems until after they happened," Dugout stammered, "but you seem to be okay."

"No thanks to you. Listen, after the visit here I am pretty satisfied there were six more nuclear bombs than the South Africans reported to IAEA. They may have been shipped to Israel years ago. I am going to go there to see if I can verify that and, if so, where they went from there. Have you gotten anywhere?"

Dugout hit the touch screen on the laptop next to the iPad, pulling up a program that the Minerva software was plowing through. "Maybe. I figure that the five remaining warheads were probably moved after their sale. Likely in shipping containers with special shielding to avoid detection by Geiger counters. So I am looking for unusual movement around then, shipments of containers originating in one place and then being off-loaded and shipped to likely target locations. Looking at aircraft, ships not operated by Maersk and the other big lines, going to the U.S. or Israel. There is a lot of data to crunch. Still running through it."

"By the way, when you have your next little séance with Winston at the Cosmos Club, tell him to keep the CIA away from me," Ray said. "Having them tailing me around is like hunting deer with a boombox by your side. Speaking of our illustrious Intelligence Community, have they or any of the others come up with anything?"

"Dry holes. Winston won't let them talk to any liaison services about it because he thinks it will leak in minutes that we're looking for loose nukes and then the bad guys could detonate once they know we're on to them."

"Well, tell Winston that the South African intel service already figured it out and their President has stepped up searches for radioactivity in shipping containers. The story is going to leak out pretty soon," Ray thought out loud. "Gotta go." The screen reverted to a game of Hearts.

Dugout checked what the search program had found for Kranstov. He hit the first entry on the short list. "This growth mechanism for thin film was first noted by Ivan Stranski and Lyubomir Kranstov in 1938." Wonderful, probably not him, Dugout thought. It had not been a productive day, so far.

As he opened the mini fridge in search of a Red Bull, the first lines of "Rhapsody in Blue" came over the speakers tied in to his server cluster. Good news, the Gershwin masterpiece was what Minerva played when it had found what it had been programmed to look for. Dugout dashed to the screen.

A consignment of five shipping containers

had left Maputo on the Indian Ocean coast of Africa four days after the double flash. Each was bound for a different port in West Africa, on a cargo ship flagged in Liberia and owned by a company registered in Vanuatu. The master was a Philippine captain. It fit the pattern he was searching for, perfectly, five bombs, five targets. "Found them," he said aloud.

Dug tapped in a query for the onward itinerary of each of the containers. They had all bounced around from port to port, ship to ship for weeks. One container had finally cleared customs at Rotterdam, another two had been trucked away from Felixstowe near London. One had entered Mexico at Veracruz. The last one was still at sea, having been transshipped eight times. It was now on a Panamanian flagged ship from Trinidad, bound for the Port of Miami, where it was due to dock tomorrow morning. "Shit!" Dugout yelled to the empty room.

Dugout swiveled on his chair and picked up the secure phone, punching the button on the console that read DHS/NAC. The Nebraska Avenue Complex was the headquarters of Homeland Security and held its twenty-four-hour operations center, connected to Customs, Coast Guard, and a dozen other DHS agencies.

"NAC, Yeoman Burke," the Coast Guard woman answered. "How can I help you?"

"This is the PEG. I have a Pinnacle event, repeat Pinnacle event. Code Empty Quiver. Give me the Senior Watch Officer." Dugout had spoken the interagency clear code for a nuclear event, Pinnacle, and Empty Quiver, the specific category of event for a missing weapon.

"Pinnacle, yes, sir. Let me look that up here a minute," she replied. "Pinnacle, oh, God, stand by, switching you to Captain Mendoza, stand by."

13

"There is a privacy screen in First Class, madame, if you want to raise it after takeoff," the flight attendant explained. "It separates you from the passenger in the next seat."

Mbali looked at Raymond, who already had his headphones on, and smiled. "Maybe I will later, but he seems like a nice guy."

The flight attendant looked askance at the big American.

"Well, the switch is right here when you decide you need it."

Mbali had looked around at the crowd boarding the plane and remarked to herself how few blacks were among the passengers. Relations between the South African and Israeli governments were still chilled and those who traveled back and forth between the two countries tended to be Jews, who tended to be whites, with the strange exception of the Lemba people, who called themselves the Mwenye, and had been shown through DNA to be directly related to the original Israeli tribes of Moses. She laughed wondering what would happen if 747s filled with the Lemba started showing up in Tel Aviv claiming their Right of Return after three thousand years.

"What's so funny?" Bowman asked.

"It's a long story?"

"Does it have to do with termites eating bars?" he asked.

"Ah, so you finally figured it out, Mr. Bartender?"

"Yes, but it took a while, and then I tried it out on my, ah, friend and she got it right away. Well, she's more than a friend. I live with her and her partner."

"You Americans are so strange to us, really, you know," Mbali chuckled.

"Well, it, too, is a long story, which I am sure we will have time for at some point," he stammered, his ears reddening in embarrassment. "I'm still getting used to it myself, but it works. Anyway, I called Emma and Linda today and I told them about meeting you and, well, anyway, Emma knew the joke."

"Well, at least she's smart," Mbali said, reaching across and touching Ray's arm. "I am so glad to hear you're not single. When I didn't see a wedding ring, I wasn't sure. I've always had problems working closely with single men. Truth to tell, with a lot of married men, too."

"Well, I'm taken, so don't worry about any ulterior motives."

"Good."

"But what about you, since we're having this talk? Is there someone in your life?" Ray asked.

"There is a man," she said, smiling at the thought. "Some people assume I must be butch to be in this job, but no, there is a man. His name is Nelson. He's almost seven years old. I thought when I was thirty it was now or never."

"That's wonderful, but do you ever get to sec him?"

"Oh, yes. Every morning and every night, except when I travel, which is rarely." She paused a moment and her expression clouded. "So, I know you want to ask who or where is his father. He died when Nelson was two, shot leading a drug raid in Joburg. Now, Nelson is the only man I have room for in my life and he, let me tell you, is plenty. Let me show you." She withdrew her Galaxy smartphone and pulled up a photo album with hundreds of pictures of her boy, many with both her and her son.

"Maybe I can meet him when this is all over?" Ray asked, handing back the phone.

"I keep him well away from my business," she said. "No offense."

"Understood," he said. He leaned back in the chair and put his headphones back on, hoping for another airborne moment of clarity. Instead, he fell asleep.

SUNDAY, OCTOBER 23
ABOVE DAVID BEN GURION AIRPORT
LOD, ISRAEL

He woke several hours later. Mbali had put up the privacy screen between their two seats. The long overnight flight from Johannesburg in the old El Al 747 had been wearing. Even in First Class the seats were uncomfortable. The only thoughts that came to him before he had dozed off were of the men in the cars, the men in Vienna, and the noise, the blood, the shooting in Camps Bay.

CIA men had been surveilling him at the café in Vienna. That meant the Agency knew what he was doing, or thought they did. Had Winston told them, had he told them to protect him? Or had they learned about

154

it through one of their people inside the NSC staff? Were they trying to get a lead from him and then swoop in and claim credit, in the process blowing the opportunity, if there were an opportunity?

And there had been the others in the cars in Grinzing.

Two sets of others, Rosch had said. Others who were watching him or watching Johann Potgeiter, or now watching us both? Maybe Mossad was watching him, too. They always had a way of showing up in interesting places when there was a whiff of nuclear something in the air. Maybe Potgeiter had protection, now that he was a Trustee, replacing his father? Protection from those who had killed the first batch of Trustees, whomever their killers were.

That was still the central question, why kill the Trustees, especially after they had delivered the bombs. If they had, in fact, delivered bombs. Perhaps because what they had delivered was defective? The buyers felt scammed and retaliated? Killing the sellers would not get you your money back. Killing the sellers might, however, wipe clean your trail, your identity. That would work, that would be a motivation, but only if the Trustees alone knew the identity of the buyer and there were no records for the successor Trustees to figure out what had happened.

Bowman could not suppress the thought that if he failed and the parallel work by the intelligence agencies did too, something so dire might happen that the world would go off in a different direction, as it had after 9/11. It was a direction to a far worse place, where large sections of cities lay in radioactive ruin, where the dead were counted not in the hundreds, but in the tens of thousands, where paranoia and state surveillance would run amok, where the economies would tank and progress of all kinds would slow or retreat.

Or not. Maybe all the fears were wrong, all the theories flawed. Maybe the double flash was not a nuclear bomb going off. Or even if it had been, maybe it was a North Korean or Pakistani experiment. Maybe the Saudis had been developing a weapon as a hedge against the Iranian nuclear program. The Trustees were real and they had all been killed after being paid huge sums of money, but maybe there was another explanation that was eluding him.

What was real was the fact that the American President, and apparently his South African counterpart, both believed that there were loose nukes and that those nukes were going to go off in their cities sometime soon. Both men were doing, or about to do, searches that would be so obvious that the media would get the story of loose nukes in a matter of days, if not hours. Then no amount of presidential rhetoric or assurances would stop people pouring out of the great cities and engaging in all sorts of disruptive and self-destructive behavior. If there were actually bombs hidden in cities, the terrorists might well decide to ignite them then, rather than risk being uncovered in the searches. As he began to drift off again, there were two pings.

"Please make sure your seat belts are buckled and your seat is in the fully upright position as we begin our final approach to Ben Gurion."

When the 747 hit the runway with a thud, Bowman turned on his iPhone and clicked on Data Roaming. As the plane taxied to the gate, the stream of e-mails that had been waiting for him poured on to the iPhone. He was definitely going to bill the government for the charges. He pulled up his Wickr app for encrypted messages and checked to see if any had come in.

There was one from Gunter Rosch in Vienna. "Ray, tracked down the two teams that were surveilling you in Grinzing. One was the South African service, your new friend Mbali. The other were hired former Wien Polizei. They swear they don't know who hired them. We are working on that with them." Wickr shredded the message on his iPhone when he closed it, making it disappear forever from any corner of cyberspace.

He looked across at Mbali, who was actually putting on lipstick and staring into a compact mirror, getting ready for their arrival. Of course she had had the younger Potgeiter under surveillance. That's how she knew he had interviewed him. She probably had all the new Trustees being followed. It was about time he saw those surveillance reports and learned everything she knew, or else he might not take her with him up into the Galilee Hills. He remembered that sharing, she had said, had to be a two-way street.

When the First Class door opened, they were the third and fourth passengers off the plane and into the jetway. An athletic-looking man stood just inside in a short-sleeved khaki shirt and jeans. "Mr. Radford, welcome to the Holy Land. Please come with me, and your lady friend." The man opened a side door in the jetway and led them out onto a stairway to the tarmac, where a tan Mercedes waited.

"Danny Avidar is sorry he could not be here himself to welcome you, but he wanted to make sure you arrived okay and got settled into the hotel. So we will just skip over the Immigration business. If I can have your passports, I will get them stamped and return them to you. You are already checked in at the Clock. They call it a boutique hotel. It's in Jaffa. Not so many tourists as the Hilton or the Dan." He paused and then looked squarely at Ray, as if to double-check. "Two rooms, as you requested."

Danny Avidar had asked no questions when Ray had called him to arrange the visit. Either Mossad already knew what he was doing, which was likely, or Danny just assumed he would find out when Ray showed up. One thing Ray knew, Danny Avidar, the head of Ops for Mossad, would not be letting him wander around Israel unsupervised. Once he knew what Ray was up to, Avidar would probably have to tell the internal security service, the Shin Beth, to keep an eye on him.

"It's quite modern, Tel Aviv," Mbali observed as the car sped through the city.

"Your first time in Israel? You expected maybe the Holy Land was still like it was in the Bible?" their driver retorted. "We fixed it up since then. Jerusalem we left old. You

159

will see it while you are here, of course. Meanwhile, Danny is waiting for you."

Knowing Avidar would be in his suite, Ray asked Mbali to come with him to meet their host. As they entered, he was pouring. "It's the Yarden Chardonnay you liked so much last time," he offered the first glass to Bowman. "Robert Parker and Oz Clarke have both rated it now, so you may have been right about it."

Ray introduced Mbali and the three of them toasted, *"L'chaim."*

"Did you know, Raymond that the Crusaders brought the Chardonnay grape to France from Israel. It's actually native here. In Hebrew it means 'gate of God.' "

"Don't tell the French," Ray laughed.

"I ask them where in France is a place called Chardonnay? There is no such place. There is Burgundy and Bordeaux, but no Chardonnay because it is not native to France. Anyway, we are all glad you came back to do this one, Ray. The Prime Minister and the Security Cabinet are going crazy. How do we keep these bombs out of Israel? It is existential for us. However many there are, doesn't matter how many. One and we are in deep trouble. Two and we are done as a nation. Everyone will leave. No one will live in a radioactive waste pile, waiting for the next bomb to go off. You need to tell us everything you know because Washington is acting like they know nothing. Nothing to share? They think the bombs are going to end up in the States? Crazy. We are the target. What do you know? Now, tell me."

Ray had almost forgotten how fast Danny could talk, how quickly he got down to business and put his cards on the table. "You overchilled the Chard," he said pulling the bottle of Yarden out of the ice bucket. "Washington does not know much and I am sure you have ways of knowing everything they have." He sipped the wine and sat on the couch. "I suspect you may actually know more than we do."

"Then, we are all in trouble. What could we know? Somebody bought something expensive from men who used to make nuclear bombs. Then he killed them all. Our guess is that it was bombs, but we don't know where they are or who is the buyer. That's it. That's what we know," Danny said, sitting down opposite Bowman.

"One of the men who died was killed here in Tel Aviv. Shin Beth must have taken that case apart by now," Ray replied. "And the sellers were all men who had worked with Israel on developing missiles and bombs.

You know them."

Danny Avidar threw up his hands. "We knew them. That was when I was in diapers, twenty-five years ago or more. We had nothing to do with them since then. Don't try to shmear this on us, Raymond. You want to talk to the boys in Shin Beth, that I can arrange. But you know those guys are not refined and cultured like my outfit. No Chardonnay at Shin Beth. Beer maybe, if they like you."

Ray moved to the edge of the couch and placed the half-empty glass on the coffee table. "Danny, cut the shit. You just told me that this is the top priority investigation from the Prime Minister, that it is about the continued existence of Israel. So don't tell me you don't know all the details of the Shin Beth and police investigation of the death of Dawid Steyn, right here in Tel Aviv."

"Blunt as ever. Are you sure you're not a Jew? Maybe on your mother's side somewhere? That way we could give you citizenship and recruit you into the Mossad." As Bowman scowled at him, Danny Avidar sat back. "You I am authorized personally by the Prime Minister himself to tell everything to, but under four eyes. Not yet for Washington, the CIA, the FBI, the

National Zoo Police." He looked at Mbali, who had perched on a barstool and was watching the back and forth between these alleged friends with fascination. "With all due respect to my new South African friend, you I am not authorized to brief."

Mbali did not move or say a word. She continued to look at Avidar.

Bowman cut the silence. "This is a joint investigation, Danny, between the U.S. and South Africa. She knows more about the Trustees than you ever will. So she's in. If you need to call the PM to ask permission go right ahead. We'll wait, but we are doing this together or not at all."

Avidar sighed. "Then it must go no further than you, miss. No reporting back to Joburg or wherever. And you, my friend, Raymond, will have to explain this personally to the PM when we see him."

"With pleasure. I haven't seen him since the Syrian reactor briefing," Ray said. "Now, you first. What have you got?"

"Less than we would like, more than we had a week ago," Danny started. "Dawid Steyn was murdered, of that there is no doubt. Pushed off the platform at the Haganah Station. We have it on the videotape. Who did it? Mr. Nobody.

"Mr. Nobody with a hat pulled low. He

wore thick glasses. He had a mustache and light beard. He had a nose like an eagle. And all of that, the hat, the glasses, the facial hair, the nose, the police found in a dumpster three blocks away. So what use is the picture?"

Ray brightened. "Great, so you have his DNA, the assassin's?"

"We do. This we now know. He was a man. He was white. His ancestors came from what was Poland or Russia. He is likely a Jew and he has a better-than-average chance of getting macular degeneration in his seventies or eighties, if he lives that long," Danny said from memory. "Did we have that DNA on file? No. Does it help us at all that we have it now? A little, not much. Not yet."

"And the place where he bought the kit?" Mbali asked.

"Actually, we thought of that," Danny replied, looking at her. "Not in Israel is our conclusion, not even the hat. But it's all stuff you could get all over Europe, even in the States some of it. No lot numbers. Now, it's your turn, miss. Tell me something about the Trustees I don't already know."

Mbali poured herself another glass of the Yarden. "You know of course that Dawid Steyn became a Trustee upon the death of

164

his father, of natural causes here in Tel Aviv two years ago. He quit his job and managed his share of the Trustee funds full time from his office downtown."

"All this we know, of course," Danny replied.

Mbali continued. "He attended eight meetings of the Trustees. We can give you the dates and locations. But he also met twice in Vienna with the late Karl Potgeiter and his son Johann."

Bowman raised his eyebrows. This was all news to him.

"He is succeeded by his wife, Rachel, the first woman on the Trustees. She continues to live in Herzliya, but no longer works at Google," she said. "I want to talk to her."

"That last part we knew," Danny mumbled. "Rachel we are listening to, watching, very closely. There is nothing to indicate that she knows anything. Shin Beth talked to her. She admitted to being a Trustee now. Says it's secret but, it's just an international charity, says she had never seen the books before her husband died, doesn't know why there was a big deposit in the accounts in Cyprus and Dubai earlier this year. But when she sneezes, we know."

Mbali continued her account. "What Dawid Steyn's father, Jacob, had worked on for the Apartheid regime at the Circle lab was the nuclear triggering mechanics in the missile warhead. His Israeli counterpart was the nuclear weapon designer Avraham Reuven." She stopped to get a reaction.

Danny Avidar looked at Ray Bowman. "You're right. She knows her stuff, this woman." He smiled and looked at Mbali. "But here we are getting into sensitive areas for us. We must tread lightly on that bad bit of history where we and the whites in Joburg did things together. It was a different era, the Cold War. We needed each other. Maybe we made mistakes then, but it is history."

" 'Maybe'?" Mbali asked.

"All right, we shouldn't have done some of what we did, but that was then and this is now," Danny said, punching the air with his hand for emphasis. "We cannot help each other as much as we need to now if there is any risk of us getting blamed again for what happened then or if it means people talking about our alleged nuclear weapons, which we may or may not have, and drawing connections between our alleged weapons and the loose nukes that might be out there."

Mbali walked toward Avidar. "Nor do we want to draw attention to the fact that somehow we missed the fact that South

Africa produced more nuclear weapons than the whites admitted to, if that turns out to be true. Both of our governments have a shared interest in finding these bombs before anything happens, destroying them and then making sure no one ever knows any of this happened. Agreed?" She thrust out her hand to shake.

"*Zeman*," Avidar said. "Agreed."

"Lovely, you have a deal. Great. Everybody's learning things. Can we get to work now?" Bowman said, standing up. "We want to go see Avraham Reuven."

"Always sarcastic you are. This Reuven, he's still alive?" Danny asked.

"Alive and living in the hills above the Galilee," Bowman replied. "In Livnim. And I want to talk to him."

Danny Avidar shrugged. "All right. You, miss, we will have someone take you tomorrow to see Rachel Steyn in Herzliya. I don't need to go with you, I will hear the whole conversation anyway." He turned to Bowman. "Raymond and I will go visit an eighty-one-year-old man on the hill of the Beatitudes and try not to interrogate him so hard he has a heart attack."

"Beatitudes?" Bowman asked.

"Heathen," Avidar replied. "You know, like 'Blessed are the Cheeze Markers.' "

As Ray Bowman wondered at that, his iPad beeped.

14

Because of the direction of the wind and the helicopters' low altitude, the crew of the MV *Indira* had not heard the motor of the Customs and Border Protection Black Hawk until about the same time that its xenon light cut the dark and lit the conning tower of the freighter brighter than a tropical sun ever had. Simultaneously, Law Enforcement Detachment fast-roped down from a Coast Guard Black Hawk onto the darkened stern of the ship.

The Law Enforcement Detachment of Coasties, carrying M4 automatic weapons, moved quickly past the containers stacked on the deck and up to the helmsman. They arrived before the ship's captain managed to come up from his state room. There was no resistance.

Twenty minutes later the Fast Response Cutter *Margaret Norvell* bounced through the waves at twenty-eight knots, flashing red-and-blue lights like a police cruiser. A second LEDAT and ship handlers from *Norvell* boarded the *Indira* and turned the freighter east, toward the Bahamas.

By late morning, the freighter was being off loaded in the state-of-the-art container terminal at Freeport, where thousands of containers were switched from ship to ship every day. The immense crane towering over the *Indira* took the containers off the deck and piled them three high in an open area in the dockyard.

Dugout landed at Freeport just after noon, aboard Coast Guard One, a Gulfstream executive jet that he was surprised to learn was based in a hangar at National Airport fifteen minutes from his office in Foggy Bottom. He was accompanied by a Coast Guard Admiral and a senior uniformed officer from Customs and Border Protection. They had pressed him on the flight down, trying to find out why the White House had been so concerned about the MV *Indira.* He said only that there had been a tip that it might have radioactive materials on board.

As they pulled into the huge dockyard,

they were met by another U.S. CBP officer, George Martinez, one who was stationed in Freeport. "We got your suspect cargo all quarantined off over there and Blue Man is standing by to scan it. We put your cargo ahead of everything else we plan to scan today. Just need your go ahead."

Blue Man looked like a robot from *Star Wars*. On eight wheels, each taller than a person, the device towered 120 feet above the dock. On top, a driver sat in a small compartment, looking down at them. Unlike the even larger cranes throughout the port area, Blue Man did not lift containers, it rode over stacks of them. The space between its two towers was slightly wider than a container and as it slowly straddled the steel shipping boxes, Blue Man shot X-ray, gamma ray, and neutron flux beams from its right tower, through the containers, to receivers on the left tower.

"What if the material in the container is shielded, like with lead?" Dugout asked the CBP man, Martinez.

"Doesn't matter," Martinez replied proudly. "We can still usually detect. If not, at least we will know there is shielding and that is a tip to open the container. With Blue Man we can do hundreds of containers a day, without ever having to open them, swab them, or use our Geiger counters."

It took twenty minutes for Blue Man to creep over the long row of containers, three high. When the wheeled tower reached the end of the line of containers, Martinez checked with Blue Man's operator on a walkie-talkie. "Got a hit on one container. The one from Maputo. Naturally it's the one on the bottom. We'll pull it out and pop it open, once we get our guys into their space suits, just as a precaution."

The one from Maputo was the container that the Minerva program had flagged. Now, Blue Man was also flagging it. Dug felt his pulse accelerate. As they waited, Dugout asked Martinez what he had wanted to know for the preceding hour. "Isn't the Bahamas like a country of its own now? How is it you guys run around in uniform with guns and badges, and giant robots like this was the U.S.?"

"Our Coast Guard protects their waters. We in CBP do preclearance of cargoes here so when they show up in the States they don't have to wait around. It's a lot faster for shippers. This port is all automated. It goes quick here. It makes money for Freeport and it creates a lot of jobs here."

"And they let us divert cargoes here that might have like nuclear bombs in them so that our giant robot detector thingee can find them here rather than in Miami? What if it goes off here?" Dugout asked. "Doesn't the Bahamas mind being our nuclear detonation area?"

"If we ever find a nuclear weapon or an improvised nuclear device, a dirty bomb, we secure the area and call in Delta Force from North Carolina. They can be here in under three hours. They're trained in what to do to render the weapon safe. We aren't," Martinez explained. "So far, hasn't happened. Maybe we'll get lucky with your tip today."

Dugout watched through binoculars as a team of four CBP agents in chem-bio-radiation suits with oxygen masks, broke the seal and the lock on the suspect container and swung the door open. Two of the agents, carrying lights and handheld detection gear went inside the container. Almost immediately there was chatter on the walkie-talkie, but Dugout couldn't understand what was being said.

"Red granite, pretty rare," Martinez said to the three men from Washington.

"Huh?" Dugout asked.

"It's a container of red granite from Africa. Granite almost always sends off the alarms. Most people don't know their countertops are slightly radioactive. Anyway, false alarm. We get them a lot."

The Coast Guard Admiral and the CBP man from Washington both looked at Dugout, silently. They could have been golfing or doing a dozen other things on a Sunday.

Dugout didn't want to give up. "You do hundreds of containers a day with this Blue Man. What percent of containers entering the U.S. are scanned with Blue Men before they arrive?"

Martinez smiled with pride, "This is the only operational Blue Man in the world. We get less than one percent of the containers going in to the U.S. to scan here in the Bahamas. Most just sail right in to Newark or Norfolk, Miami, Seattle, LA Long Beach. Scary, huh? You guys want to hit the casino for lunch before you fly back?"

CLOCK HOTEL
JAFFA/TEL AVIV, ISRAEL

Danny Avidar walked into the little gym carrying a bouquet of flowers. Mbali Hlanganani stopped running on the treadmill in astonishment. "For me?" she asked.

"I didn't feel that we welcomed you appropriately on your first trip to the Holy Land," he said. "The girl at the front desk

174

said you were down here, working out."

"That's so nice of you. I must say your hospitality has been superb," she said, stepping off the machine and grabbing a towel and water bottle. "I look forward to working with you."

"Well, that's the thing. We haven't worked closely with your service before," he shrugged. "I guess because we had been close to the anciene regime, but that was when I was a young man, when I was just a recruit in the paratroopers."

"And when I was still in school," she added. "I don't blame you, I don't blame Israel, for all of this. It was, after all, South Africans who made these bombs and, I am pretty sure, South Africans who just sold them."

"True, but Israel helped the Apartheid government with its defense and intelligence needs. In some ways they helped Israel. It is not something we are proud of," he said and opened a water bottle for himself. "Of all peoples, we should not have supported Apartheid and we didn't, but we did support the government, against the Communists, but nonetheless."

"Danny, may I call you Danny?" she asked. "Let us put it behind us. We face a common challenge. These people, whoever they are, who have the warheads now, they could use them against either of our countries, we don't know which one is the target. We have to work together."

"The Americans think it's al Qaeda and they are going to bomb New York and Washington again," Danny Avidar observed.

"The Americans always think it's about them," Mbali said.

"And they always think they can solve the problem with money and technology," Avidar added.

"This time it's going to take more than that, and less," she agreed. "It's about people, getting to the right people, and getting them to reveal what they know."

"I promise you, Miss Mbali, I will tell you everything I learn about this case as we develop it, if you will do the same with me," Avidar said, offering his hand to shake.

"Then, Danny, we have an intelligence partnership of our own."

15

"Call it Lake Kinneret. That's its name," Avraham Reuven scolded.

"I told you Mr. Avidar, my father is sometimes not good with guests. His mind, well, it wanders." Benjamin Reuven looked to be in his fifties. He had explained that he lived on the nearby kibbutz Hokuk, where he ran a specialty plastics factory. He came into town almost every day to see that his father was all right.

The kibbutz had not been "comfortable" enough for Avraham. To be near his son and his grandchildren on the kibbutz, Avraham had moved to a villa in nearby Livnim, complete with a pool and a great view of the Sea of Galilee. Now, the grandchildren were at university in America, but he didn't mind, Avraham said. "This view from this

177

restaurant is like the view from my house down the street. I love it. Lake Kinneret."

They sat outdoors at the Roburg, the gourmet restaurant in Livnim, the Sea of Galilee glistening in the near distance. "Lake Tiberias, the Romans called it, after their perverted emperor, but it's Kinneret in the Torah, not Galilee. The Galilee is the region," Avraham insisted.

"We came to talk about South Africa," Danny Avidar began.

"Operation Peace for Galilee, that's what they called it when they invaded Lebanon the last time," the elder Avraham went on. "A piece of the Galilee for the Army, but *peace* for Galilee didn't happen, of course. No peace. Peace in Galilee, that would be a real miracle."

"Dad, Mr. Avidar wants you to remember about your time in South Africa," the son tried. "He's from the Mossad, high up."

"The Christians think miracles occurred in the Galilee, of course. Over there in Capernaum. Down the road in Cana. That was a good one, the one in Cana. They claim a Jew made water into wine there, in Cana, not just wine but high-quality wine. No high-quality wine in Cana now," Reuven Avraham said looking at Bowman. "Not bad here though, at Roburg's." He sipped his

178

glass of dark red wine.

"Do you recall a man named Potgeiter? Or one named Roosmeer?" Avidar asked.

"Yes, Potgeiter, yes. He liked tunnels, built tunnels," Reuven Avraham recalled.

Danny Avidar perked up and leaned forward. "Tunnels for what?"

"Simeon bar Yochai, he built tunnels, too, up here in the Galilee region. Did you know that?" Avraham asked.

"No, I didn't," Danny answered. "I don't know him. Was that when you came back from South Africa that he built the tunnels up here? Why did he build tunnels?"

"No, before that," the old man scoffed. "He built them to escape from the Romans. He was a Tannaim. You're obviously not."

Ray Bowman couldn't help it anymore, he broke out laughing. Avidar gave him an evil look.

"It is good wine," Bowman began, "for a blend." He rolled the red around in his glass. "I saw Johann Roosmeer two days ago. He said if I saw you to pass on his best. He said without you, he could never have redesigned the warhead to fit on to his missile. He makes wine now, Johann does, with his two sons in Stellenbosch."

Avraham Reuven turned and stared at Bowman like a falcon contemplating its prey. He pushed his glasses up from the tip of his nose. "His missile? It was a Jehrico II, just like ours. You use a little warhead, but you boost it with tritium. Simple. That's what we did. What they did, too, with the few they made in the tunnel."

"Potgeiter's tunnel. That where they made the tritium gas, in the tunnel?" Ray asked.

"Of course," the old man said, disdainfully.

"And then Potgeiter built another tunnel to store the missile warheads in when he left South Africa?" Ray guessed.

"Yes. The man loved his tunnels, like the Nazis," Reuven answered.

"What did you think of his second tunnel, the one where he moved the warheads? Was it well designed?" Ray asked.

"Never saw it," Reuven admitted. "Think I'd go to Madagascar? Even Potgeiter got sick there. Lucky he didn't get bitten by the bats. Huge things. Built nests in his tunnel. Had to chase them out. Bloody mess. Guano everywhere," Reuven said laughing, as he took another sip of the wine.

"Potgeiter told people he sent the missile warheads here, you know," Ray continued.

"*Pfft . . .*" Reuven chortled. "He never even offered. We didn't need them. We had two hundred and forty-eight nuclear warheads.

Why would we want theirs? No, they never came here. Went straight to the bat cave. Think they moved them lately? That why you came, find out where they moved them? I wouldn't know. I haven't talked to any of them in years, the South Africans. Not in years. Wouldn't know, not me, no."

"They still send you the good South African wine though, I hope?" Ray took a shot in the dark.

"Roosmeer does. A case every year at New Year, their new year, not ours," Avraham Reuven admitted. "Much better than the piss we make in this country. Haven't made high-quality wine here since that boy did his magic trick over in Cana."

As they left the Reuvens and walked to Danny's car in the parking lot, the Mossad man stopped and looked Bowman in the eye. "Forget two hundred forty-eight. He never said two hundred forty-eight, all right? Besides, he's demented, obviously."

"I don't think he's demented at all. He just didn't like you. Or Mossad. Or both," Ray said, and began walking again. "He knew what I needed and he gave it to me. He confirmed that there were secret bombs that the South African whites did not reveal to the UN. He said they never came here. And he told us that they went to Madagascar for safe storage in a tunnel. The coup de grâce? He confirmed the weapons were boosted with tritium."

"That's important, the tritium part?" Danny asked.

"Damn right. It's a limited life component. It decays. By now, it's dead," Ray thought aloud. "If the bombs were detonated now, they would not be fifty kilotons, more like five kilotons."

"Raymond, even a handful of five-kiloton nuclear explosions in Israel and the Exodus happens again, but in the other direction."

"Wouldn't do good things for Manhattan and DC, either," Bowman replied.

16

MONDAY, OCTOBER 24
HERZLIYA, ISRAEL

"Oh, you're black," Rachel Steyn said as she opened the door. "Oh, forgive me, I didn't . . . I just assumed a South African policeman would be, well, a white man. Please come in, I am awfully sorry for that greeting."

"My name is Mbali Hlaganani," the guest said, stretching out her arm on the doorstep.

"Well, if they had told me that, I would have known, please, do come in."

Mbali stepped into the luxurious villa on the beachfront.

"Most police and security services in South Africa are black. Some are colored, some Indian, a few are whites."

"Yes, of course, I haven't been there since I was a child," Rachel admitted. "I thought we would sit out by the pool. I have lemonade and biscuits."

"First, Mrs. Steyn, I want to express my sympathy on the death of your husband. I want you to know that my organization is working hard with the Israeli government to determine who killed him and why."

"Killed him? So you think it wasn't an accident?" Rachel asked.

"Most definitely. Haven't the police told you that?"

"No, they just said they were investigating, but I suspected it as soon as I got the call."

"May I ask you why you were suspicious?" Mbali asked.

Rachel exhaled and paused, briefly. "Dawid thought he had been followed a few times in the week before, before he died." She paused again and looked at the ground. "I told him he was being silly, paranoid. Who would want to follow him?"

Mbali took a cookie from the platter. "Well, that is the question, Mrs. Steyn. Your husband was involved in international finance and controlled very large sums of money."

"Yes, but so do many men."

"Maybe the Trustees have made enemies, Mrs. Steyn. Now that you are a Trustee, it may be important that you know who your enemies are."

"So, you know about the Trustees. Of course you would, wouldn't you," Rachel Steyn said, more to herself than to Mbali. "The others have suggested bodyguards for me and the children, but I have said no. It would scare the kids and I don't even know who they would be protecting me from. Do you think I should have bodyguards? Do you know who or why?"

"It's such a lovely view from here," Mbali replied. "Maybe we should walk along the beach," she said pointing to her ear and then raising a finger to her mouth.

Rachel understood immediately. "Yes, I was going to suggest that. You may want to leave your shoes here." Mbali did and also left her mobile. Seeing that, so did Rachel.

As they strolled down the sand on the empty beach, Mbali wrapped her silk scarf around her chin, covering her mouth in case they were being filmed and a lip reader might be used later. "I am going to tell you a story that is true, but hard to believe. It is why your husband was murdered and why many more people may be soon.

"Your husband's father was one of the original Trustees, men who had worked on the South African nuclear bomb project. When they left the country, they took some bombs with them. Earlier this year, after

185

two decades, they sold them to somebody. That somebody killed them to wipe his traces, so no one would know who had bought the bombs."

Rachel put her hand to her mouth. "So that's where the half billion dollar deposit came from?"

"Yes, from Dawid's killers. And they are likely to use the bombs to kill thousands more, here in Israel, or in South Africa, or in the U.S. We don't know where yet. But maybe you can help us figure out who they are."

They turned and began slowly walking back to the house.

"I gave the police all of Dawid's records, all of his computers. I only have copies, but I have been over them a thousand times. There is nothing that even suggests where the money came from or why. Do you think Dawid knew about the bombs? I do not believe that."

"We assume all the Trustees did, but maybe not. I doubt he would have willingly been part of a plot against Israel or a plot to kill thousands of people." As she said that, Mbali thought that she really knew very little about Dawid Steyn and whether he would have agreed to sell nuclear bombs.

"How can I help you find his killers?" Rachel asked as they approached the villa.

"Maybe you ask for an emergency meeting of all of the new Trustees. You have talked on the phone, but you have not all met each other before? If you got together maybe we could get someone to say something, or do something. Let me do some planning and bring a proposal back to you." As they walked onto the pool deck, Rachel's mother appeared, having picked the two children up at their school. The two girls ran to their mother and then looked up in amazement at the tall, black woman. "You are so pretty," the younger girl said to Mbali. "What's your name?"

"My name is Mbali and I have a little boy about your age. His name is Nelson. What's yours?"

When, a half hour later, after a tour of the kids' rooms and artwork, Mbali prepared to leave, she whispered to Rachel, "Don't tell the others about me, but I will stay in touch." Mbali handed her a mobile phone. "If you need me, hit speed dial #1. Anytime. Don't use it for any other calls. Check the voice mails every day. The PIN is the month and day Dawid was killed." Rachel grasped the phone and Mbali's hand and squeezed them.

"*Toda raba*," Rachel whispered.

187

17

MONDAY, OCTOBER 24
POLICY EVALUATION GROUP
NAVY HILL, FOGGY BOTTOM
WASHINGTON, DC

"Even a five-kiloton nuclear detonation devastates Manhattan," Dugout said into the modified iPad to Bowman. "I pulled up a model that Homeland uses, developed by Oak Ridge nuclear lab." He described to Ray what he saw on his desktop monitor. "Detonate it on the south end of the island at Battery Park and the blast is felt as far north as Canal Street.

"It's a smaller bomb than Hiroshima and the buildings are now built much better, so only knocking over buildings within a couple of blocks of the blast, but setting fires and sending glass flying for many more blocks.

"The electromagnetic pulse fries all circuitry in Lower Manhattan and over in

Jersey City so cars don't work, ambulances, fire trucks, phones, any computer, any engine."

"Does the computer model give you casualty figures?" Ray asked.

"Detonated at midday during the week and you get twenty-five to forty thousand prompt deaths from incineration, burns, building collapses, flying debris," Dugout read off the chart. "An equal number of nonprompt deaths from burns and radiation poisoning over the following thirty days."

"And if the tritium gas had not decayed, what would happen?" Bowman asked.

"Exponentially worse," Dugout said, switching screens. "The explosion is ten times as big, so more buildings collapse, buildings up to Central Park are damaged, the EMP fries equipment in every hospital on the island, first responders all over Manhattan and into Brooklyn could not communicate or likely even get their vehicles to start. And the long-term radioactivity makes most of the city uninhabitable for a century or more."

"Even if that weren't the case, nobody would want to live anywhere near New York, or any other big city after that," Ray added.

Dugout paged down through the

Homeland department's model. "Listen to this: 'At fifty kilotons, first responders should not attempt to go within at least two miles of the blast site. Those still alive within the hot zone will perish within hours or days even with medical care and by entering the area first responders will only become fatalities themselves by exposure to high doses of lethal radiation. Establish a perimeter and prevent anyone from going into the hot zone.' It means there will be thousands of people dying in great pain, but no one should go to ease their pain. What a horror.

"Fewer deaths in Washington because the concentration of people is less, fewer high-rises, but it still takes out all the government buildings and makes the place too hot to ever use again. Fifty kilotons at the Washington Monument turns the Potomac into steam."

They sat in silence for a moment, thinking about what would happen if they failed. "How is the election campaign going?" Ray said, breaking the quiet.

"Well, the debates are finally over, but the ads are all over the TV. It's going to be close," Dugout said.

"What about what Reuven said about Madagascar. Any leads there?" Ray asked.

"Well, there we have a bit of good news,

potentially. Seems like land ownership is a big problem there, knowing who owns what. Leads to a lot of conflict and also makes it hard to sell land, which hurts the economy. So USAID gave the government in Antananarivo a grant to bring in Oracle and create a digital database, going back thirty years, of land sales. That gave Minerva a lead and data to trace.

"In 1989, the Springbok Mining company of London, England, bought a tract in the north, including a big hill. Springbok Mining dug a diamond mine into the hill, according to an old mining magazine from the time, but came up dry. Want to guess who one of the principal stockholders of Springbok was?" Dugout asked.

"The late Karl Potgeiter?" Ray asked.

"Along with the late Mr. Merwe and the now-departed Marius Pleiss, all of them Trustees," Dugout replied. "Sloppy in covering their tracks."

"Well it was in 1989, before they actually started the Trustees, so they probably bought the land with ARMSCOR money they could not repatriate from weapon sales to Singapore or wherever. I will bet Springbok no longer owns it," Ray guessed.

"You win the teddy bear," Dugout said. "They sold it in 1991 to Gazelle Trading of

Sydney, which, of course, had the same address in Sydney as Mr. Merwe. As far as I can tell, Gazelle still owns it, but it looks abandoned and largely overgrown on the satellite imagery I pulled up. Want me to send you the photo?"

Bowman was walking along the Tel Aviv corniche, carrying the iPad, using headphones and a mouthpiece to chat with Dugout, hoping that even Mossad and the Shin Beth could not hear the conversation. "No, just tell me the date on it."

"Shit, it's two years old. Guess we don't have much need to do strip photography of Madagascar."

"Get NGIA to target it for a close-up right away. If the cave looks like it's been opened up in the last few months, then we will need Winston to talk to the Pentagon," Ray told Dugout. "It may be time for JSOC to drop a little team into northern Madagascar for a look around, complete with Geiger counters."

He stopped and watched the sun sinking into the Mediterranean. For the first time in eight days since he had started this goose chase, he felt he was getting closer to an answer. At least, he might now know where the bombs had been. He had six days to find out where they went, before the

President ordered Operation Rock Wall to look everywhere for a nuke. And fourteen days to the election.

Winston Burrell had assumed the bombs would go off just before voting day.

The last ray of the setting sun refracted through the sea and for an instant, Raymond Bowman thought he saw a green flash. He wondered if, when it happened, he would see the nuclear flash.

18

Unusually for a back country road, there were streetlights on the telephone poles every hundred meters as the road meandered from an abandoned mine near Cullinan, east toward Mamelodi. Just before the Bedford step van turned at the bend, the streetlights went out.

"What was that noise?" the guard in the truck asked.

"We ran over something," the driver said.

The truck made a flapping sound and slowed.

"I've got a flat," the driver said.

"You've got more than one, my man," the guard said, and drew his Beretta from its holster. As he did, the bullets came through the window, two in his head, two in the driver's.

The three men in the Range Rover escorting the truck did not hear the shots, since the shooters used silencers. The Range Rover hit the same set of spikes on the road, but the driver did not stop. He swung the wagon into reverse, but not in time. The bullets that sprayed the Range Rover came from three automatic weapons, also with sound suppressors. The Range Rover kept backing up and fell off the road into a ditch. The shooters shot out its lights. Then they moved quickly, in two teams of two, to give each of the five men in the two vehicles a coup de grâce in the head. A third team, of three men, blew open the back door of the Bedford van with a small charge. Then they took one small black case, containing five special bottles. They left two other cases with similar content. They only needed five bottles.

It had taken four minutes and then they were gone. The cars that had been blocking the road up ahead and behind, left quietly without ever seeing another vehicle. The Mercedes S-Class and the ambulance carrying the heisted material drove south to the N4 and then on to the airport at Midrand, where a medevac flight was waiting. The chartered Boeing Business Jet, a modified 737-800, took off with a "patient," his family, his aides, and one small black case.

MONDAY, OCTOBER 24
POLICY EVALUATION GROUP
NAVY HILL, FOGGY BOTTOM
WASHINGTON, DC

The speakers on the server began playing the opening stanza of Beethoven's Fifth Symphony. It was a sound that Dugout did not want to hear. He had programmed that music to play when one of a handful of unwelcome events were observed by the scanners he had set up looking for key words in the flood of raw intelligence that the United States vacuumed up around the world, all day, every day.

He walked to the monitor connected to that set of servers and woke up the screen. There were reports from South Africa: the police, security service, the Interior Minister's office, the Prime Minister's office. They all seemed to be about a hijacking or a robbery from a truck east of Pretoria. What had triggered the alert was the phone call to the Prime Minister's office in which the Interior Minister had said the word "tritium."

Dugout picked up his Bowman-paired iPad and tapped a red app with a white exclamation point in the middle. The app

196

was labeled ALERT. It was after midnight in the Clock hotel near Jaffa in Tel Aviv, when Ray's iPad made a noise he had never heard from it before. It woke him from the first deep REM sleep he had enjoyed in a week. When he woke, he knew neither where he was nor what the awful buzzing sound was. In a minute after talking with Dugout, he knew both. In five minutes, he knew that a different clock had just started ticking.

19

"You were going to tell me when?" Bowman bellowed in the private breakfast room that Avidar had the hotel set up for them.

"I found out about the heist around the same time you did," Mbali protested.

"The heist, yes, but how long have you known about Potgeiter's tunnel at Cullinan and its secret, little research reactor still making fucking tritium."

"I wasn't authorized to tell you. I asked for permission, but the President said no," she said.

"Wonderful. Here I am running around, wasting time trying to confirm that there was a secret facility in South Africa where the extra bombs were stored in the nineties and where there was a tritium production facility and you already knew. Better yet, the fucking thing is still running, still making tritium. For who? For what?"

"It's a secret contract with the Pakistanis," she admitted. "That's why I couldn't tell you."

"The Pakistanis, oh, joy. No wonder they're cranking out H-bombs like sausages. They have a reliable supplier of tritium boosters," Ray was yelling as Danny Avidar walked in. "Well, the poor Pakistanis are not getting their shipment this time, are they? Because some bunch of lunatics heisted it an hour outside of your goddamn capital city. And your people have not a clue where it went."

"Where what went?" Avidar asked.

"Enough tritium to blow Israel to the moon," Ray boomed. "Or to blow up the U.S. just before our election, which by the way, is two weeks from today."

"We are looking everywhere. The tritium can't get out of the country," Mbali said. "Keep your voice down. People will hear."

"He owns the damn hotel. It's a Mossad proprietary. Everyone here is cleared," Ray said, more quietly.

"Really?" Mbali asked, looking at Danny Avidar.

"Yes, of course," Avidar said. "Who has tritium?"

199

Ray answered, "Whoever the hell has the bombs. Now we know what they were waiting for, the tritium to boost the yield by a factor of ten. Now they don't have to wait anymore. Now their South African bombs have South African tritium. *Boom.*"

"I'm going to have to tell the Prime Minister," Avidar said, moving back toward the door. "He'll want to seal the borders."

"Tell him he can't do that. It won't do any good and it will tip them off, they may go sooner," Ray said.

"You tell him," Avidar replied.

"Good, let's go." Ray looked at Mbali. "You, stay here. We'll sort this out when we get back."

WEDNESDAY, OCTOBER 26
MORONI, COMOROS ISLANDS

Two hours into the twenty-sixth, the Boeing Business Jet took off to the northeast, resuming its flight plan to Dubai. It had been on the ground in the Comoros for less than fifteen minutes. Air Traffic Control and Customs had not recorded the arrival, or the departure. As far as the records showed, the BBJ had left South Africa on a nonstop to Dubai.

At the request of the South African government, the aircraft would be searched by Emirati customs officials in Dubai. All aircraft that left South Africa around the time of the tritium heist were being searched, but the BBJ would be cleared because the tritium had been off-loaded in Moroni, where a little money went a long way.

The tritium gas had been "bottled" for Pakistan by the South Africans at their secret "research" reactor. Pakistan had provided the containers, which were specially designed to fit into Islamabad's missile warheads. They would, however, also fit into the larger cavity in the older South African missile warhead design. All five bottles would easily fit in one large suitcase, but in the villa on the hill above Moroni, they were carefully placed into five separate, appropriately lined, briefcases.

The next day they would be flown again, this time to where they would be mated with the five 1990s-era nuclear missile warheads. The tritium gas would act as steroids for the aging bombs, giving their relatively small amount of highly enriched uranium a destructive yield almost ten times what it would otherwise have been.

ANTSAKABARY, MADAGASCAR
Almost three hundred miles north of

Madagascar's capital, an old Dauphin helicopter landed on a cleared space outside of the town. Marcus Stroh emerged from the backseat of the aircraft and stretched. It had been a bumpy ride. He grabbed his backpack from the helicopter and walked toward his waiting hosts from the Madagascar Central Intelligence Service, the CIS. They had a new, four-door, Hilux pickup. Not bad for the local CIS, Marcus thought, as he prepared to make his introductions.

"The boys in Antananarivo said to be sure to give you this package," Stroh said after the handshakes. "It's from my boss lady in Cape Town, Mbali Hlanganani. It's her way of saying thank you for all of your help, from a brother African service." Wrapped in newspaper and coarse rope, the five hundred 5 euro notes were clearly visible. Stroh had left ten times that in the CIS headquarters in the capital, Antananarivo.

The two local officials drove Stroh up the dirt main street of the town toward the mountain that dominated the horizon. The road quickly became rutted and then more or less disappeared into grasslands. The three-mile journey from the town took almost an hour of circumnavigating creeks and boulders and then, inexplicably, a dirt road appeared near the base of the mountain. In one direction it lead off down the east side of the hill. In the other, it led past several small, abandoned, cinder block buildings and, after a turn, to a gatehouse where they parked the Hilux.

Stroh could see the tunnel entrance ahead, sealed with a poured cement wall and, in the middle, two metal doors. Someone must protect that, Stroh thought, or that metal would be long gone for its scrap value. He also noticed an electrical line running in from the poles along the road.

His hosts, who spoke a version of French with some English thrown in, explained that there had once been thousands of fruit bats inside. Marcus took some comfort in their use of the past tense. The locals were taking in no special protective equipment. They did, however, produce three dim flashlights.

Marcus Stroh opened his large backpack and produced a strap-on headlamp, a camera, and then some sort of electronic device about the size of a large laptop. When he turned the device on, it buzzed and lights flashed, giving rise to nervous laughter in his hosts. Stroh went first into the tunnel, followed by his guides. Inside, it was cool, but dry. It was also lit by neon tubes every ten feet. They provided only a dim illumination, but Stroh thought, the point was that they were still working.

When they emerged twenty minutes later, the South African removed the last of his devices from the backpack, a satellite phone. With it, he beamed photographs and radioactive readings back to Cape Town. Then he called Mbali in Tel Aviv.

"Well, boss, you were spot on. There were five sort of shelve things, purpose built to store something. And each of them lit up the sensor," Marcus explained. "Nobody around here today, but it looks like they may still be paying some locals to guard the place, otherwise it would have been stripped bare by now. I also spotted something interesting on the way up to the cave. There's also a truck road, which my hosts either did not know about or didn't want me to see."

"And I suppose nobody in the town remembers seeing a bunch of trucks two months ago?" Mbali asked.

"No, of course, not," Stroh laughed. "But I will see if the guys will ask around again. I'll also see if we can drive back down the hill on the truck road and find out where it goes, but I've only got the chopper for a few more hours and I do not, repeat not, want to spend the night up here."

"Is where you're staying in Antananarivo that much better?" Mbali asked from her suite in the Clock.

"As Paris is to Soweto, boss," Stroh said before he powered down the Satcom.

20

"Why do I want to meet this woman, Margaret Taylor?" Mbali asked Danny Avidar as they drove through the narrow streets toward the sea.

"You don't. And you won't, she's not there today," Avidar said, as he steered the car through the traffic. "And it's Tayar, not Taylor. It's a good, little restaurant, with a nice view. That's all."

"Does Mossad own the restaurant, too?"

"No, but we rented it today so there will be no tourists, just us," Avidar explained and then added, ". . . and Raymond."

She glared at him.

"You two have to work together. This thing is too important. So we will all have a nice meal and you two will work it out and we will get back to business."

Mbali started to protest.

"No, don't say it. You are my prisoner. You must come with me," Avidar joked.

Bowman was waiting on the restaurant's rear patio. For late October, the weather was warm and lunch by the sea was a good break from his hours on the iPad with Dugout. He expected Danny to bring Mbali; for an intelligence officer, Avidar was adept at overcoming strife, or at least trying.

Over the stuffed sardines, eggplant, peppers, and couscous, Ray offered an olive branch. "I forgot to mention that Avraham Reuven may have provided us with a lead."

"Really, what was that?" she asked.

"Well, he's an old man, maybe suffering a little Alzheimer's, but he seemed to say that Karl Potgeiter had moved the bombs from South Africa directly to a tunnel somewhere on Madagascar. We're going to check it out."

"Don't bother," she said.

"Why not?"

"I already did. I can show you the photos from inside the tunnel taken this morning by Marcus Stroh. He said the radioactivity readings in the storage bays were what the experts said to except if bombs had been stored there for years."

"How did you . . . ?" Bowman sputtered.

"Danny told me," she said.

207

"I told her," Avidar concurred.

"Last night," Mbali added.

Danny Avidar nodded. "We have an intelligence liaison relationship now, our two countries, information sharing," he said with his mouth full of sardines.

"You . . ." Bowman started. "I have a team of Delta Force commandos getting ready to HALO into there. How did you even know where on Madagascar?"

"You're kidding, right, about the commandos?" Avidar asked.

"No."

"Americans," Mbali said, shaking her head. Avidar rolled his eyes.

"But how?" Bowman pressed.

"My people called up their service. It's called the CIS, not CIA. The French helped them set it up," she explained.

"And so did we," Avidar added. "Help set up their service, that is."

"Madagascar has a state-of-the-art database on all property records, digital," she said reaching for the hummus. "You think only Americans have technology? Africans do, too. It wasn't hard to track down names like Potgeiter and Merwe. Not too many of them on that island." Both Danny and Mbali laughed.

"We're days away from a nuclear warhead

208

detonating in one of our countries and you two are laughing?" Bowman said.

"Raymond, in this business, as you should know, of all people, you have to sprinkle in some dark humor, or else you go crazy, with all the killing and the killers, the madmen," Avidar said. "Try the Barkan. It's their Special Reserve Chardonnay. I noticed you didn't finish the Yarden, so I got this. Maybe you like this one. Drink."

"So what did you find in Madagascar?" Ray asked.

"I'll give you Marcus's report when it comes in, but he found a cave that pretty obviously had been modified to securely store something very radioactive."

"All right, let's talk about Rachel calling for the emergency meeting of the Trustees," Ray responded. "When is it?"

Mbali glared at Danny Avidar. "You told him."

"I did."

She sighed and shook her head. "Rachel asked them to gather at Robert Coetzee's place on Saturday. They've almost all agreed already."

"Dubai?" Avidar asked. "I can't go to Dubai again after, eh, last time."

"Hong Kong," Bowman corrected him.

"Hong Kong," she nodded.

209

"Meanwhile, I don't suppose that your people have found the missing tritium in their dragnet of the country," Ray asked Mbali. She shook her head, no.

"Well, I have tasked all of our technical collection platforms to scan all shipping and aircraft departures from South Africa," Ray said. "And we are running the results through our Minerva big data correlation analytics package. I should have the results in a few hours."

This time it was Danny Avidar who said, "Americans."

Mbali nodded.

"By the way, how did you two do with the your meeting with the Prime Minister last night?" Mbali asked.

"He ordered all aircraft and ship cargoes to be fully searched at the point of departure outside of Israel or when they arrive. All containers, all cargo. He's mobilizing some Army Reserve units to help," Danny answered.

Bowman shook his head, obviously disappointed.

"When does that start?" she asked.

Avidar looked at his watch. "An hour and ten minutes ago."

Something bleated. Mbali grabbed for her large Dior bag and withdrew a mobile phone. "Yes, Marcus?" She listened for several minutes and then signed off.

"Is that encrypted?" Bowman asked.

"No, why would I care if the Israelis intercept the call?" she replied. "I'm going to tell Danny here anyway."

"Tell me what?" Avidar asked.

"Marcus, my man in Madagascar who found the weapon storage tunnel. Before he left town, he went to the little Catholic church on a hunch. Marcus thinks priests know the secrets in any town. There was a priest there who told him that everyone in the town actually knew about the tunnel and the CIS guys had helped to guard it.

"The priest remembered a big convoy of trucks that went up and back to the tunnel on the road that goes around the town," Mbali went on.

"When?" Avidar asked.

"The priest said something I don't understand. Maybe it's some sort of code," she said. "Something about St. Lawrence."

"St. Lawrence Day? When was that?" Ray asked.

"August tenth. And when was the mysterious double flash?"

Avidar was looking at the calendar on his own mobile.

"August ninth," Ray replied. "So the one

test bomb worked and then they moved out the others the next day. The buyers must have been impressed with the test and moved fast."

Mbali pushed her chair back from the table. "I have to go meet with Rachel. She wants help on what she says at the Hong Kong meeting, how she can figure out if any one of the new Trustees know who their predecessors sold the bombs to."

On the narrow street, the small white Hyundai Accent pulled up quickly outside the restaurant and onto the sidewalk. The young Arab driver sat there, with the engine running. A woman across the street began yelling at him.

As the trio walked back from the rear patio into the little indoor dining area, there was a sudden large, blinding light, the furniture came flying toward them, plaster fell from the ceiling, and then an overpowering noise engulfed them, and an invisible force field pushed them to the floor. Outside automobile alarms began wailing.

Two minutes later Bowman pushed himself up. His vision was blurred, but he saw Mbali, dusting herself off. His own blue blazer was covered in white plaster, but he saw through it on his right shoulder where the spot from the brain matter from Cape

212

Town had not completely come out in the hotel's dry cleaning. From behind him, he heard, "Car bomb. We are lucky."

It was Avidar talking, and coughing. "It went off a little early."

COSMOS CLUB
MASSACHUSETTS AVENUE
WASHINGTON, DC

The National Security Advisor was not one for formal greetings. Dugout had been on time and been waiting for twenty minutes. When Burrell sat down his hand went out, not to shake, but for the glass of Macallan, neat, that had already been placed on the table. "I talked with Bowman. He says he's fine, just some ringing in his ears."

"I talked to him, too. He said the Israelis have begun searching everything with radiation sensors," Dugout replied as he sat down at the small table between the marble columns. The Heroy Room could hold thirty for dinner, but it was often just National Security Advisor Winston Burrell and a few guests. When it was a one-on-one, he sat in the alcove by the fountain, as they did now.

"Glad to see you remembered to wear some sort of jacket and tie this time," Burrell greeted him. Even in the private dining rooms, Cosmos enforced the dress code. "I know about the Israelis searching. The Prime Minister called the President this morning to explain. Said he couldn't wait any longer."

"The media are already speculating that there must be intelligence about a loose nuke or an improvised nuclear device," Dugout added.

"I know. The President wants to say it's a bilateral exercise, with our part of the drill beginning within forty-eight hours."

"That's earlier than planned," Dugout noted. "I told Bowman you had agreed to wait until November first."

"That was before the tritium heist, before the Israelis jumped the gun. Tell me what you know about the heist."

Dugout opened his iPad and read from his notes. "South African security thinks the heist was done by a gang of eight to ten men, most or all of whom were probably white. Probably not Arabs. The kind of professional hit that trained military or ex-military commandos would do. They've begun searching outbound cargo for the tritium, but it is a small container. The searching is drawing media attention there, too. Their cover story is that there was a diamond heist, but it's a thin cover."

A waiter appeared with the dinners that Burrell had preordered, Dover sole and Brussels sprouts. "You know the Cosmos Club actually started across the street from the White House in Dolly Madison's town house. Moved here over sixty years ago, but this mansion is twice that old."

Dugout played along. "Ray took me to the Metropolitan Club once. He's a member there. Much closer to the White House."

"Yes, but it's all goddamn lawyers and lobbyists from K Street. Cosmos has had three dozen Nobel laureates and twice as many Pulitzer Prize winners."

The waiter finally departed and Winston Burrell got back to business. "The Israelis say the car bomb was driven by an Arab. Could be al Qaeda showing its hand, trying to kill Bowman."

"Could be, but was it them trying to kidnap him in Cape Town? Did they bring a boat or a plane to Madagascar to pick up the warheads? Did they do a truck heist outside of Pretoria?" Dugout asked.

"You're asking me? It's your fucking job to find connections among all of these threads," Burrell yelled. "You don't think al Qaeda has enough money to buy people to do all of that?"

"Probably, or they could get the money

from their friends in Kuwait and Qatar," Dugout agreed. "I'm looking at money movements from their backers. They handle hundreds of millions in cash. They use these unofficial exchanges called *hawalas*. They don't leave a lot of electrons behind them for me to find."

Burrell put his fork down and put his hand of Dugout's shoulder, squeezing the corduroy jacket. "I know you are doing your best and it's better than all the rest of the agencies put together. They got nothing." He resumed the dissection of the sole. "Do you buy Bowman's fear that when we start searching cargo with radiation detectors the terrorists will know we know about them, will move up their schedule, will . . ." He had a hard time getting out the last word. ". . . Detonate?"

"Election Day is coming up fast. If they want to affect it somehow, maybe, but I'm not sure we know their motivation with the election," Dugout replied. "I have Minerva running through all sorts of data on the heist, the car bomb, the people who tried to kidnap Ray, the Trustees, the way the money was moved, how the warheads were moved. There must be a correlation there I am missing, a motivation."

"Well, I know my motivation. It's to get

through the next three months without a disaster, so it does not happen on my President's watch and so I can hand this job off to the next sucker," Burrell said. He pressed the SERVICE button to call the waiter. "And so far it doesn't look like I am going to make it."

21

THURSDAY, OCTOBER 27
OUTSIDE MORONI, COMOROS ISLANDS

As the disappearance of Malaysia flight 370 in 2014 had proved, the Indian Ocean is vast, largely empty, and infrequently traveled. Even on some of its island nations, the world seldom took note of what happened and, in truth, little ever did happen.

The test of whether the South African bombs would still work had been a detonation on August ninth in a part of the Indian Ocean almost never transited by ship or plane. The MV *Octavius* had vaporized almost three thousand miles east of the South African coast, almost twenty-five hundred miles from either India or Australia. Most spots in the Indian Ocean are like that, a long way from anything.

Yet, immediately off the coast of Africa, the Indian Ocean is filled with small island nations and one very large one. Less than three hundred miles from the African coastal nation of Mozambique is the island of Madagascar, a nation as large as Texas, but with nothing like that state's big cities. Scattered around Madagascar are several of the smallest and most beautiful islands in the world. Some, like the Seychelles, the Maldives, and Mauritius are nation states. Some, like Reunion, Tromelin, and Glorioso are territories of France. One, Diego Garcia, is owned by Britain and rented to the Pentagon.

It was in the isolation of Madagascar that the South African Trustees had stored their bombs for over twenty years without anyone noticing. From there, the test bomb had sailed east in July on the MV *Octavius*. Also from there, after the test, the remaining bombs had been flown out immediately by their new owners. The bombs had been flown back toward the African coast, to a cluster of islands in the Mozambique channel, almost halfway between the African coast and the giant island of Madagascar. That island cluster, once owned by France, is now the nation of Comoros, where three quarter of a million people eked out a living by farming and fishing. Comoros has a million people if you count Mayotte, the one island in the cluster that France had retained.

Shortly after midnight on October 27, on one of the islands in the Comoros, they inserted the tritium bottles into the bombs. That was the last step in getting the weapons ready to be placed on the ships. For two months they had been slowly and carefully replacing the wiring and the batteries. Although the weapons were over twenty-five years old, with the new tritium, wires, and batteries, they were as good as new. The key part of the weapons, the highly enriched uranium, was as good as when it had been first made. HEU took over a thousand years to decay.

The Pakistani-designed tritium container was smaller than the old South African bottle it replaced, but it rode securely in the larger cavity designed for the original booster. The consensus was that it would work well, giving a forty-kiloton yield, maybe more. Even if the gas was defective, the HEU would provide an explosion larger than any conventional weapon. And they had seen with their own eyes what that looked like on August 9. It was a sight like nothing they had ever seen.

Even from the aircraft so many miles away, it had seemed immense and threatening, but also oddly beautiful, almost like something natural, perhaps the way the Big Bang appeared in the first nanoseconds of the birth of this universe. When the next five went off, it would, the men who now owned the bombs assured each other, also be the beginning of a new era.

EILAT, ISRAEL

A half hour after the sun had set, the thirty-four-foot twin outboard left the marina near the cluster of high-rise hotels and moved slowly toward the opening in the seawall. It was a cloudless night, but the lights from the town drowned out most of the stars. When the boat passed the break wall, the young Israeli at the helm increased the speed and turned east.

Ray Bowman smiled, feeling the cool breeze on his face as the boat sped up and the wind blowing his hair around. He was glad to be wearing a warm leather jacket, courtesy of the Mossad office in the town. The sound of the engines was loud and steady, as the boat bounced over the perfectly flat sea, passed the King Herod and then the Dan Hotel.

His escort from the local office was chatting on a mobile phone, in Arabic. "There they are," he said in Hebrew and pointed for the boat's driver. The boat moved out farther away from the shore toward a set of small, blue lights.

As they approached the blue lights, Ray made out the speedboat laying still in the water. The running lights on Ray Bowman's boat blinked twice and then went out. The driver cut the engine back and the two boats coasted together. The Mossad man threw a rope to the only man on the other boat and called out *"As-salamu alaykum."*

"Shalom," came the response. The two boats pulled together side by side. The Mossad man helped Bowman step from the Israeli outboard to the slightly larger Jordanian craft. He passed Bowman his two small bags.

Abdullah al Shahwan grabbed Bowman, as he jumped down to the deck. The two men embraced. "Welcome back to Jordan, Raymond," Abdullah said in English.

"You shouldn't have come out on the water yourself," Bowman replied.

"It's my boat. I almost never get to take it out. The King doesn't come to Aqaba as much anymore, but tonight he's in the palace here so I am here." Behind them, the Israeli boat opened up, heading back to Eilat. Ray noticed the red and green running lights were back on. "I used to fish at night for hammour. Now I fish at night for al Qaeda and ISIS."

"I'd rather have the grouper, the hammour, tonight. I am famished," Ray said, sitting down in the chair next to the helm.

"The Israelis didn't feed you? And they almost get you killed by a car bomb? We'll treat you better." He pulled back on the control for the big inboard diesel and the boat almost stood up as it headed toward the shore where a giant Jordanian flag, fluttering in the spotlight, flew above the port once liberated by Lawrence of Arabia.

SDE DOV AIRFIELD
TEL AVIV, ISRAEL

"It's an old Hawker, but trust me it's all new on the inside. New engines, glass cockpit, like a new plane it is," Danny Avidar was making small talk while he waited plane side with Mbali and Rachel. "From Cyprus, you will be on a charter. A Falcon. French, very nice. Bigger than my Hawker and owned by Greeks. Really. No one in Dubai will ever know you started from a small airstrip south of Tel Aviv.

"You will spend the day in Dubai, Rachel, on the South African passport, while Mbali drives to Abu Dhabi to get on an Etihad flight to Hong Kong,"

Mbali picked up the story. "I will actually

223

arrive a day before you. You fly out the next day to Hong Kong on Emirates from Dubai."

Rachel looked concerned. "You are worried, don't be worried," Danny Avidar assured her. "You're looking at the big smoke tower at the end of the runway? No one has ever hit it."

Rachel smiled. "It's the first time that I have left the girls overnight with my mother since, since Dawid," she said.

"I told you, I have my people watching the house, watching the girls. They will be fine until you get back. And Mbali will be around the corner from you all the time in Hong Kong to make sure you get back."

Mbali pulled Rachel close. "And it won't just be me. Danny's people will be helping me. And I have some other friends who will be in town working with me. You go to Hong Kong, have the meeting with the new Trustees, and be back here in four days. Don't worry."

Rachel looked at Danny Avidar. "I consider myself to be Israeli. This is the only country I have ever really known. There is no other home. Nowhere else to go where I would feel safe. I may not practice, but I am a Jew, as are the girls. If there is any chance that a nuclear bomb might come here . . ."

Avidar reached out his hand to her. "You are doing your duty. You may be able to help us find the bombs and the bombers."

"I just can't believe that Dawid would have knowingly been part of a plot to sell a nuclear device to anyone," she said to Avidar.

"I'm sure he didn't know all of the details," Avidar assured her, "but that's what we need you to find out, the details. And I know you will, dear, I know it." He escorted the two women to the plane, a Zulu who stood just over six feet tall in flat shoes, and a young Israeli mother who was five foot eight in heels. He had sent odd-looking teams undercover before, including men dressed as women, but he had trained those teams well. This mission was more important than any of those, but this one was being put together as they went along.

He stood by his car on the apron and watched the Hawker take off and bank west, the taillights blinking as it passed the power plant smoke tower.

22

FRIDAY, OCTOBER 28
OUTSIDE AQABA, JORDAN

Abdullah added new wood to the fire, as his "tea boy" changed the tobacco in their hookahs. The lights of Aqaba below were as bright now after midnight as they had been in the early evening. No one on this side of the border was conserving on electricity or fuel.

"You have a magnificent home here. Why are we sitting on a patch of dirt above it freezing our asses off," Bowman observed, "after a sumptuous meal with some truly outstanding Montrachet."

"I told you my wife won't let me smoke the hubby bubbly in the house," he said holding a small battery powered fan over the tobacco as his aide lit the coals. "This is the good apple cinnamon from Turkey. They make good tobacco for the hookahs, the Turks."

"Your wife is in London. You just like pretending you're a bedouin or a desert Arab when you have never been on a camel in your life," Bowman laughed. He took a drag on the water pipe, tasting the flavored tobacco on his tongue. "The only things you ride are Bugattis and Black Hawks."

"Did I tell you I qualified on the Osprey? Boy was that hard. You think flying a helicopter is difficult?" Abdullah asked. "We have three Ospreys now in the Royal Wing."

"I don't trust those things," Ray replied. "Secret Service will not let the President ride in one."

"Speaking of your President, who is going to replace him? They say it is so tight, neck and neck. His Majesty watched the debates. He loves switching between MSNBC and Fox," Abdullah said. "We couldn't believe they were still talking about climate change and abortion. How can anyone still not believe in climate change? And abortions? We just go to London for them."

Ray poked at the fire, stirring it up. "I have no idea who is going to win the election. Until a little while ago I was safely off the grid, or almost. My job now is to make sure the election happens and is not canceled because of nuclear bombs going off a few days before."

Abdullah put down the hookah. "So it's real then? We saw the Israelis starting to inspect all their cargo with Geiger counters. There are nukes on the loose? North Korean? Pakistani?"

"No, old ones from South Africa. Somebody just bought them. Spent two and a half billion U.S.," Ray explained. "The President is about to start holding up all of our cargo, too, looking for nukes. I was hoping you would tell me that al Qaeda just spent that kind of money on something and where I might look for that something."

"If I knew anything like that, Raymond, Washington would already know from me. Besides, how would I know?"

Bowman took a long gasp from the hookah and exhaled a cloud. "Because you and two other royal Arab houses have pretty good intelligence services and you have each penetrated al Qaeda and its branches, AQAP, AQIM, ISIS, and the rest of the alphabet soup of sickos. You all share what you get with each other, but not always everything with Washington."

"Raymond, who do you think pays my bills? I tell them everything, of course I do."

"No, Abdullah, you tell them most things, you tell them facts, you don't tell them sources. Because you fear Washington will leak to the press or some perv like Snowden will tell the Russians and your sources will be slowly flayed alive. I know because you were telling me more than you have been telling the Agency. You knew it wouldn't leak from me and it never did."

"Okay. I've heard nothing about a WMD. Neither have my brothers in the Gulf. Nothing," Abdullah insisted.

"Tell me about the money. Could AQ come up with that kind of money to buy nukes?"

"Once maybe, not now. Their bank rollers in Qatar and Kuwait are spent out on ISIS, the Muslim Brotherhood and Egypt, the Nusra in Syria, their tribal militias in Libya, the Houthi down in Yemen, even Shabab in Somalia," Abdullah replied. "It would take a major effort to get that kind of money and we would have heard about it."

Bowman added sticks to the fire. "Can you double-check?"

Abdullah stood. "Walk up the hill a little, so we can see the stars, farther away from the villa." Raymond Bowman followed him.

They looked down on Abdullah's villa, the lights in the pool making the water seem like a floating blob of baby blue. "I do have a very special source, which I hear from time to time. You are right about him.

Washington does not know about him. He is too precious."

"Why is he so special?" Ray asked.

"Ray, AQ is not as fractured as Washington thinks. The big man still calls the shots on major policy decisions. Using a WMD would be a major policy decision. No one would act on a WMD without his knowledge."

"And your source would know?"

"He is a very precious source, Raymond."

"He calls you?"

"He communicates."

"You have an emergency way of initiating communication?" Ray asked.

Abdullah looked up at the stars. "There is Orion's Belt. You see it?"

"If a WMD bomb goes off, or several do, and you had a way . . ." Ray began.

"I understand. I do, truly, Raymond, *habibi,* I do." Abdullah began to walk back down the hill. "It may take several days. It may not even work."

"Please try," Ray Bowman pleaded.

"Of course. Anything else?"

"Are you or the King using the Gulf-stream 650 tomorrow? I need to get to Hong Kong."

"But you're white," the drummer said.

"White dudes can play tenor sax," Dugout insisted.

"Name the great tenor saxes in history," the drummer asked.

"Okay, okay. Charlie Parker, Coltrane, the Hawk, Dolphy, Sonny Rollins, Lester Young, and Stan Getz."

"And how many of them was a white dude?" the drummer asked.

"Stan Getz."

"You play like him?" the drummer asked.

"No, man, I play like Charlie Parker," Dugout answered.

The four guys in the group laughed simultaneously. "This I have to hear with my own damn ears," the bass player said. "You're in. Besides, our man Harold is sick and there ain't no other tenor sax players here tonight."

"Yeah, okay," the drummer agreed. "Besides it's just an open jam after the midnight show. Let's call it practice."

"Or we could call it integration," the bass player joked.

"What you know, Mr. Parker, or what you

231

say your name is."

"They call me Dugout. Why not start out hot and then go blue. So, maybe 'Mercy, Mercy, Mercy' then switch up to 'Mood Indigo'?"

The group looked around at each other, nodding. "Let's try it," the bass player agreed.

As the blue lights came up on the little stage and the group appeared from the darkness, the bass player spoke into the mic. "We had a little problem tonight with Harold Rainman Rollins. His appendix done burst this afternoon. So, in the spirit of brotherhood, we are integrating the group tonight. So on tenor sax, we have Dugout. And because we haven't played a lot with him before, we ask of you 'Mercy, Mercy, Mercy.' Hit it."

After the first two bars, the drummer hit the cymbals and the room started to clap, Dugout leaped into the sax solo, and handed off to the piano player amid a round of applause. The drummer gave Dug a wink and a thumbs-up. As the piece ended with Dug squeezing out a high note, the bass player intoned in a deep voice over the audience's approval, "Mercy, Mercy, Mercy."

"Mood Indigo" gave way to "Green Dolphin Street," "Desafinado," "I

Remember Clifford," and "Isfahan." Dugout had soaked through his black T-shirt under the lights and was wondering how long a set these guys played, when the bass player stepped up and explained to the crowd. "We appreciate that it seems like none of you all have left during this set. That's always a good sign. So, maybe we found us a good sax after all." There were hoots and clapping. "So, we're going to close out with a piece that will let him strut his stuff. A piece made famous by his hero Charlie Parker."

Dugout felt a moment of fear, not knowing whether this was a setup, whether this was going to be something he knew how to play.

" 'A Night in Tunisia,' " the bass player exclaimed.

It was the classic Charlie Parker piece, written by Dizzy Gillespie. He knew it cold. Dug hit the opening bar and it was all his after that.

After the set, the group sat around in the audience, drinking on the house. "We're hoping to get Harold back next week, but you are welcome to join us anytime," the bass player said as they were closing the hall.

"Yeah," the drummer agreed. "After all, you can never have too much sax."

It was after three in the morning when

Dugout got on the red Capital Bikeshare bicycle on F Street and pedaled past the White House toward Foggy Bottom. The streets were far from empty. Students from George Washington were finding their way back to the dorms from 14th Street, from H Street, from wherever they had eaten a grease burger to sop up the booze after the bars closed. As he dodged them on his way to Navy Hill, the breeze giving him a little chill after the heat of the club, Dugout still felt the high of the music, the audience, the group. His good feeling was reflected by the fun the college kids were obviously having that night. He thought of texting a friend to see if he was still up, to see if he wanted a late-night visit.

Then he thought of the work he had to go in to do, and why. He had needed the break of playing his music, but he also felt guilty taking any time off, with Ray out there with people trying to kill him. He really should not have a life of his own, Dugout thought, until he had cracked the problem. And he had thought of new ways of running the correlations, new databases to add. As he passed a knot of students horsing around outside a fraternity, he sensed sobriety overtaking him. Unless he could crack this jumble, find out who it was they were up against, there might not be many more fun nights in this city.

He flashed his badge at the gate into the Navy Hill complex and punched in his PIN. The guard in the gatehouse knew him by sight and waved. Dugout showed up a lot in the middle of the night.

23

SATURDAY, OCTOBER 29
GULFSTREAM 650
TAIL NUMBER JY-RF3
FORTY-THOUSAND FEET OVER KUWAIT
Not flying over Iran added a few miles to the flight, but this was one of the King's private planes that could fly over eight thousand miles without touching down for fuel. They could make it to Hong Kong without a full fuel load. As he explored the cabins and amenities on the aircraft, Ray wondered how many electronic intelligence services would be tracking the aircraft: the Saudis, the Russians, the Chinese, the Israelis, obviously the Americans, and the Brits. The Paks and the Indians would take note when the aircraft went through or near their air space. How many of them would wonder why the King of Jordan was flying to Hong Kong? How many would know that he was actually in his palace near the Red

Sea planning the moves involved with dumping yet another Prime Minister?

"Finding everything all right?" It was the blonde flight attendant, or rather one of them. She was Dutch. The other one had said she was Estonian. "We've made up the bed in the rear cabin and, if you are going to try to sleep, I can give you some Ambien," she said.

"Oh, no, thank you," Ray replied, "I've sworn off the stuff. Better off being jet lagged and groggy. Besides, I prefer the natural method. Do you have any single malt?"

"There are three bottles of the Macallan twenty-five-year-old," she said.

Of course, there were. With a bottle retailing at a little under a thousand dollars, Ray Bowman found himself wondering why you would need three bottles on any flight.

He shuddered at the thought of the sleeping pill and the memory of his own Ambien horror three years earlier. He had woken, or semi-woken, in the middle of the street three blocks from his condo in Foggy Bottom, naked. He had no idea how he had gotten there, but later deduced he had sleepwalked from his bed after taking an Ambien to deal with jet lag.

In one very quick instant, he had

calculated his options: skulk back home through back alleys, where he might be arrested as a lurking rapist; saunter nonchalantly down the brick sidewalks, acting as if he were some protesting nonconformist; or run as fast as possible, hoping that no one would notice that he had no trunks on. He chose the jogging option and, since it appeared to be deep in the middle of the night, and he ran faster than he ever had in his life, a blur of a six-foot-two man with very white, hairy skin, he had made it to the town house without seeing another human and, more importantly for his career, not being arrested for indecent exposure. There he had another moment of fear stabbing at his stomach, as his hand went to his pocket for the keys.

Another flash and he remembered that the backup key was in the dirt around the little fir tree in the giant pot. Later as he sat on his deck, wearing running trunks, watching the sun begin to turn pink the distant sky over Maryland, he sipped a twelve-year-old Balvenie single malt and told himself he would never again use Ambien.

"That would be great. The Macallan. Three fingers, neat," he told the Dutch woman.

As he sipped the liquid mahogany, he

thought how well he was dealing with the fact that there were people trying to kill him, people whose identities he did not know. He had focused instead on the more important fact that those same people were probably trying to kill a lot more people than just him, that they were even at this moment probably moving nuclear warheads into place in some great cities.

When they did that, there was no way of knowing what the consequences would be beyond the immediate disaster area. They would, however, be momentous and negative. And when exactly they would do that, Washington thought in its collective, classified wisdom, was sometime in the next week, the last week of the presidential election campaign. He tried to find hope in a scenario in which the Hong Kong meeting would reveal that some of the new Trustees knew who had bought the nuclear devices. Just a lead, that was all he needed, a thread that he and Dugout, and Dugout's machines, could pull on.

The Gulfstream had climbed to forty-two thousand feet as it headed out of the night and the Arab Gulf into the Indian Ocean, racing toward the sun.

He sipped the single malt and thought of what was waiting ahead when the Gulfstream touched down. He knew the last Police Commissioner of Hong Kong, but not his replacement. At least the new guy had agreed to meet with him. What a story the Commissioner was going to hear.

24

"You should let me win once in a while. Maybe you would get promoted, Richard," Stephen Cheung joked as they walked toward the clubhouse.

"I don't think I am ever being promoted again, Commissioner," Richard Taylor laughed. "There is a glass ceiling for people with English surnames and I have hit it. So, after thirty years on the force here, I take my little satisfactions where I can."

"You must be our guest for drinks," Commissioner Cheung said, looking up at Raymond Bowman, standing on the steps of the clubhouse. "This is Assistant Commissioner Richard Taylor, Crime and Security. We have reserved a private room. Follow me, if you would." The threesome walked past portraits of English military officers and colonial officials from earlier centuries, up a narrow back stair to a perch atop the clubhouse, looking out and down on a city in the distance, in the smog.

"We know who you are Mr. Bowman. The American Consulate has explained who you report to," Commissioner Cheung began. "My predecessor, Peter Wong, recalls you fondly from his year at the Kennedy School. He sends you his best. I did not get to go to Harvard. My year it was the Royal College of Defense Studies, which made my wife happy. You see we met twenty-two years ago when I was a bobby for two years in Scotland Yard. She still loves London."

The Assistant Commissioner was mixing two gin and tonics at a drinks dolly. "Will you join us in a G and T?" Taylor asked. "Can I make a third?" Bowman nodded agreement.

The Commissioner waved Bowman out on to the small balcony. "Don't let all this British atmosphere fool you, Mr. Bowman. We are ruled by Beijing. Our semiautonomous stature goes only so far. That city in the distance is in China."

"You seem rather unlike the People's Armed Police," Bowman replied.

"Very unlike them, yes," Richard Taylor agreed, joining them on the balcony. "Hong

Kong Police are independent. We get no help from the mainland. We have to have our own little navy of boats and our own little air force of helicopters to secure one of the most densely populated cities in the world and its many islands. But the Ministry of State Security and the People's Liberation Army stay in their compound in Central, where the British Army used to be. Beijing knows what goes on here, although not always in real time."

"So it is I who will decide whether to assist you, not Beijing," the Commissioner asserted. "Tell me why I should."

"No city anywhere in the world has been destroyed by a nuclear weapon in over seventy years. That may be about to change," Bowman began. He told the two Hong Kong policemen most of what he knew. "What I am asking your help with is surveilling the new Trustees and their meeting."

The two Hong Kong officers looked at each other in a way that said they were used to being told bizarre stories that were unfortunately true. "Do you know where they are now?" Commissioner Cheung asked.

"I know where their mobile phones are. All at the Upper House, the five-star hotel

243

owned by Robert Coetzee, one of the new Trustees. They are waiting for the last Trustee to arrive and she gets in late tonight. Their meeting is scheduled for tomorrow morning."

The Assistant Commissioner laughed, "You just want us to get into Mr. Coetzee's hotel tonight and bug the conference room he plans to hold his secret meeting in tomorrow morning. Is that all?"

"Yes, and we need to get a man into the hotel's server and telco room," Bowman replied. "And you always have two off-duty officers working security at the hotel at night. Naturally, we will pay them for their cooperation."

"Naturally, you will not," Cheung shot back. "This is not Shanghai. We are a clean police force. No bribes. They will help you because I will order them to help you."

"Thank you, Commissioner," Ray said.

"You want them all under physical surveillance when they leave the hotel?" Taylor asked.

"Yes, if possible. Three men, two women. But we have a few of our own people who have been picking them up at the airport and following them to the hotel."

"CIA men stand out in Hong Kong," Taylor observed.

"But the people they hire do not. And six South Africans flew in to help."

"Blacks will stand out even more," Cheung laughed.

"Yes, sir, but they are not black, although they work for a black woman. I think you might like to meet her and I know she would like to meet you. She is the Director of their Special Security Services. Right now she is running a little ops room we have set up."

"At the American Consulate?" Taylor asked.

"Ah, no," Bowman admitted. "We are using a company in a high-rise in Central."

"We will pretend we don't know that," Commissioner Cheung said. "Now Richard will help you get all of this in place and will get you some bodyguards, while I go home to see the grandchildren before they go to bed."

"Bodyguards?" Ray protested.

"Mr. Bowman, you just told us they have tried to kill you in two countries. Third time may be the charm. They, these unknown bad guys, must be here, too, and they may eventually kill you, but they will not do so in my city. I like to keep my murder statistics low." With that, Cheung left the two men to their nightwork.

25

MONDAY, OCTOBER 31
FORTY-SIXTH FLOOR
PACIFIC TRUST TOWER
CENTRAL, HONG KONG

"There is a great view of Kowloon across the bay," Mbali said, "or at least there was before they put up the blackout curtains. Welcome to our upscale offices."

"CIA spares no expense when it comes to their own real estate needs. They'll say it adds credibility to their cover, whatever that is," Ray replied as he walked into the conference room filed with computer monitors, television screens, headsets, and other electronics.

"We're a hedge fund, Emerging Opportunities," a man with Mbali explained. "Peter Mason, Base Chief Hong Kong." He looked like he might have been an Assistant Professor of Economics, in a blazer, bow tie, and horn-rimmed glasses. "They've finished the small talk over breakfast and are convening in the hotel conference room on fifty-two. The audio and video feeds are working well from the room and we are running the audio from their cell phones as backup. All set."

"I wish we were closer, in case anything goes wrong," Mbali said to Ray. "Pacific Place, where the hotel is, even though it looks near, would take us almost half an hour in this traffic."

"We're fine. You have two guys in the hotel and two guys outside. Peter, here, has twice that number. And Hong Kong Police have undercovers everywhere, including doing counter surveillance to see if anybody else is here."

"You mean besides Danny Avidar's team," she said.

"I told the Commissioner they were ours. No need to complicate things. Where are they?" Ray asked.

"In the next room," the CIA Base Chief answered for her.

"A nice young couple. They live here full time. He actually does work at a hedge fund, when he's not doing errands for Mossad. They are getting the same audio feed we are, but they have some special link back to Tel Aviv so they wanted their own space."

"So we have Israeli, South African, American, and Hong Kong agents all set up on this meeting. I am sure no one will ever notice," Ray deadpanned.

They could see the meeting beginning. Five people arranging themselves around a round table, placing their coffee mugs and teacups next to their papers. "Amazing that Coetzee is using a room with videoconferencing," Mbali noted.

"All of his conference rooms have videoconferencing," the Base Chief observed. "He just thinks the camera is off. He unplugged it. We swapped it out for a lookalike with a battery pack and a wireless feed."

Robert Coetzee began. He was still a large man, even though he was in his late seventies, with a pink head of thinning white hair. "We meet as the Trustees of a charitable foundation, created to care for the needs of those who became exiles after the fall of the government of South Africa. We are fiduciaries of that fund. Yes, we are compensated for managing the fund's investments, but fundamentally we are the leaders of a global fund that is housed in several different countries. We each manage a portion of the money individually, but we decide together how the funds are spent."

Coetzee continued. "As you know, the tradition among our predecessors was that there was no chairman. The meetings rotated among the five cities and the host always played the role of informal chair. So, it falls to me under these sad circumstances to welcome us all as new members of the Trustees, to our first meeting. Rachel, I am glad that you asked for this session. I am sure that we need it. Before we hear from Rachel, however, maybe we could each introduce ourselves and say a little about what we do, who we are. Paul Wyk, will you start? You are the youngest."

Wyk looked even younger than the twenty-nine years that he was. Tall and thin, with the wiry look of a tennis star, he was in fact an investment banker. "I live in Wellington, New Zealand. I replace Willem Merwe of Sydney, who replaced his father before him. My late father was the head of Army Research and Development in South Africa. He resettled in New Zealand when I was little. I have no real memories of Africa. The books I have taken over from Merwe show that we have slightly over 1.8b U.S. dollars under management from the Sydney office, some of it newly arrived. I can go into the details of how it's invested when we get to that part of the meeting."

"Hesitant, very matter of fact," Mbali observed to Ray Bowman in their observation post a half mile away.

"Like he's not sure what it's all about," Ray added.

"Liz Pleiss, from Toronto. I replace my father, Marius, who lived, and, ah, died in Dubai." She looked to be in her early forties, dressed in a gray business suit. She looked like she felt at home in a boardroom. "I have been a management consultant, specializing in making mergers work, but now I think I may have to leave that work to do full time on these investments. I have an MBA from the Sloan School, but investing is not my expertise. My father's data show a book value of 1.3b U.S. dollars, although much of the original 800 million dollars is tied up in real estate."

"Notice that she didn't mention what her father did in South Africa. Didn't mention South Africa at all," Mbali said.

"What did her dad do back then?" Peter Mason, or whatever the CIA man's name was, asked.

"He was the CFO of ARMSCOR, their big defense industry," Ray Bowman replied.

"I am Rachel Steyn, a mother of two girls. I worked at Google in Israel. I managed databases and had a small R-and-D team

250

on new projects in data storage. I served in the Israeli Army before that. My late husband, Dawid, who was murdered, was the investor. He had 2.1 billion dollars in the accounts. His father made nuclear bombs in South Africa, but I will wait to talk about that."

"Nicely done," Bowman observed. Mbali nodded, pleased.

"Johann Potgeiter, Vienna. My father also worked on the nuclears, lately for the UN. I had been working with him on the assets for some time. We have 3.1 billion U.S. dollars under management, much of it in real estate."

"Short and sweet," Mbali said.

"From a man who told me he was not a Trustee," Ray added.

"Well, back to me," Robert Coetzee began. "I was a South African Special Forces officer. My brother was in intelligence. He was the Trustee. With the new money, we have almost three billion dollars in book value, which, if I have done my sums, gives us collectively slightly over ten billion dollars U.S. in assets under management. We are going to have to discuss at some point what we do with it all, because it must kick off far more than we need to pay for the widows and orphans. But, first, Rachel, you wanted to

251

discuss the, ah, recent events."

"My husband was murdered," she began. "Your father was, too, Elizabeth, as was yours Johann. And your brother, Robert. And Willem Merwe."

"Well, Rachel, we can't be sure of that yet. The police think that the deaths in Dubai, Sydney, and Vienna may have been accidents," Johann Potgeiter replied. "Although I admit it would be an extraordinary series of coincidences."

"They were not coincidences, Johann," Coetzee said. "That is why I am willing to provide for all of your protection at home in your countries using the global security company we own. All former Special Forces and Special Branch types from several countries. Very good. Very solid."

Rachel resumed. "They were all murdered shortly after they received large deposits of half a billion dollars each. They were killed by the men who paid them that money, who paid them for something."

"What? I don't understand," said Wyk. "Why pay and then kill them. Why not the other way round? What did they sell them?"

"Nuclear bombs," Rachel said.

No one replied, for a moment.

"How do we know that?" Robert Coetzee asked.

252

"Mossad. They told me. They have proof," Rachel said confidently. "Proof that the original Trustees took with them when they left South Africa not only cash, diamonds, and gold, but also six nuclear missile warheads. There are five left. One they tested secretly to prove they work still. Then they sold the five."

"That's incredible," Wyk said.

"No, I think it could be true," Robert Coetzee interjected. "Cornelius always told me there was a secret program that he could not read me into. He also told me before he died that they had made what he called a Deacquistion Decision that would result in a great deal of additional cash. They sold something to somebody."

"But, as Paul asked, then why would the buyers kill them? Maybe it was someone else who killed them because they sold whatever it was they sold?" Liz Pleiss thought out loud.

"They killed them to cover their tracks. Now no one knows who bought the bombs," Rachel said looking around the table. "Unless one of us does."

Johann Potgeiter squirmed in his seat. "It is possible," he said. "My father and I used to have long discussions about his work at the IAEA, over schnapps, after my wife and

253

the children would retire." He seemed reluctant to go on, but then added, "I remember him asking me whether the best way to deal with Iran's nuclear program would not be to give the Saudis nuclear weapons."

"That's crazy," Paul Wyk said.

"Maybe, but if Iran has the bomb, they can intimidate everyone in the region. Unless another equal power also has the bomb. Just like India's program balances Pakistan's. Like America's balances Russia's and China's. I think he wanted Saudi Arabia to have the bomb. He believed the answer to nuclear proliferation was balance."

"Lovely," Rachel observed.

"Well, you already have nukes in Israel," Johann replied.

"Balance could mean someone else," Robert Coetzee interjected. "It could mean South Korea getting some to counter what the North has made."

"Or it could be al Qaeda," Rachel noted.

"My brother would not have done that," Coetzee shot back. "Never. If he did this, he must have thought the buyer was a responsible party."

"Responsible for killing him," Liz Pleiss added. "So, let me get this straight, we are all accepting the fact that we have about 2.5

billion dollars in dirty money, money made from selling nuclear bombs? That makes us all criminals, even if we didn't know, they could arrest us, or at least seize the assets, or both. This explains why they raided my office yesterday. I heard about it just after I landed here."

"Who?" Johann Potgeiter asked. "Who raided your office?"

"Apparently the RCMP, the Canadian police," Liz Pleiss replied. "They took all my files, according to my secretary."

"The Shin Beth took mine," Rachel answered.

"God, the Mounties going through everything. That's all I need with my taxes as they are," Liz said.

"Taxes? Is that all you are worrying about, your taxes," Paul Wyk asked. "Don't you get it? Somebody is getting ready to blow up bombs. Nuclear bombs that we, our organization sold them. Shit. We need to turn ourselves in."

"To who?" Robert Coetzee asked.

"The UN, I don't know," Wyk stammered.

"No, it's not that we sold them," Liz Pleiss insisted. "We did nothing wrong. We knew nothing about this. We just inherited the money as fiduciaries of a charity for South African exiles. No, we did not sell bombs.

We did nothing."

"Who could arrest us?" Wyk asked.

"The Americans certainly," Liz Pleiss answered. "They have all sorts of laws related to anything they think is national security. Christ, we are going to need some good lawyers."

"Maybe we give the money back," Paul Wyk offered.

"To who?" Rachel asked.

"To the Americans, for starters," Liz Pleiss suggested. "Maybe they can trace it."

"Mossad couldn't," Rachel replied. "They told me they tried."

"Do you work for them?" Johann Potgeiter asked. "You said you were in the Army."

"Ten years ago I was in the Army. We all do that in Israel," Rachel answered. "The only intelligence service I worked for was Google. We collected intelligence so we can sell ads to people. The first time I met Mossad was when they came to tell me that my husband's dying was no accident."

"It's all so incredible," Paul Wyk repeated. "How have I gotten involved in all of this?"

"Rachel, if there were bombs somewhere, they must be ancient. Did Mossad say that they think they would still work?" Liz Pleiss asked.

"Yes. They say the test bomb worked in

the middle of the Indian Ocean. And then, recently, something else happened."

"What was that?" Robert Coetzee asked.

"In South Africa, there was a truck hijacking, ah, what do you call it, a heist," Rachel explained. "Someone stole some special material called tritium. That is what is needed to make the old weapons work. Around the same time, Mossad thinks, the bombs left their storage area on Madagascar."

"Oh, dear," Robert Coetzee replied. "That does sound like al Qaeda or some group, not Korea. Korea would just have made its own stuff, Trit, whatever it was."

"We need to find out who they sold the bombs to because we need to stop them from being used," Rachel interjected. Her voice was higher now, her pace faster. "What if it is al Qaeda? I know Dawid would not knowingly have sold to someone who would threaten Israel, but what if they were al Qaeda pretending to be somebody else? I love Israel. It is my home, my children's home. If it is a risk, I must do everything I can to save it."

It was Paul Wyk who broke the ensuing silence. "If any country is at risk of a nuclear attack, we all must do everything we can to save it and not just because we personally will be to blame."

Robert Coetzee had his head in his hands. He looked up, ran his fingers through his thin white hair. "Yes, of course, but the question is how can we help. We have all been through our predecessors' records. I assume no one found a receipt for the sale of a nuclear bomb? Or anything else that might lead us to who the recipient was?"

"So," Johann Potgeiter said, "we are all assuming Rachel's story is right. That what the Mossad told her is true?"

"We have to," Liz Pleiss answered. "We have to assume it's true, for now. It's certainly not impossible and it does answer the question of why we suddenly have so much new money." She opened her laptop. "We need a timeline, a unified timeline. Where were our predecessors in the month or two before they died? Did they meet together somewhere? Did a couple of them go somewhere first to negotiate on behalf of the group?" She tapped the keyboard. "I have all of his travel records."

"I have Dawid's, too," Rachel added.

"In the two months before he died, my father went to New York twice, Taipei once, London once, and Vancouver twice," Liz Pleiss read from the screen.

"Taipei?" Robert Coetzee queried. "My

brother was in Taipei as well. Was that your father's first trip there?"

"As far as I know," Pleiss answered, staring at her records.

Paul Wyk was busy tapping on his iPhone. "We may be on to something here. I just checked with my office. Merwe also went to Taipei six weeks before he died."

"That's it, that's the balance my father was talking about," Johann Potgeiter interjected excitedly. "Taiwan was one of the examples he used. He said they were building a nuclear bomb in the eighties, but the Americans caught them and made them stop. He said if they had gone ahead, they could have stood up to China better. He talked about that after he returned from a trip to Asia. I didn't know it included Taipei, but it must have."

"Rachel?" Coetzee asked. "Was Dawid in Taipei?"

"Not that I know of," she said. "But it does make sense that he would be willing to sell nuclears to them. They would be no threat to Israel. And Dawid hated Communism."

"Well, it seems plausible that our predecessors as Trustees sold old nuclear devices to Taiwan. There would be nothing dishonorable in that, just helping an ally of

259

old South Africa to defend itself. Taiwan is peaceful, doesn't threaten anyone," Robert Cotzee mused aloud. "And I suppose perhaps the Taiwanese could have been somewhat duplicitous and killed off the men who sold them the weapons, just to make sure no one knew about the deal. They have a large intelligence service."

"So, is that what we think?" Paul Wyk asked the group.

"It explains it all rather well, actually, fits all the pieces together," Johann Potgeiter added.

"And it may not even have been illegal," Liz Pleiss suggested. "You said, Rachel, the bombs were stored in some African country?"

"Madagascar, it's an island, a country, off Africa."

"Okay, I bet they don't have laws there against selling nuclear bombs," Liz said, gaining in enthusiasm for her own theory. "Maybe the bombs were stolen property, but I bet that can be argued either way. Maybe our fathers and brothers owned the bombs when they moved them from South Africa. Anyway, it could all be a legal transaction, maybe violated some UN resolutions, but nothing that could cause us to be arrested. A sovereign government did a transaction with our funds and paid us for goods received. We're off the hook."

"That's a relief," Wyk replied. "It does leave the fact that the Taiwanese may have ordered our predecessors murdered, but maybe we just forget about following up on that."

"That would be wise, Paul," Coetzee suggested. "If we try to do anything about it, we will be telling Taiwan that we know who bought the bombs. Then they could come after us. No, I think we remain silent about our suppositions about whether there were bombs, who they were sold to, and who ordered the hits on our people. Silent."

"I agree," Liz Pleiss replied. "Completely. And I suggest that we also all agree that this conversation never took place." There was murmured concurrence around the table.

"Then, let's take a break and go out on to the roof deck for some tea and coffee," Robert Coetzee suggested. "When we come back, we can deal with the issue of how we spend what these funds earn, in a way that benefits the diaspora that we represent."

From their little war room, Mbali and Ray watched on their screen as the new Trustees pushed back and got up from the conference table. Mbali looked at Ray without a

261

word, but with a face that asked for comment.

"Taiwan? I doubt it, but let's check with Dugout and see if the records match up," he said. He tapped on a keyboard and another image appeared on the large screen in the room, a long-haired man, with glasses, wearing a black T-shirt. "I assume you were listening to all of that Duggie."

There was a brief static as the audio connection from Washington was established. "Yes, good evening to you, too. It's evening here, of course. And thank you for introducing me to Miss Hlanganani. Pleased to meet you. My name is Douglas Carter and I have the pleasure of working with the gentleman to your right."

Ray Bowman rolled his eyes. "Delighted to finally meet you," Mbali said to the video camera.

"As to your implied question, Raymond, I'm not buying it," Dugout continued. "Yes, Pleiss, Coetzee, and Potgeiter were all in Taipei at the same time six weeks before they were murdered. The others weren't there. Those three gentlemen were there to close on an investment in a large, new hotel and high-end retail mall that each of them put some money in. But we would know if the Taiwanese had bought bombs and there is no indication that they did."

"How would we know?" Ray asked.

"First of all, we have their government fairly well penetrated and second, there is no record of funds like that leaving any Taiwanese accounts around then. And do you think the Taiwan intel service could stage everything else involved: murdering these Trustees all over the place, the tritium heist, the covert shipment from Madagascar, the attempted hits on you?"

"Probably not," Ray replied. "But it wouldn't hurt to confront them with the story and see what happens, see if they panic and say something internally, something we can pick up."

"You two are forgetting something," Mbali interjected.

"What's that?" Dugout asked over the video link.

"We just had Rachel do something to see if anybody panics. She laid out the fact that we know what is going on, or at least Mossad does." Mbali was proud of how her newly recruited agent had done as an actress in the meeting. "If you two are right and it's not really Taiwan, then somebody will panic shortly when they find out that we are on their trail and we are closer than they thought."

"Well, one of them better panic quick. 'Cuz we got an election in eight days and a lot of people at CIA, FBI, and DHS are telling the President that nukes are going to go off in this country between now and then," Dugout answered.

"Patience," she said. "You Americans need to learn patience and the skill of laying in the tall grass, waiting, listening, like a lion. You are all flapping and flying like your eagle. We are like the cat. Still, 'til we pounce."

26

She looked uncomfortable as her press secretary made brief introductory remarks to the hastily assembled news conference. She had not left governing a huge state to do this. It was borderline dishonest and unethical, but the President had persuaded her that sometimes for the greater good, temporarily, some amount of truth could be withheld.

"Last night I ordered a no-notice operation to exercise sovereignty over our borders, specifically, the cargoes crossing our borders.

"Congress has, for years, insisted that the Customs and Border Protection agency, CBP, inspect every container and shipment coming into the United States for drugs and other contraband. That is what we are now doing as of this morning.

"This is the first in a series of no-notice exercises that I will be ordering in the next few weeks, testing each of the components of DHS, testing their ability to surge in an emergency. I want to be able to identify any remaining weak spots or deficiencies we still have so that I can report on them to my successor, whom I assume will be taking office on or about January twentieth. Thank you."

With that the Secretary of Homeland Security left the podium without taking questions, but questions were thrown at her as she walked out of the room, questions she ignored.

UPPER HOUSE HOTEL
CENTRAL HONG KONG

Johann Potgeiter returned to his suite just after midnight, only slightly tipsy from the spectacular dinner party Robert Coetzee had thrown for his colleagues at his villa in the New Territories. Clearly, Coetzee had been spending a lot of the Trustees' funds on living expenses.

He did not begrudge Coetzee the extravagance. Indeed, he was planning a very nice, new life for himself very soon. The day had gone well. What had started out as a potential disaster with the Israeli woman revealing the plan, had turned into their acceptance that Taiwan had probably ordered the hits on their predecessors, and a consensus the best path was to forget about all of that. They had agreed to build a high-end retirement village and health-care facility in Australia, with priority given to South Africans, white South Africans, who would be heavily subsidized and given every comfort. A good day's work had been followed by a good night's dinner and drinking. Suspicions had been eased. They were all good chums now.

Before he crawled into the bed, he needed to report in. He would have preferred to send a text message, but the old man was old school and would want to talk, so he extracted the German E-Plus mobile from within the lining of his computer bag. They had put a compartment in the bag, lined so it did not show on X-rays, big enough to hold his German identity of Wolfe Baidermann, his mobile, his passport, some credit cards, and euros.

He had memorized the number of the proxy, the phone switch in Los Angeles. When he dialed it, anyone tracking calls would see a German mobile somewhere in Hong Kong, using data roaming, contacting a number in America. What they would not see, was that as soon as the connection was made in California, the call bounced out from a Los Angeles area code 310 number to another phone in area code 236.

"I've been waiting for your report," the voice on the other end said.

"I could not break away sooner. It would have raised suspicion."

"Was the meeting a success or do we have problems?"

"Both. The Taiwan story worked."

"Then why do we have problems?"

"Because they know. They know about the test, the sale, Madagascar, and Pretoria."

"Don't say anymore," the distant voice scolded.

For a moment, there was only the sound of breathing on the connection. Then the distant voice resumed, "Come to me. We may need to act sooner than we planned and I will need you to help with my part of it. You have your extraction planned?"

"Yes," he sighed. "I can be there in three days."

"Good." The connection was severed.

He set the alarm for five o'clock and then let the jet lag take him. Five hours would be enough sleep. And when he woke, he would become Wolfe Baidermann and begin his next journey.

27

"What do you mean they lost him?" Winston Burrell's voice boomed over the videoconference speaker in Dugout's high-tech man cave. "How the fuck could they lose one guy when they had intelligence agents from half the nations in the world in and outside the hotel?"

"I don't know. Neither does Bowman," Dugout explained. "They know he was at the dinner and returned to the hotel, made the call, slept, then disappeared. Never checked out of his room at the hotel. Hong Kong Police say he hasn't flown out of the city or crossed into Macau or Mainland China, at least not under the name Johann Potgeiter. My search of their databases shows the same thing."

"This guy is now our one lead at the moment to whoever bought the bombs," Burrell said. "It's great we have a lead finally, but not so great that you have no fucking idea where he is. You have to find him."

"Well, I did trace the call. It was not really to somebody in LA, so it does not mean that there may be somebody in LA with a bomb."

"It doesn't mean there isn't, either," Burrell replied. "Where did the call go?"

"The 310 number was a bouncer, it switched the call to a mobile with a 236 area code number: Vancouver. And it was actually moving around downtown Vancouver when it took the call. Since then, it's been off," Dugout explained. "I don't know where it is."

"Fucking find Potgeiter. Either in Hong Kong or in Vancouver, if that's where he's going. Does al Qaeda have a cell in Vancouver? Didn't they do something up there during the Millennium rollover?"

"We think that's where he's going, based on our transcript of his conversation and the guy on the 236 end saying 'Come to me,' " Dug answered. "I'll look into any AQ cells in BC, but I doubt it."

"Well, this just means we were right to extend from the air and seaports to the land crossings," Burrell seemed to be talking to himself, reassuring himself that his decision to all but close the borders with Canada and Mexico was the right call. "Of course Ottawa and Mexico City are going batshit. Violation of NAFTA, blah, blah."

"I don't think it's going to be sustainable for long. GM won't be able to assemble cars or trucks. They ship parts back and forth, to and from plants on both sides of the Canadian border. Same with the maquiladoras, the factories just over the border into Mexico," Dugout said.

"I know. Half the Cabinet is waiting in the Roosevelt Room to complain," Burrell admitted. "We're going to have to deploy National Guard troops to augment Homeland Security doing the inspections. And after I get battered by the Cabinet, I have to go see a gaggle of Allied ambassadors who are complaining that containers are backing up already in Rotterdam, Tokyo, and everywhere else. I know it's not sustainable to search everything coming in to the U.S., but that's what the Homeland Security Secretary announced last night and that's what we're doing until you find the bombs. So find them, before the entire world economy dies of constipation." Burrell clicked off at his end.

Dugout swiveled in his chair to look for guidance from his boss, Grace Scanlon, who had been sitting off camera listening to the video call. "So, I am very glad that when I replaced Bowman, I did not inherit the care and feeding of the National Security Advisor. Very glad that Burrell chose to give that job to you. And you get all those meals at his Club," she said smiling at Dugout.

"You know that not a single person in the world thinks that the Homeland Security Secretary decided on her own to conduct a ten-day Border Control Exercise nine days before the election," Dugout observed. "Every media outlet thinks there is some threat that they won't admit to."

"I think it was the White House that leaked the story that there may be al Qaeda hit teams coming to poison water supplies," Grace Scanlon said. "That's better than people guessing that it's actually nukes we're looking for."

"The media will figure that out fast enough," Dugout countered. "They've deployed all of the Nuclear Emergency Support Teams. They're using Geiger counters at all the ports, airports, land crossings."

Director Scanlon walked to the window and looked down on the river. "The Republicans are loving it. Shows that we need a hard-line President. Strong on defense. Tough on terrorism."

"They will love it even more if all the Democrats in the cities realize that the urban areas might be nuked and flee to the countryside without voting," Dugout said, walking up to the window and standing next to her. "That's my fear, millions of people clogging roads and falling all over each other to get out of Dodge. That could be next."

"There's something wrong with this. Something we're missing. I know you and Burrell don't buy the Taiwan idea. I'm not there yet, let's wait to see what happens in Taipei when we confront them."

"Winston is convinced it's al Qaeda," Dugout noted.

"Maybe he's right." She looked straight at Dugout. "If a nation state bought themselves a ready-made nuclear arsenal, why would they be operating out of Canada? Only a terrorist group would be up there, getting stuff ready to come down here."

"I know, Ray and Mbali are going to get on a Cathay Pacific flight to Vancouver because they think Johann Potgeiter is en route there," Dugout said. "I think that's largely because they don't know what else to do. Don't just stand there, fly on."

"The new Dynamic Duo," Grace laughed. "They must make an odd-looking couple. Meanwhile, keep running Minerva, have the software find the correlations that humans can't see. It's there somewhere. Who hired the off-duty cops in Vienna to follow Ray, the hit team in Cape Town, the car bomber in Jaffa? Who paid for the heist near Pretoria? How did they get the tritium out of the country? When the bombs left Madagascar, where did they go and how? You have a lot of leads there, Duggie. Run them down. You have to give the Bowman some arrows."

Dugout began with the audio recording of Johann Potgeiter making the call from the hotel room in Hong Kong. Dug checked the time the call was made, precisely. Then he examined the record of the mobile telephone tower closest to the hotel and checked what calls were made from the area of the hotel at the exact time of the recording. There was a German mobile calling Los Angeles.

Next, he checked on the telephone number in Los Angeles. Then he began to trace the movement of the German mobile phone. He pulled up the name of the owner of the German mobile from a database in Frankfurt and then he checked airline reservations for flights booked in that same name. There was one, originating in China, going to Korea, and then to Vancouver. The passenger had also booked a rental car for Vancouver.

As he kept monitoring the phone owner's movements, Dugout started the process of hacking into the video surveillance system of the Vancouver airport and the Canadian immigrations system. Then he hacked into the Hertz reservation system and then into an SUV through its GPS navigation system. He was ready to see where it would be driven.

28

"I am not your errand boy," the General said to the gardener inside his walled yard. The villa was modern, but in a South Asian motif, like a small version of a Bengal palace, complete with turrets and cupolas. The large garden in the back, on the other hand, was pure England, a bit of Britain that a colonial master would have loved during the days of the Raj.

The gardener, who had been on his knees in the dirt, stood and dusted himself off. "No, General, you are not and I am not the gardener. I am the man who pays you in cash every month. For that tidy sum, my head office thinks they have the right occasionally to ask a question on their schedule, not yours."

"Mohammad, we are both intelligence officers. You know as well as I do that I put myself at risk when I have to ask them a specific question at a specific time. It's too obvious," the General protested. "If al Qaeda doesn't figure it out, my colleagues at ISI will."

"Nonetheless, you did ask, didn't you?" the gardener queried.

"Yes, after the Americans announced their border inspection operation. Then it seemed logical to ask, 'Are you guys trying to slip something into the home of the Far Enemy before their election? Did you get your hands on some WMD?' I told them we would not like to be surprised by something like that. No more 9/11s. The last one has cost us dearly."

"And?" the gardener asked.

"They laughed. They wished they had capability in North America. They wished they had some WMD, even sarin, or ricin."

"And you don't just take their word for it, do you, General?" the gardener asked.

"If they were planning to do something crazy like that in the next few days, they would all have gone to ground. Instead, they are in their villas in Quetta, in the Swat Valley," the General reassured the Arab pretending to be his gardener.

"General, if you think the Americans went running around like rabid dogs after 9/11, what do you think they will do if one of their cities goes up in a mushroom cloud, or two, or three?" The gardener moved closer to the General. "And what will happen if they think that the bombs that went off might have come from your arsenal of nuclears? They will team up the Indians and turn your country into an incinerated wasteland."

"We have our nuclears well hidden now, well secured," the General insisted. "But I know what you are saying. We do not want it to happen. So I squeezed them. I told them we have to know who recently got the bomb."

"And they told you what?" the gardener asked.

"Hezbollah. They think the Iranians gave them nuclears," the General said, proudly, puffing out his chest. "There. That kind of information justifies your money. In fact, I think I shall be asking for more."

"Where, when, who? Details, General, details that can be traced, acted on, corroborated," the gardener asked.

"Well, you cannot be expecting to get that kind of information. That work you must do yourself. But now you know where to look. Now, I must get back to say the prayers with my sons. Be gone."

29

THURSDAY, NOVEMBER 3
VANCOUVER INTERNATIONAL AIRPORT
SEA ISLAND, RICHMOND
BRITISH COLUMBIA, CANADA

"I reserved an SUV," he said in English with a slight German accent.

"Yes, Mr. Baidermann, I have the reservation here," the Hertz man replied. "We have a Yukon for you, in space 87, just through those doors. I'll just need your driver's license and credit card."

Not even my passport, he thought. The Canadian immigration officer had also been friendly, unsuspicious. To her he was what he seemed, a German businessman arriving from Seoul on KAL, visiting for a week, staying at the Four Seasons downtown.

The Yukon SUV was very large, he thought, but he was told that it would fit in well here and it would do well in the snow. They all seemed to drive big cars here.

Canada had so much gas and oil, with even more untapped in the arctic reaches. As he sat in the parking garage, he turned on the navigation system and entered his destination near Whistler. The town was apparently a ski resort that had been expanded to host an Olympics.

He would need to stop at a café for coffee to help him stay awake. It had been a tiring trip, crossing from Hong Kong into China proper at Lo Wu, walking across the covered bridge, waiting in the concrete block passport control buildings on each side, then taking the taxi to Shenzhen. The hotel he used there was best described as a businessman's lodging. It was not as clean as he would have liked. Then, that night, he had flown to Shanghai and changed planes for Seoul.

The Incheon Airport had been sparkling and the hotel there was a place where he could relax, however briefly. Then the flight to Canada, which seemed short by comparison with the long flights he had known from Europe to Asia. He knew before he told the old man about the Israelis that the news would upset him. He should have guessed that he would summon him, but he might have done that anyway. He wanted Johann's company. He didn't like being alone with just the guards, waiting, waiting for the bombs to get in place.

It would happen soon enough. There would be chaos and disorder. Then there would be a new order and new opportunities. They were ready to take advantage of those new opportunities, ready to shape the world that emerged. The traffic thinned out after he left Vancouver and headed north. It was a beautiful region, with pine trees and mountains, and deep fjords like those in Norway. Now, in early November, it was cool, brisk.

The navigation system talked him toward the ski lodge, on a side road outside of Whistler. The pine trees and firs were thicker along the road. Finally, he saw the small wooden sign that he had been told about, pointing to the dirt road. THE WIL-SONS, it read. PRIVATE ROAD. When the road took a sharp left, he came upon the men in the truck, blocking the path.

"He's been expecting you," one man said, after looking at the passport. "I'll radio ahead." The other man backed the truck up to let him pass. Three minutes farther down the bumpy road, the trees gave way to a wide green lawn, and the large ski lodge on the hill.

His passport was checked again by men

outside of the lodge. They all seemed to be Canadians, or Americans. It was hard for him to tell the difference. "Just go up the stairs. He's in the Great Room at the top."

The stairs were wide and opened into a lofted space that filled the entire second floor of the log cabin–motif building. At first, he didn't see the old man in the vastness of the room. Then, he spotted him sleeping in a large wooden chair by the fireplace. As he walked toward the fire, the old man stirred and looked up. "You are finally here." They embraced. "It is good to have you here, good to have you here. The weapons have been mated with the tritium. After all of our work, not long now."

30

Raymond Bowman was always impatient, but especially now with the clock running down and the election only four days away. He had arrived at the meeting site early and they had put him and Mbali in a Visitors Office, offered him tea, and showed him how to work the television remote. The Deputy Commissioner would be with them shortly, they had reassured him.

"The Canadians and Americans are very close, part of the Five Eyes, so I assume they know everything you know?" Mbali asked Bowman.

"You are fixated on the fact that South Africa is not part of that club. Yes, we and the Canadians are as close as anybody is. We share a lot," he said, "but not everything,

284

not with anybody, not with them, or the Brits, or certainly not with the Israelis."

"So, what have they already been told?" she asked.

"Not much, that's why we are here," he said. "We have not told them that the guys we're looking for may have some nuclear weapons with them. And we certainly are not going to tell them that Dugout hacked their government computers and their phone company's servers. We are going to let them discover that Potgeiter's here and where he's hanging out."

"You're confident that they'll do that, in time?"

"Yeah, they're good," he said. "And we will lead them as to where to look if we have to."

"Then what?"

"Then we tell them we have to act immediately. They won't be able to, so we say, no problem, we just happen to have a JSOC team en route in a bunch of Black Hawks," he said smiling at her.

"Jay Sock?"

"Delta Force?"

"Oh, those guys. In Canada?" she asked.

"Flying in from Washington State. They're trained in dealing with nuclear weapons. No Canadians are. If we're right and there are nukes in Whistler, the Mounties will very gladly yield the job over to us. JSOC will hit the house and grab the bombs and it will all be over, *inshallah,*" he said.

"When did you become an Arab?" she asked.

"It's a long story," he replied. "For when this is over and we are drinking beers somewhere."

Mbali checked the time and then turned on CNN to hear the press conference that Dugout had texted them about. Winston Burrell lifted his corpulent frame up to the podium in the White House press briefing room. Standing next to him was the well-coifed, stylish Secretary of Homeland Security. She was not looking pleased. Mbali turned up the volume.

"The Secretary has just briefed the President on Operation Rock Wall, a no-notice border control surge, which concluded this morning," Burrell began.

"Concluded?" Mbali asked Bowman.

"The President had asked the Secretary earlier this year to conduct surprise exercises involving emergency management, disaster recovery, and other functions falling within the purview of her Department. We believe it is essential that all first responders and enforcement officers be able to mount major operations on a moment's notice. Rock Wall was such an exercise. No one but the Secretary knew when it was coming. It demonstrated our ability to ramp up security and inspection of cargo bound for the U.S. whenever necessary. It was a success. And now it's over," Burrell read from a script in front of him.

"Does that mean they already found the bombs somewhere else?" Mbali asked Bowman.

"It means the heat was too much on the President," Bowman replied. "They were hurting the economy badly with the customs inspections and the backups at the borders and ports. And the media were beginning to speculate that there was something they were looking for, something that they weren't telling the public about."

"Dr. Burrell, *The Washington Post* quoted senior White House national security sources as saying that Rock Wall was really looking for an al Qaeda operation to poison water supplies. Is that true?" the CNN reporter blurted out before Burrell was finished.

Burrell scowled at him, but answered. "I just said it was an exercise. If you had let me finish I was going to tell you more about it, but let me just spike any rumors right here and now. We have no intelligence about any al Qaeda plot to poison the water supply or do anything else in the homeland. Isn't that right, Madam Secretary?"

"Don't think about a blue elephant," Bowman chuckled.

The Secretary of Homeland Security looked surprised to be called on, but moved to the microphone on the podium as Burrell shifted somewhat to the side. "We have no such information, nothing to indicate that al Qaeda was planning to poison the water supply," she said and then added, "I'd like to know how these rumors start. It does no good to have these false stories going about." She did not look at Burrell as she said it.

"Madam Secretary, why did you choose to have this first surprise exercise so close to the election?" the ABC reporter asked her.

"At the Department of Homeland Security, we operate twenty-four seven, every day and night of the year. We have to be ready at any time," she vamped.

"But were you aware of the damage it would do to the economy of the United States and its partners?" the NBC reporter called out.

The Secretary looked at Burrell, who took

a half step away from the podium. "Any economic effect is entirely temporary and I am sure will be recouped shortly," she replied. "The economic cost of not being ready would be higher than anything we could cause by an exercise."

"Can you confirm that teams from the nuclear labs, NEST units, were involved in the operation?" The *Washington Post* reporter yelled out.

"While most of the exercise was carried out by my Department, led by CBP, Coast Guard, and ICE, this was a whole of government exercise, involving the National Guard in several states, the Navy, other DOD assets, and elements from other departments including Justice, Energy, Transportation, and the Intelligence Community," she replied.

"So, just to be clear," the *New York Times* correspondent asked. "You, Madam Secretary, by yourself, chose the timing for this exercise?"

"That's what the statement said," the Secretary replied.

"Thank you all," Winston Burrell added. "Thank you very much. That's all we have time for now. Thank you." He escorted the Secretary off the platform and they moved together quickly to the door into the secure sanctuary of the West Wing, where reporters could not follow. They ignored the questions yelled at them as they left.

"Totally threw her under the bus," Bowman observed to Mbali. "He does that."

Mbali shook her head in confusion. "So they have given up looking just because of long lines at the borders?"

"No, they have canceled the overt part of the operation because the true story was about to leak out and they didn't want to panic everybody," Ray explained. "Now Burrell will leak a story saying that the Secretary overreacted to intelligence about al Qaeda and the water supply, which turned out to be inaccurate upon further analysis."

"And I thought South African bureaucracy and politics were bad," she said.

"They were never going to find the warheads with the overt searches. No terrorist group was ever going to put its nuclear warhead in a truck or boat or plane bound for the U.S. in a way that it was going to get inspected," Ray said aloud, looking out the window at the forest that surrounded the gleaming new headquarters of the Royal Canadian Mounted Police in British Columbia. "But now that they think we have stopped looking, they might move the bombs. I wonder how much the Mounties spent on this palace?"

"Less than a billion dollars Canadian," Deputy Commissioner Lyle Deveaux answered as he walked through the door. "Nine hundred ninety-six million and not a penny more. That's our story and we're sticking to it. Welcome."

Deveaux was in uniform and was followed by a small gaggle of others. He introduced another Mountie in charge of the Border Integrity Unit, a man in a different uniform from something called the Canadian Border Services Agency, and men in suits from the Canadian Security Intelligence Service and the Canadian Communications Security Establishment. They sat in a circle on the couch and stuffed chairs while tea was served on RCMP china.

"I got a call from Privy Council in Ottawa, very high up, this morning, asking me to convene this group and meet with you, to give you all the help you need. Frankly, Mr. Bowman, that's all I know, other than you work somehow for the White House and you, miss, run a security service for the South African President. Can you tell us more, so we can try to help you?"

"We need to find this man," Ray Bowman began by passing around a set of pictures.

"His true name is Johann Potgeiter, he was South African and is now an Austrian citizen. We believe he came here recently, to the Vancouver area, possibly from China, or elsewhere in Asia, probably under a different name. He is likely meeting with several people here who could be involved in smuggling nuclear material into the United States, or elsewhere."

Bowman was sure that the Canadians would find Potgeiter quickly, but if they did not, he would reveal more to them. For now, he did not want them to know the United States had hacked into Canadian networks. Their cooperation would slow or dry up if they knew that. There was a brief silence while the men examined the photos. "If that's all you wanted, you should have said that, instead of tying up the border in knots for a week," the man from Canadian Border Service said.

"Eric, let's be civil now," Commissioner Deveaux scolded.

"No, he's right," Ray admitted. "I had nothing to do with the border screwup, but I am sorry it happened."

"If you will excuse me for a few moments, I will see if this man entered through a legal point of entry," the Border Service man said. "May I borrow this picture?" The

Communications Security Establishment civilian left with him.

"Well, while they are doing that, why don't we show you around the new palace," Deveaux offered. "Eric will meet up with us in the Command Ops Room."

After a brief walk around what a billion Canadian dollars can buy in the way of a police station, they entered on to the Command Balcony of the Operations Room, which stretched below them the length of a hockey rink. Maps and live images appeared on giant screens on the far wall of the Center and officers and civilians sat in banks at consoles below.

"He's been here for less than twenty-four hours," the Border Services commander announced as he rejoined the group. "Landed in Vancouver on a legitimate German passport from Seoul on a KAL flight. Here, we can call up the video," he said picking up a control.

"That was fast," Mbali whispered to Bowman.

The windows into the Operation Center suddenly turned a milky white, an opaque barrier created electronically. The largest screen on the Command Balcony came on and showed a video clip of Johann Potgeiter responding to questions from the CBSA officer in a booth at the airport.

"Wolfe Baidermann, is the name on the passport," the Border Services commander explained.

The video then switched to a scene of Herr Baidermann walking down a narrow corridor toward the exit from the Customs and Immigration Control zone. The video then froze the frame and a number popped up: 49 171 891 3636.

"That turns out to be a German mobile number, registered in Munich to a Wolfe Baidermann," the Communications Security Establishment man explained. "We pick up active mobiles on people when they enter the country."

"How hard would it be to track where that mobile is now," Mbali asked.

"We could do that for you," Ray answered, thinking of calling Dugout.

"No need," the Communications Security man replied. "Already done. Exigent circumstances. Warrant to follow. He's in Whistler, the ski area, looks like he's in one of the big private lodges just outside of town."

"Do you have a SWAT unit available quickly?" Ray asked the Commissioner. "If not, I can get one here fast."

"SWAT is a very un-Canadian sounding

name," Deveaux replied. "I have an Emergency Response Team, but its French language designation is more informative. We call it the *Groupe Tactique d'Intervention.*" He pulled up an image on the screen. It showed ninjas in black body armor with automatic weapons, the title RCMP ERT, and the slogan, "You don't need a red uniform, cool hat, and horse to kick ass."

"Do they have training in handling nuclear materials?" Ray said.

"Limited, but, yes, they do. We will need a warrant for this, however," the Commissioner explained. "So, if you two could prepare a statement in writing, we will find a judge."

"You could have just asked us to find this guy in the first place," the Border Service officer said.

"Eric," Deveaux snapped.

"Would have saved a lot of time and money. We don't all wear red suits and ride horses, you know."

"I am sorry," Ray Bowman nodded. "I am sure you can handle it all very well by yourselves, but I do need to be in on the interrogations."

"I am sure we can work something out. But you are right that we are quite capable ourselves. In fact, I think we will get the helicopter assault unit on this one, too," Deveaux offered. "May give us some greater element of surprise. Besides, we need to justify ERTs having the helos in the first place."

31

It was supposed to be his day off, but he never had one.

He did, however, insist on going in late on Saturday, first having a late breakfast with his wife at the country club across from the office. It was a little tradition, just the two of them, a time to discuss things without the children, or now the grandchildren, around. Sometimes they just sat quietly, smiling at each other, eating, sipping the cheap Champagne, glad that they had made it this far.

After brunch, he dropped her off next door at the Cineplex, where she would meet her friends for an afternoon movie. Then, he would drive through the double gates into the compound. It was a nice neighborhood, he thought, country club, cineplex, intelligence headquarters.

He dreaded this Saturday. While his wife was watching some comedy about young Americans in love, he would be interrogating the prisoner. He hated interrogations. In fact, he actually didn't really do them, never had. His approach was straightforward, reasoning. If that failed, what happened after that was the prisoner's fault, not his. He didn't do what happened after that. Someone else did. Sometimes it worked and he got what he wanted. If he didn't, what followed was never very productive, or useful.

"Leonid Klishas, you are an Israeli citizen, emigrated from Leningrad, excuse me, Petersburg, when you were fifteen," Danny Avidar began the questioning. "Klishas, is that a Jewish name?"

"No, my mother was Jewish," the handcuffed man at the table said, looking at his wrists. "Why am I here? What is this place?"

"You know the answer to both those questions, Lenny, don't you?"

"Is this Mossad?" Klishas asked. "Why am I talking to you? You are not the police, or even Shin Beth."

"No, but we can introduce you to them. Shin Beth's facilities are not so nice. Nor is their technique, not so nice."

"What do you want with me?"

"Actually, it's more like what do you want with me, Lenny. Why did you try to kill me and my luncheon companions in Jaffa? What did I ever do to you? Nothing yet," Danny said, walking behind the prisoner. "He was no fool, the boy. He followed you, after you gave him the down payment. Got the number off your car, maybe just in case you didn't pay the rest. Nice picture on his mobile. The mobile survived the bombing. He, of course, did not."

"I don't even know who you are or what you are talking about."

"Of course you do, Lenny. You hired that poor Palestinian boy to drive the car bomb. You told him it would go off after he cleared the area. You lied, Lenny. You lied to him, just like you are lying to me now." Avidar came around and sat opposite the prisoner at the small wooden table. "I have no time for liars. When you decide to tell me the truth, why you hired him, why the car bomb, why you tried to kill me and my friends, you can just say my name and they will hear you. My name, by the way, is Daniel."

Avidar's tone was matter of fact, unemotional. He could have been a doctor talking to a patient, flat, to the point. "You have thirty minutes to do that. Then they will come for you. The Shin Beth, not the police. See, if the police had taken you, there would be an arrest record. There is no record at all that you have been taken. And when your dead body is found, in poor condition, maybe, then the police will be called. They will conclude that you were the victim of a brutal killing by other Russian mobsters like yourself and dumped in the sand dunes where the whores ply their trade. Thirty minutes from when I walk out the door. You can see the clock?"

Klishas stared at him. Avidar moved to the door. "That's it? That's all you are going to say?" Leonid asked as Danny opened the door.

"You won't have to raise your voice to yell for them to get me," Avidar said softly. "They will hear you. If you call out. Not, if you don't." Avidar walked out and shut the door quietly behind him.

OUTSIDE WHISTLER, BRITISH COLUMBIA
"They've got two guys out front in a van and two who walk around the sides and the back of the lodge. The guys out back are carrying long arms. They also have several cameras on the building, maybe some in

the woods. Four cars and two vans in the parking lot. There are eight bedrooms, it was built for the Olympics. A TV network rented it out. So there could be a dozen or more guys inside," the ERT commander explained to Lyle Deveaux. Ray Bowman and Mbali Hlanganani stood next to the Deputy Commissioner on the road half a mile from the lodge. It was 0315 in the morning.

"How will you achieve surprise?" Deveaux asked.

"We have been authorized to designate the target hostile, so we will sneak up as close as we can and then launch stun and smoke grenades. At the same time, we will cut the electricity. While we are charging in from the woods, the helos will come over the hill. One will drop a team by rope onto the parking lot. Number two will hover over the roof while four men rope down and enter through the balcony on the third floor. That will give us two dozen men on site in the first minute."

"Everyone in full body armor?" Deveaux checked.

"Yes, Commissioner, and then the three Tactical Armored Vehicles will race up from the road below and unload another dozen men."

301

The ERT commander was making a point of ignoring the American and South African standing next to the Deputy Commissioner. Bowman interrupted. "If there is anything that looks like a bomb or an electronic device, do not touch it. And we will need to interrogate the guests at the lodge as soon as possible after the raid."

The commander kept looking at his boss. "Is there anything else, Commissioner?"

"No. Very good. Whenever you are ready," Deveaux replied. He turned to Ray and Mbali. "Let's go inside the truck so we can watch it on the video link."

"All units, status check, prepare to move, sound off in order," the ERT commander said into his radio. As the Deputy Commissioner and his two foreign guests climbed up into the mobile command post, the commander hit the PUSH TO TALK button again and said, softly, "On my order now: Go, go, go."

The Mounties in black tactical gear, who had crawled on their stomachs the last hundred yards through the woods toward the lodge, leaped up, some ran straight for the building, while others provided covering fire from the tree line. Smoke canisters fell on the meadow on all sides of the lodge, sending up walls of colored clouds: green, yellow, black. Two small helicopters, with their lights out, were suddenly hovering over the lodge, with men rappelling down ropes, and crashing through windows. Simultaneously, the lodge's guards down the road were jumped. Then three black, tanklike trucks roared past the guard post and up to the lodge, with blue lights strobing. More men in black tactical gear jumped from the trucks.

In seconds, half a mile away, Ray, Mbali, and Commissioner Deveaux could hear muffled explosions and a whirring from the helicopters. On a video monitor they could see flashes and smoke around the ski lodge. The radio loosed a torrent of crisp, coded chatter, as ERT men described what they were doing.

At the lodge, the guards outside had raised weapons toward the rushing commandos and been dropped by the shooters from the tree line. The first wave of ERT Mounties burst into the building, through the front and back doors, through ground floor windows. Nine of the assault team charged up the grand staircase, exchanging places with each other as they moved forward, hit the landing, and moved up, providing protective cover as the point team dashed forward.

In the darkened Great Room, only the fireplace provided light. There were brief flashes as the first of the assault team threw four stun grenades about the room. Then the first four ERTs into the room saw the shooters, two men who rose from behind furniture with long guns. Both were taken out before they could fire. As other ERT commandos entered the darkened room, one of them yelled, "Gun, three o'clock." They all looked right and saw two more men with handguns near a large desk. Five of the ERT fired at them, riddling the bodies and the desk.

At the command post down the road, the chatter on the radio and the noise of the assault seemed to let up and then, they could hear the burst of gunfire again and the chatter resumed on the tactical radios. The ERT commander came back into the mobile command post to report to Deveaux. "The building is secure. There are casualties, but none of our boys. We've told the ambulances to drive up now, although I doubt they will do much good. I'm going up there now, Commissioner. I'll radio you after I get there, but you all should be able to come up in a few minutes."

After the ERT commander left, Bowman sat down next to the Deputy Commissioner.

"Sir, you have done everything we could have hoped for here," he began, "but if there are nuclear weapons on site, there is a U.S. military unit from JSOC standing by just over the border in Washington State. They can be here within the hour on their Black Hawks. By agreement between your Prime Minister and our President last night, this will become a NATO military operation and the JSOC unit will take control of the area."

Deveaux looked crestfallen. "I suppose your JSOC Black Hawks have already taken off?"

"Yes, sir, they are circling near the border now and will come in if I see nuclear weapons on site," Bowman admitted.

Deveaux looked at Mbali. She shook her head, "Americans."

"Let's go up to the lodge then," Deveaux sighed. "We will have to do this carefully so that if your guys do come in they don't see my ERT and shoot them."

The lodge was now lit up like it was part of a television show. Spotlights from the little tanks and police cars were augmented by mobile light stands that were being set up by the Mounties. The electricity had been restored and every light in the building was on. Ninjas in tactical gear, uniformed police

305

officers, and men and women in civilian clothes moved around purposefully, like a swarm of ants going in all directions.

There were two bodies on the lawn, the men who had been in the truck in front of the building. The air still stank of cordite from the gunfire and sulphur smoke. Flashes went off as police photographers started to document the raid. A choir of radios at full volume blurted out in uncoordinated dysphonia.

The ERT commander escorted Deputy Commissioner Deveaux, Mbali, and Ray up the grand stair to the Great Room on the second floor. There were four bodies on the floor. Each had a rifle or a gun nearby.

"They were about to shoot at my men," the ERT commander explained. "We had no choice."

"Goddamn it," Ray spit out, looking at the ERT commander.

Ray moved closer to the bodies and recognized one of the dead men as the man he had met in Vienna, Johann Potgeiter, who had briefly become Wolfe Baidermann. Next to him was the body of an older man who bore a striking resemblance to Johann.

Bowman turned to Mbali. "Remember the man who died in the car crash with the tram in Vienna, who was identified by dental records because the body was too charred by the fire?"

"Karl Potgeiter, why?" she asked.

Ray pointed at the corpse in front of him. "The dead man in Vienna was not who we thought. This dead man is the real Karl Potgeiter, South African nuclear weapons expert."

She knelt down to examine the dead bodies more closely.

"Ah, so it's father and son," she replied. "Well, now at least we are getting somewhere." Ray frowned at her. "Think about it," she said. "We now know one of the buyers, one of the group who wanted the bombs for . . . something."

Two men approached the ERT commander, one in tactical gear and one in civilian clothes. "Tell them," the commander said, to the civilian.

"There are no signs of anything resembling a bomb or a warhead and there are no unusual readings from the radioactivity sensors," the civilian explained.

"Swell," Ray replied.

"I think you have some Black Hawks to turn around, Mr. Bowman," Deveaux said. "Now."

Ray took his secure iPad out from its case. As he did, he noticed that on the large dining room table where the two Potgeiters had apparently been sitting when they were so rudely interrupted, there were two Mac-Book Airs. "Okay, no JSOC, but I am going to need those laptops and, since you don't want my Black Hawks to fly in here, could I ask you to loan us one of your helos to run us and the laptops over the border?"

"They're evidence," Deveaux replied. "There are chain-of-custody concerns. They need to stay here for the trial or coroner's inquest."

"Commissioner, there's not going to be a trial. Your highly capable team just killed the people I needed to interrogate. Now all I have left to interrogate are those laptops. And I am taking them with me. And since you are keeping my Black Hawks out, I will need one of your birds to take me to Washington State. You can send someone to accompany the computers if you like and you'll get them back when we have imaged them," Ray said. "Promise."

After the Deputy Commissioner relented, Ray called Dugout, who suggested they take over the largest parallel processing computer complex in the country to crack the encryption on the laptops and to give Minerva extra speed and power.

Dugout proposed they meet above San

Francisco's East Bay at a national laboratory that, coincidentally, also knew a lot about nuclear weapons. Winston Burrell had, after all, promised him "Whatever you need."

As they walked toward a pair of Canadian Air Force twin engine Hueys a half hour later, carrying two laptops, Mbali looked at Bowman. "You're always borrowing other people's aircraft. Some people would see that as presumptuous arrogance in a man."

"In my case, it's just expediency. I'm operating without the usual American support structure," Ray said to her. "As a result, there has been a fuckup. We let the Canadians do the raid and they killed the only lead we had. Those two knew where the bombs are."

"Maybe. But sometimes even laptops can tell a story," she said, looking back at the house. "It's just harder to ask them questions, but the guy you keep calling, the one I met on the video, what's his name, Sand Trap, he is some sort of computer whiz, isn't he?"

"Dugout. His name is Dugout. He devised this great predictive algorithm for the Red Sox. They're a baseball team. All he wanted in return was to sit in the dugout, where the players sit when it's not their turn to be on the field. So we call him Dugout. Yeah, if anyone can make those Macs talk, Dugout can. But it may not be fast. And right now we need fast."

"Then let's go to the Dugout," she said. "Now, which one of these is our chopper?"

32

In the hills of Virginia, Maryland, and West Virginia, as the sun came up and cast a yellow light on the remaining leaves west of Washington, there was more traffic than normal for a late autumn, early Sunday morning. It was not enough for anyone to notice, unless they were perhaps an intelligence officer from an embassy in Washington, sitting by the roadside, drinking coffee, reading the paper.

Such a person would have noted the unusual number of cars with Washington, DC, plates, with only a passenger in each car. Unlike the local traffic of pickup trucks and older Chevys, this trickle of vehicles was made up of Priuses, Hondas, and the occasional BMW. Tracing the plate numbers, the agent would have been able to confirm that there was something going on. They were senior government officials driving west at a time most of them would normally be at brunch in Georgetown.

Quietly, while the nation focused on the last few days of the frenetic presidential election campaign, while the locals in the little Shenandoah and Blue Ridge towns went to church, senior federal bureaucrats had been activated. The day they hoped would never come seemed to be in the offing. They were told to pack for a week away and to tell their families only that they were going on a surprise and secret trip. With that, they drove west trying to find the cave, or the bunker, or the old Forestry Service facility where they would wait to see if a nuclear bomb went off in Washington. If it did, their impossible task would be to try to govern the country from the bunkers. None of them really thought that would work.

LAWRENCE LIVERMORE NATIONAL LABORATORY
NEAR SAN FRANCISCO, CALIFORNIA
"The bombs will go off today," Bowman said. "It's Sunday now, right?"

"It has been Sunday for an hour here. In California. We are in California, in case you were wondering. Why today?" Dugout asked, distracted, while he watched data whizzing by on a screen in front of him. "Why not tomorrow?"

"They'll want Washington to call off the election. If they explode today, there will be time to react, to cancel the presidential election," he replied, laying on the couch with his eyes closed.

"Why don't you just let it happen, just go to sleep?" Dugout asked.

"I'm taking a power nap, just twenty minutes, then I'll be all rejuvenated."

"You know Mbali is smarter than you?"

"Probably, but why do you think so?" Ray asked.

"Lots of reasons. One of which is she had enough sense to go to sleep. You can't possibly think straight when your body does not know what time zone it's in. You realize you have flown all the way around the world?"

"Not completely," Ray replied, sitting up. "I have only done twenty-one time zones, I still have three time zones left. How long till you crack the encryption?"

"I told you it doesn't work that way. It's not a microwave, you don't just put something in for five minutes on high. It's a massively parallel processor array, the largest and fastest in the world, which is why we're here, which is why I bumped the climate change guy off this system, which is why he hates me," Dugout babbled as he moved from screen to screen in the computer control room.

"How long 'til you crack the encryption, then?" Ray repeated.

"Any time between now and never, since I don't know what kind of algorithm they used, I can't answer that, so we are making multiple different assumptions and trying them all simultaneously, hence the massively parallel part."

Bowman yawned and poured a mug of black coffee for himself. "Well, if you don't do it today, it may not matter."

"NSA is working on it, too, back at the Fort," Dugout observed, taking the mug out of Bowman's hand, "but I think this hunk of junk has a better chance of getting there first, or ever."

Bowman poured himself another mug of black coffee. "I talked to your boss."

"Which one? Winston, Grace, or did you just talk to yourself again?"

"Grace," Ray replied. "She thinks we're missing something, thinks we're too close to the forest or something. Taiwan did not pan out. When the State Department confronted them, they denied they had bought nuclear weapons and then they had a high-level meeting to try to figure out why we would ask them such a crazy thing like that. They didn't seem to be acting."

"So why were the three Trustees there in Taipei six weeks before the test blast?" Dug asked.

"They actually seem to have been buying a hotel and shopping mall," Bowman reported. "But, according to Taiwan's National Security Bureau, their spooks, Karl Potgeiter did meet with some retired generals while he was there. Even after the meeting, the generals weren't sure why they met. Potgeiter said something about looking for ways of investing together, using their expertise."

"That doesn't add up," Dug replied.

"It does if the late old man Potgeiter was telling the other Trustees that he was arranging the sale of the nukes to Taiwan. Maybe the meeting was just a show, an act, to convince the other Trustees that the buyer was acceptable, that it was Taiwan," Ray thought aloud. "The others see him meet with Taiwan generals, but they don't sit in on the meeting. Potgeiter says the Taiwan guys are the buyers."

"When actually it was someone else?" Dugout asked.

"Someone who Potgeiter was dealing with, someone who the other Trustees would probably not have agreed to sell nukes to, maybe," Bowman continued.

"Like al Qaeda?"

"No, I'm pretty sure al Qaeda is not involved. CIA and NSA are all over the AQ groups. They would have picked it up. Besides, I have my own special source, who came back to me this morning. Said they weren't doing it, said maybe it was Hezbollah."

"Special sauce, what are you, Ronald McDonald?" Dugout laughed. "By the way, Winston called earlier. He wants us to do a video link with him at eight his time. You might want to, uh, comb your hair or something."

"I can't believe I heard that coming from you," Ray said, as he wandered off to the men's room.

Two hours later, Winston Burrell appeared on the large monitor in the computer control room, looking as strung out as Ray and Dugout were. It appeared he was in his West Wing office, alone.

"It's decision time, boys. The President wants to know first thing this morning if he should order evacuations in New York, Washington. If we think that nuclear bombs are going to go off before the election Tuesday, now is the last time to order the evacuations. It's all prepared, FEMA has activated all of its response teams for an exercise, the Vice President has already come off the campaign trail allegedly because he lost his voice. He's actually gone into a bunker in Virginia. The President has been holding off deciding on evacuation orders until he saw if you found anything on the computers."

"Oh, God, blame me, go ahead," Dugout muttered while they were still on mute. "Dugout couldn't crack the code in time and so they all died."

Bowman pressed the TALK button. "Winston, we don't really know that there are bombs in the U.S. There was no trace evidence of bombs at the site in British Columbia. If there are weapons in New York and Washington and you start to evacuate, the terrorists will decide to ignite them before the cities empty out. If there are no bombs in those cities, you will have killed dozens of people who will get run over in the panic of an evacuation, to say nothing of what you will do to the economy and the election."

"I know all that, we have been saying that to each other for weeks now," Burrell replied. "I was hoping for a recommendation from you."

Bowman bowed his head for a brief moment and then looked into the camera. "I have a report that maybe the group buying the bombs was Hezbollah, but I don't believe that. Doesn't make sense and besides the subsource really wouldn't know if Hezbollah was doing it. He's not in a position to know what they are up to."

"Not al Qaeda, not Hezbollah, not Taiwan. Telling me who it isn't doesn't help," Winston Burrell said, gesturing with his hands in the air. "Tell me who it is that has the bombs. Tell me what I recommend to the President, what does he do now?"

"Do nothing," Ray responded. "You have insufficient grounds for knowing what a prudent course of action would be."

"That is the same situation I was in a week ago. You were supposed to put some facts on the table to help with the decision," Burrell snapped. "Sorry, I didn't mean it like that. I mean, you have actually added lots of facts, it's just that they haven't got us to the fundamental questions of who, where, when, and why." Burrell stood up. "I have to go give my recommendation to the President."

"What's it going to be?" Ray asked.

"I don't know yet." His image faded.

SIXTY-FIFTH FLOOR PENTHOUSE
CENTRAL PARK
SOUTH MANHATTAN, NEW YORK CITY

"I think this Park view was worth every penny," he said looking down at the last leaves of autumn, falling off the trees in the middle of the city, leaving little color to counteract the grayness of the sky. "I'll miss this apartment, but I did make a huge profit on it in less than two years."

"It was an extravagance and it drew un-needed attention to you," she said, moving up next to him. "You always have to have the newest, the best, the most expensive, and that's what it was when you bought it. Now it's not the newest anymore."

"You're wrong. I don't always need the newest, but always the best," he said and kissed her briefly. "Which is why I leased the 787. We'll be flying that today to the meeting in London. What did Sergey tell you? Did he find out what happened?"

"Their source in the Mounties in Vancouver reported that the Canadians essentially found nothing. The Americans, Bowman, took some computers, but the disks were encrypted and they won't be able to get anything off them," she told him.

The older man nodded at his daughter. "When I heard from Potgeiter that Bowman knew about the test blast, and the storage area at Antsakabary, and the tritium heist, I thought for sure the President would order the evacuation of the cities before the election, but they didn't," he said. "They have no balls."

"It's just as well the Potgeiters are gone," she said. "They had no real role going forward. And for Bowman, the trail will end there."

A breeze swept down 57th Street, knocking more leaves down, pushing the ones on the ground into piles around benches. For almost eight on a Sunday morning, there were few runners out. Perhaps it was the early chill, the hoar frost on the grass that deterred some from venturing out too early in the day.

"They have no balls," he repeated, "and they have no idea. Our ships are out there, and they are not looking for them. Instead, they have people driving around the docks in Jersey with radiation detectors."

"Think of it as a Rorschach test, Father," she said. "They see the evidence that something is going on and they think it's al Qaeda, or they think it's about their election. In Israel, they think it's about Arabs wanting to destroy Tel Aviv. In South Africa, they thinks it's about whites wanting to blow up Joburg. We all see in things the issue we are already working on, or what we secretly fear most, not necessarily what we should fear. People in this city, if you tested them, would fear snakes, but there are no snakes in this city. Of course, there are people with guns, but that seems almost normal to them. They are blind to the real problems because they decided long ago there was nothing they could do about them. Too hard."

"Yes, Professor, you are quite right," he said, turning his back on the city. "And for that blindness, they are about to pay a price."

"Who do you think will win the election Tuesday, Father?" she asked.

"Given what is about to happen, what difference does it make?"

33

Voting began shortly after midnight in the handful of little towns that vied to be first to report their election results. In twenty-one states, early voting had been going on for as long as two weeks, meaning that millions of Americans had already voted. They did so at a time of rumors in the media of some vague, terrorist threat. Less than two weeks before Election Day, the Homeland Security Department had, bizarrely, initiated a no-notice exercise to conduct 100 percent inspection of all cargo entering the country.

Homeland Security claimed it was part of a bilateral exercise with Israel, something the Prime Minister's office in Jerusalem was slow to confirm. The media grew quickly skeptical of the official explanation, especially as major corporations began hollering. Just-in-time delivery of parts for cars, of Apple computers and iPhones, of almost anything you could name, failed to be on time. The U.S. Chamber of Commerce claimed that the cost to the U.S. economy was twenty billion dollars a day in lost sales and the expenses of keeping facilities idling.

Photos of miles-long lines of trucks in Mexico and Canada were on every newspaper's front page. Both presidential candidates demanded a clear explanation of what was going on. Shortly thereafter *The Washington Post* headlined a story, attributed to senior Administration officials, that Israeli intelligence had reported an al Qaeda plot to smuggle poisons into Israel and the United States with the intent of attacking water supplies. Shortly thereafter, police and National Guard troops were seen standing around city reservoirs and treatment facilities. Some blogs noted that among the federal units seen in New York were elements of the Department of Energy's Nuclear Emergency Support Team, or NEST.

Undercover trucks and unmarked helicopters from NEST had been crisscrossing the New York City and National Capital Region metropolitan areas, searching for signs of nuclear radiation. NEST had placed sensors on bridges and tunnels leading into Manhattan and on the Potomac bridges from Virginia to Washington. The alarms went off with regularity on all of the sensors, cases of false positives, of medical-related radioactive material, or natural materials, that emit signals similar to uranium.

No media sources reported the secret activation of the Government Continuity program that had sent senior bureaucrats into caves and other clandestine facilities. Some noted that the Vice President had appeared healthy just before his office announced that a flu had caused him to cancel his planned rallies in support of Democratic candidates throughout the country.

FEMA, the disaster recovery agency, had alerted and moved many of its units, including the mass mortuary team, under the guise of hurricane preparations. Since what was likely to be the last of the season's hurricanes was aiming at Florida and could move up the East Coast, no one saw through to the real reason why the FEMA units were activated and relocated.

The President insisted on staying in Washington and having his family remain there with him. He could not sleep as midnight came and Election Day began on the East Coast. He had become convinced by his National Security Advisor, as well as the intelligence agency heads, that the possibility of nuclear explosions in the United States on Election Day was nontrivial. Two hours into the day, actually at 2:12 a.m., he appeared in the White House Situation Room to visit the Crisis Task Force that had quietly been stood up. He peppered them with questions, looking for any intelligence that would confirm the nuclear risk.

Winston Burrell was more than just his National Security Advisor, he had been with the President since his unlikely announcement of candidacy nine years earlier. When Burrell said he could not recommend evacuating New York and Washington because the intelligence was too vague, too unspecific, the President had actually been relieved. He readily accepted the recommendation.

The first polls closed at 7:00 p.m. in a few states in the Eastern Time Zone. Florida, North Carolina, Ohio, Michigan, Virginia, and Indiana were all too close to call, according to the television networks' exit polls. Heavy voter turnout was reported across the country, including in Florida where the hurricane's effects were beginning to be felt in the south. Long lines were still waiting to vote in three of those states. That meant it was going to be a long night.

On the West Coast, in their temporary headquarters at the High Speed Computing Center at Livermore National Lab outside of San Francisco, Ray Bowman, Mbali Hlanganani, and Dugout tried to focus on their mission, to find what they had become convinced were five loose nukes. Using Dugout's Minerva big data analytics software, now running on the massively parallel computer, they tried to find connections, patterns among all the events that had happened. Who was behind the string of murders, thefts, clandestine movements, and other activities that stretched from South Africa to Europe, to Israel, and Hong Kong, and now to Canada? The only two men they knew for sure had been involved in the central conspiracy were both in a morgue in British Columbia.

Using another part of the big computer at the lab, Dug was systematically trying to crack the encryption codes that the Potgeiters' had used to lock the files on the Mac Air laptops. At Fort Meade in Maryland, NSA was also going at those codes. Dugout admitted that it was theoretically possible that the number crunching could go on unsuccessfully for decades.

After literally running around the world chasing leads, Ray Bowman was beginning to feel not just physically exhausted, but emotionally strung out. He had been convinced that the nukes would have gone off by now. The fact that they had not left him with no theory of the case, no idea what to do next. Although he had not opened up to either Dugout or Mbali yet, he knew he would have to admit to them soon that all he could think to do was wait for a lead, wait for the computer, wait for the enemy to make a mistake and reveal themselves. Maybe the bad guys, whoever they were, already had slipped up, he thought, and they had missed it.

His mind raced through possibilities, coming up with nothing.

"Do you think the President will tell the winner what has really been going on?" Dugout asked Bowman when he caught Ray's attention focusing on the muted TV news coverage. "Congratulations on your election, and by the way we really have been looking for some loose nukes and we can't find them?"

"Whichever one of them wins tonight, the incumbent is still the President for the next ten weeks and he gets to call the shots till then," Ray replied. "You'd better believe he's going to want us to solve this puzzle well before he steps down."

"But what if we don't?" Mbali asked. "What if we just keep hitting dry holes? You know there is a scenario where these bombs are like the lost Rembrandts. Nobody knows where they went. Somebody just paid a lot of money to get them, just to have them. Or maybe just to have them to take out and scare people if and when they ever feel threatened?"

Bowman opened a Diet Coke and sat down next to her on the couch. "I thought of that, like Saudi Arabia or Taiwan, or even South Korea. Thing is that the U.S. Intelligence Community, as often as it screws up, would really probably know if one of those three countries had done this. Even if some wealthy, weird little place like Qatar had done it. We would know by now."

"Which, again, leaves us with a bloody rich terrorist group that we have never heard of," she said.

"Or a bunch of Luddites who wanted to throw the world into reverse, or maybe just slow it down?" Dugout added. "You know, people who are afraid of robots and genetic engineering, and drones."

"And have billions of dollars and have hired some seriously good hit squads and other operators?" Ray asked.

"Hmm, seems unlikely," Dugout admitted and went back to his search models. It was just before midnight and into Wednesday on the West Coast. "We have a winner," the announcer intoned as marching music played on the television screen in the lounge and the image on screen shifted to a presidential seal spinning over a map of the United States. "We are declaring a winner in Ohio and with those electoral votes assigned, we can now declare the forty-fifth President of the United States." The screen shifted to scenes of wildly celebrating supporters in a giant ballroom and then to an outside shot of a crowd of people cheering in front of Jumbotron screens in New York's Times Square.

Ray, Mbali, and Dugout sat quietly in the scruffy lounge of the computing center, surrounded by stained couches and empty vending machines, looking at each other, like mourners at a wake, or the last wedding guests after the bride and groom have been long gone. The candidate that all three supported had won, but they were not feeling like celebrating. Dugout hit the MUTE button.

"I know what those guys at the losing candidates headquarters feel like, just

329

empty. I should be glad we all survived and nothing happened, no bombs blew up, but this just feels like the biggest letdown ever. We didn't find the bombs, but they didn't go off. We failed, but it didn't matter. I'm spent, just like tapped out," Dugout said, looking at the television coverage. He shifted his gaze across the room to Ray, who was sprawled out on a battered-looking couch. "Are you going back now, to the bartending, to the island?"

Mbali looked quickly at Bowman. It was a question she had wanted to ask, but had not.

"I feel like I just woke up from a binge, without the fun part of having been drunk," Ray announced to himself, as much as to the others in the room. "Yeah, I thought that the bombs would go off before yesterday, before the election, but when I think about why I believed that it was because that's what you and Winston told me when you recruited me. I just bought into it, uncritically."

"So, if your mission was to stop the bombs going off and preventing, disrupting the presidential election, you failed. But there was no plot to blow up bombs before the election," Mbali spoke in a tentative way that sounded like she was asking a question.

330

The television coverage was showing the new President-elect, beaming, about to make a victory statement. "She's right," Dugout said. "The United States succeeded in running an election, but not because of us. We failed."

Ray looked at Dugout and then at Mbali. He put his hands on the couch and forced himself up and then stood, looking at the other two in the room. "That was never the task. It wasn't just about the elections. The task was to find the bombs. We haven't failed. We still have to go find the nukes before someone uses them for whatever it was that they're meant for."

"Good," Mbali said, "but what do we do now? Maybe it was never about the U.S. Maybe it was about South Africa, or Israel. We still don't know anything."

"No. Look, we know a lot more than we did twenty-one days ago when I left the bartending job. We know for certain that there were South African nuclear bombs, that they were stored in Madagascar and they left there, that the Potgeiters were part of a plot to transfer them to somebody who paid a lot of money for them," Ray said, sounding like he was trying to motivate himself. "Most importantly, we know that there are loose nuclear bombs out there somewhere and not in the hands of good owners. It may not have happened in the last forty-eight hours, but something awful will happen as a result of that. That is a wealth of information, we have developed."

Mbali laughed. "You sound like a coach giving yourself a gold star, an A grade? Good, you uncovered a lot of leads, but I repeat, what are we going to do now? I cannot go home to my President without knowing where the bombs went."

"We clear our heads, we get some sleep. In the morning we take a day, walk around San Francisco, whatever, and we come back tomorrow and start again from scratch," Bowman declared. "And meanwhile, Duggie, you keep that massive thing cranking away trying to decrypt something on those laptops and run down all those leads. One of them will give us what we need. It has to."

WEDNESDAY, NOVEMBER 9
UNION SQUARE, SAN FRANCISCO
In the morning, Bowman took his own advice and drove into the city, parked, and began to walk in a city he loved. He wanted to think about nothing, the old technique that had always worked for him, the way he let his subconscious speak to him above the

din, tell him what it had figured out while he was distracted. He parked in the garage under Union Square and planned to walk up Post Street, turn right on Van Ness, and march to the sea. It would take a while, but he was in no hurry. He needed the exercise. He had spent too much time in airplanes.

He emerged from the underground parking garage and entered the plaza. A cable car was moving down the hill.

Skateboarders were dodging pedestrians. Four elderly Chinese were doing stylized exercises on the grass. Businessmen who had been up late the night before watching the election results and were now late for work, moved purposefully across the Square. For early November, it was warm and the sky was empty of clouds, a bright, cerulean blue. His head was clear and he felt ready for the long walk across the city.

The phone in his pocket vibrated. He thought about turning it off, but he recognized the country code 972, Israel. "Mbali gave me your number. She said this number is new, it should be clean. Nobody knows it." It was Danny Avidar calling.

"Well, that was true," Bowman said as he sat down on a bench.

"Do you know a man named Sergey Rogozin?" Avidar asked.

"Never heard of him," Ray said, stretching to recollect. "Should I have?"

"Well, he knows you," Danny replied. "He hired the guy who hired the guy who was outside the restaurant. You remember the restaurant we went to?"

The scene of the car bombing in Jaffa flashed in front of him, the sound, the smell, the invisible hand smacking him to the ground. "And we know things about this Sergey guy?"

"I can't say more on this line," Danny answered. "I just sent our file on him securely to Mbali."

"Securely? How did you do that?"

"I gave her a device when she left here. We have a partnership now, sharing. We call it the four eyes, hers and mine. So maybe, you should get back to work now, yes?" The connection broke.

Bowman sat on the bench and repeated to himself what he had just heard and what he thought it meant. One thing it clearly meant was that he had to go back to the lab, where evidently Mbali and probably Dugout were still at work. The head-clearing walk had lasted three minutes. He headed back to his rental car, into the underground.

34

"The Purpose Fund is pleased to announce the grant recipients for this year's research program," Professor Victoria Kinder spoke from the podium. A bank of video cameras were in front of her to her right. She looked down and smiled to the board members seated in the first row of seats to her left. Behind them sat many of those who had applied for the funding.

"The Hospital for Tropical Diseases, London, will receive fifteen million pounds for a three-year study in emerging viruses," she read out. "The Byrd Polar Research Group of Ohio State is awarded twelve million dollars for its continuing work exploring the polar regions." Small groups gasped, hugged, or clapped with each reading. "Moscow State University's Institute of

Agricultural Genetics is granted fifty-two million rubles for further work on adapting crops to grow in tundra regions."

The attractive, young American academic went on, announcing funding for laboratories and research teams in India, Iceland, China, Norway, Canada, Austria, Australia, Switzerland, Korea, Chile, and Japan. Programs in alternative energy, biogenetic engineering, geological exploration, and multispectral satellite sensors were among the diverse recipients of the private largesse. In all, the fourteen awards totaled a quarter of a billion dollars. Each of the five board members had given fifty million dollars for this year's Purpose Fund research grants.

"And now, I want to call upon the Chairman of the Board, a man who makes me so proud every day, my father, Jonathan Kinder." The man, with a thick head of silver hair, swept back from a high forehead, stepped forward. He kissed his daughter on the cheek, as she stepped away from the podium. For a man in his seventies, he seemed trim and fit in his double-breasted blue pinstriped suit. He removed the microphone from its holder on the podium and stood in the middle of the stage, looking out at the appreciative audience that continued its applause for him.

"Thank you, thank you very much," he began. "It is, after all, you who we, the Board of the Purpose Fund, should be applauding, you who do the hard work to advance our knowledge as the human race. You do the work that matters, that will make it possible for us to live better lives in the face of the ever-changing conditions on this planet.

"For me, the Purpose Fund gives reason for the many years that I have struggled in the fields of private equity, real estate, energy, and agri-business. Those years of effort made me a very rich man, as you know, but what good does it do a man to have money unless there is a purpose for acquiring that wealth?

"That is why I was so pleased to join Zhang Wei, Sheikh Arbaaz, Konstantin, and Sir Clive in coming together to create the Purpose Fund several years ago. We each initially contributed the equivalent of three billion pounds to the foundation's science and research programs, which include our own laboratories, exploration teams, and even satellites. We are also proud to sponsor some of the most cutting-edge work at many of the world's most prestigious institutions through these annual research grants.

"We have also over the years created a series of joint corporations, to invest together in ventures, which we believe will over time create a continuing stream of revenue, much of which will go to the Purpose Fund in the out years. We also believe that these investments will help assure that the world's peoples will have a continuing supply of energy, food, and raw materials to support a global economy well into this century and out into the next."

Following his remarks, the grant recipients joined the board members for a Champagne reception in the mirrored ballroom next door to the hall in which they had held the press conference. Tuxedoed waiters poured Krug into crystal flutes, Krug Grande Cuvée 2012 for the researchers, Krug Clos d'Ambonnay 1995 for the board members.

As Victoria Kinder guided her father from group to group of scientists, other board members hung back, subtly separated from the crowd by bodyguards in Savile Row suits, tailored to hide the small arms under the Super 150 weight wool. Konstantin Kuznetzov looked impatient, checking his Richard Mille Tourbillon wristwatch. He turned to the tall thin man at his side. "Sir Clive, shall we leave this show now and go upstairs and start our meeting? We have much to discuss. Are you sure this hotel is a safe place to have these discussions?"

"Your man Sergey says it is," the Brit replied. "He had his people sweep it and install the protective electronics. The hotel manager tried to stop him from ripping things up, but it is, after all, the Sheikh's hotel."

Kuznetzov smiled. "Vladimir," he called to one of the bodyguards. "In a minute, tell Kinder we have gone upstairs to the meeting. Ask him to join us as soon as he can break away. Discreetly, Vlad, discreetly this time."

35

*WEDNESDAY, NOVEMBER 9
LAWRENCE LIVERMORE NATIONAL
 LABORATORY
HIGH SPEED COMPUTING CENTER
LIVERMORE, CALIFORNIA*

"I don't know how long they will let us stay here now that the election is over," Dugout said, as he tapped away at his keyboard. "They have a lot of high-priority work backed up that needs the high-speed computer." It was almost noon and Ray Bowman had returned from across San Francisco Bay to what had become their temporary headquarters, a room in the High Speed Computing Center at the Livermore National Lab.

"You said it has the best chance of any computer to crack the encryption on the Potgeiters' laptops, so we need it until it does," Bowman said. "If they give you trouble, call Winston and have him tell the

Energy Secretary to have the lab rats back off. What did your Minerva program find on Rogozin?"

An image appeared on the large wall monitor, a series of annotated boxes with lines connecting them. "It did this link analysis based on the information Danny provided Mbali." Ray glared at her, still upset that she and Avidar were exchanging information and that she was carrying around electronics that the Israeli had given her. Mbali smiled back at him.

"Rogozin, the name Danny Avidar gave us, is CEO of Olympus Security, a security company headquartered in Cyprus, with offices around the world. They provide security to oil companies, celebrities, laboratories. He's linked to a Polis Holdings Corporation of, wait for it, Polis, Cyprus. They own or lease ships, tankers, and freighters, as well as aircraft, cargo, and executive jets. It looks like Polis may own Olympus."

Bowman stared at the chart, with its array of corporations and different-colored links connecting them. "So who owns Polis?"

"A company in the British Virgin Islands, which, you can see, links back to a company on the island of Jersey in the English Channel, which traces to a company in

Bulgaria. That's where I hit a wall. Not great corporate records online in Bulgaria."

Ray Bowman sat down, continuing to stare at the chart. Mbali had been making notes on a legal pad. "Just a hunch," she said. "Olympus Security has offices around the world? Is that what you said?"

"Yeah, here's their home page. The picture is of Mount Olympus, the one in Cyprus, not the one in Greece," Dugout explained.

"Do they have a list of their branches?" she asked.

"At least some of them, yeah."

"Do they have offices in South Africa?"

"Yes, Pretoria," Dugout answered.

"And Austria, Australia, Israel, the UAE, Hong Kong, Singapore?" she asked.

"That's seven of the twelve," Dug replied. "Since you are on a roll, do you want to guess the rest?"

"London, everyone needs an office in London."

"Right, go on," Dugout urged.

"New York?" she guessed.

"No, nothing in the U.S."

"That's interesting," Ray muttered. He looked like he was about to doze off. It had been a late night and his body was still unsure what time zone it was in.

"Give up?" Dugout asked. Mbali

shrugged. "Russia and the three Cs: Chile, Comoros, and Canada."

"Comoros?" Bowman said, coming alive. "Major commercial cities of the world, countries with interesting raw materials, and then the Comoros Islands? The ones in the Indian Ocean? The ones near Madagascar where the nuclear bombs were kept?"

"Not only, but offices in Vienna, Tel Aviv, Dubai, Singapore, and Sydney. All of the cities where our five Trustees had their untimely departures," Mbali added. "I'm calling back to my boys in Cape Town. We need a little nocturnal visit to the South African offices of this Olympus Security group. Perhaps we also make a visit to the Comoros. And I'll ask Danny to examine Olympus in Tel Aviv, if he hasn't already."

"Good, I'll ask our friends in Hong Kong to do the same and Commissioner Deveaux to have the Mounties check on the Canadian office," Ray added. "He owes me one after his guys killed the Potgeiters before we could question them."

"Let me ask Deveaux," Mbali suggested. "He may owe you, but I think he likes me a little more. I haven't tried invading his country with my special force commandos, unlike some other person I know."

"Nine days away," Sir Clive Harcourt said to Konstantin Kuznetzov, as he looked across at the dinner's detritus, spread over the long table — half-eaten desserts, emptied wine bottles, stubs of cigars. "I can't believe, Konny, that we made it this far. I must admit, when you first proposed this, I thought you were crazy and would get us all arrested."

The two men were a study in contrast, the Brit tall and thin, the Russian short and squat. What they had in common was great wealth and, despite that, greed; greed and a desire to control things. Both men had failed to rise up to where they thought they should be in their national political systems, although they were each associated with their nation's ruling elite. Although they had never discussed it with one another, both felt underappreciated in their societies; after all they had done to support the right charities, the proper political parties; after all the success they had achieved in making money, they were still essentially unknowns in their own countries and certainly around the world.

They would still be unknowns after what was about to happen, but they would have exercised power like few men ever had, changed the direction of things in bigger ways than all but a few men in history. And when the dust settled, it would be these two men and their partners who would dominate the world's new economy, for what they owned now would be immensely more valuable then. Their hand in the creation of the chaos would have to remain secret, always, but they were confident that it would. None of them had any desire to claim the credit, or the opprobrium, and they had covered their tracks very well. The Americans, the Israelis, even the South Africans had all tried to track them down and failed. It looked now like they were almost giving up, after running down so many dead ends.

"Don't worry, Clive, my friend, we will not be arrested. They will never figure out it was us, even though, regrettably they do now probably know enough that they will figure out what happened after the fact. They just won't know who did it," Kuznetzov reassured him, as he poured out the last drops of the claret. "We have spread all sorts of rumors in the right places. The latest is that Hezbollah has the bombs, with help from Iran. The Americans and Israelis think Hezbollah are going to use the bombs in Tel Aviv and New York, the two biggest Jew cities in the world."

Sir Clive, whose maternal grandmother was Jewish, winced at the Russian's description. "But, Konny, why would anyone believe that? Surely, Iran has its own nuclear bombs by now. Why would they need to buy the old South African bombs to give to Hezbollah?"

"Deniability, Sir Clive, deniability," the Russian said, sounding more than a little drunk. "The story we spread is that Iran didn't want to use its own bombs because they could be traced back to Tehran and then America would fire off its nuclear missiles and turn the Persian sands into a sheet of glass."

"Well, I'm glad that won't happen," Sir Clive said, looking about the table for a bottle with some sparkling water left in it.

"Oh, but it will, Clive, it will. That is the best part, it will."

The British lord stood halfway down the table pouring himself water in an attempt to prevent what he feared was going to be a bad hangover. "I don't understand, Konny."

"You see, even though New York and Tel Aviv will not blow up, we will still spread evidence that it was Hezbollah and Iran who used the bombs, enough evidence that America will retaliate. They will need to attack somebody. They always do after a big disaster. It doesn't matter if the evidence isn't one hundred percent. Look at 9/11. They needed to attack somebody big time after that. So they accepted the theory that it was Iraq, that Iraq was involved in 9/11. There wasn't much evidence and what there was, it was all a lie, but they destroyed Iraq. Iraq may never recover. This time they will destroy Iran, nuke it probably. Better that than they figure out it was us."

Sir Clive returned to Konstantin's end of the table and sat down next to him, pulling his chair close to the Russian. "Konny, my old friend, there is something I have to ask you and I don't want you to think me a weak sister when I ask."

The Russian looked uncomfortable and pushed his chair back a little, creating some space between him and the Brit. "Yes, what is it you wish to ask me?"

"How do you deal with the deaths?" Sir Clive asked. "I know what we are doing is the right thing in the big picture, in the long sweep of history, but if the Americans nuke Tehran, if everything else goes as we expect it to, there will be many, many deaths. Many of them, most of them, innocent people. It doesn't seem to bother you. I need to get there, so it won't bother me when it happens and afterward. How do you think about it that makes it possible for you to sleep at night?"

Kuznetzov sighed, relieved at the question. "Oh, is that all? Sir Clive, we lost twenty million dead in World War II in the Soviet Union. Stalin, he killed another twenty million Soviet citizens. This is what happens at great moments in history. This is going to happen with or without us. The only questions are when, how fast, and who profits from it, who is left standing after it happens."

"I suppose you are right, Konny, it's just going to be hard to watch."

"Clive, when you have a wound and you put a bandage on it, the wound heals and the bandage is still there, still sticking to your skin. Do you peel it off slowly or rip it off quickly? Which will hurt more?"

Sir Clive Harcourt looked at the billionaire Konstantin Kuznetzov as if he were a drunken schoolboy. "Well, I suppose it would hurt more if you pulled slowly, wouldn't it now."

Kuznetzov's fist darted out and hit the Brit hard on the knee. "Exactly, you rip it off quickly. It hurts, but it is over fast. That is what we are going to do, Sir Clive, we are going to get it over faster so the pain will last a shorter time. And when it is over, what we have will be worth a lot more, a lot more."

36

THURSDAY, NOVEMBER 10
MOSSAD HEADQUARTERS
GLILOT JUNCTION
OUTSIDE TEL AVIV, ISRAEL

"You are lucky we maintain all the phone records for a year," said the Brigadier General from Unit 8200, the Israeli equivalent of America's NSA, the signals intelligence unit. "It takes a lot of storage to keep all of those records."

"Thank you for coming, General, as the deputy of one intelligence agency to the deputy of another, I thank you," Danny Avidar said as the two men sat in Avidar's dimly lit office.

"Not a problem. Next time you will visit our house, maybe come to see our base in the Negev."

"Perhaps. So, the question was last August fifteenth, at 0726 in the morning at the Haganah train station a man, Dawid Steyn, was murdered. We gave you his mobile number. Were you able to see if there were any mobiles of any interesting people at the time near Dawid Steyn in the station?"

"We got the list of all the people Shin Beth thinks work for this Olympus Security you mentioned. We pulled up all of their mobiles. None of them were in the Haganah Station at 0726 on fifteen August. Or if they were, they had their mobiles turned off," the General said.

"Shit."

"But wait, it's not over," the General added. "We did what you asked us to do and what do we get, we got nothing. But we are the experts on these things, yes? So, we do what we would do. We expand. We expand the time period we are looking at and we expand the radius of where we are looking. This is what we do. You see, Danny, you asked the question wrong. But not to worry, we corrected the question for you, even though you did not know enough to ask us to do that. We did it anyway."

Avidar endured it. "Well, of course, you know much better than we how to do these things. Thank you for correcting the question. If we had asked the question right, what would you have found?"

"If you had asked the question right, what

we would have found is what we found when we asked the question our way. At 0734, a mobile called a number in Cyprus. The mobile was moving at the time and at the speed of and in the direction traveled by a local bus, probably the Dan line fifteen, which leaves the Haganah Station at 0730. I know your next question. Was the mobile one that belonged to someone from this Olympus? Yes, it happens that it was. Mobile number 52 612 is registered to Efrim Brodsky who is on the list of Olympus employees given to us by the Shin Beth."

Danny Avidar leaped up and struck out his hand to shake with the general from the 8200. The General remained seated and held up his hand to indicate *stop.* "It's not over, yet. Do you think we at 8200 stop when there is more to collect? Never."

Avidar sat back down. "Of course not."

" 'Of course not' is right. We are very professional. We may not get all the credit and all the fame that you guys do in the Mossad, but often it is us that provide you the leads that you need to do what you do. Without us, many times, Danny, you know you would not be able to track these bad guys."

"We appreciate all that you do," Avidar said, quietly, politely. "As an intelligence officer and a professional, you know that often what we do, what you do, must never be known, and no one can get the credit."

"Exactly," the General agreed.

"So tell me what the fuck more you know, all of it, now."

"All right, all right. No need to be nasty," the General replied. "That mobile was last heard from when it pinged a mobile tower on October twenty-sixth. It didn't call anyone. It just was turned on and it pinged the tower."

"Where?"

"Odd. The tower was in the Comoros Islands."

37

FRIDAY, NOVEMBER 11
HIGH SPEED COMPUTING CENTER
LAWRENCE LIVERMORE NATIONAL
  LABORATORY
LIVERMORE, CALIFORNIA

"When will you be done?" the man in the lab coat asked, grabbing him by the arm as he entered the building.

"Who the fuck are you?" Dugout asked, pulling away.

"The guy who was scheduled to use High Speed. The guy you stole it from."

Dugout remembered him now. It was the climate change guy who had some huge model he was running simulations on, simulations that could only run on something as massively parallel as the Livermore High Speed computing array. Dug wanted to explain that he appreciated the importance of the man's work, but that there was at present, an immediate need that trumped it. If nuclear bombs went off in our cities, the economy would so badly crash that any and all scientific research would be retarded for a century. No one would be able to do anything about climate change until it was too late, which would just compound the new Dark Ages started by the bombs. All of those thoughts dashed through his head in an instant, as well as the realization that he couldn't explain that to a scientist who was not cleared to know about the mystery of the missing bombs.

Instead, Dug just said, "I don't know yet. Soon, maybe soon. I can't promise you."

The short man in the lab coat did not look like the type to pick a fight, especially with someone who was about six inches taller and about twenty years younger. Yet, he placed a finger on Dugout's chest and pushed it hard, tapping it as he spoke. "What I do is important. I need my machine."

Dugout grabbed the man's hand and placed it down by his side and held it there. "First, it isn't yours. It's the government's. Second, what I am doing is important, too. If you have a problem, take it up with the Lab Director."

With that, Dugout took the elevator up to the fourth floor.

He normally took the stairs, but he didn't want that guy following him, yelling at him. He waved his badge over the access control, punched in a PIN, and placed his palm on a glass plate. The three-factor authentication complete, the door to the computer control room opened. Ray and Mbali were already there.

"Comoros, I knew it," Ray said.

"Good morning. Knew what?" Dugout asked.

"The Comoros Islands. They're involved. Something happened there. What was going on around October twenty-sixth?" Ray asked.

Dugout sat down at the computer control console. "Did you look at the timeline? We have been keeping a timeline. Standard procedure." He hit a few keys and a chart appeared on the large screen. "The tritium had just been heisted from outside Pretoria."

"They flew it to Comoros," Ray asserted.

"How do we know that?" Mbali asked. "We checked all the flights that left around then. None went to the Comoros."

"Efrim Brodsky. He was in Moroni, in the Comoros on October twenty-sixth, according to Danny," Ray answered.

"Like the angel Moroni?" Dugout asked.

"You a Mormon now?" Ray said, looking at Dug.

"I saw the show. *Book of Mormon?*"

"So he was in Comoros, so what?" Mbali interjected.

"So, his phone shows up as having been on in Pretoria for the week before that, according to Danny."

"Danny knows what phones are on in South Africa?" Mbali asked.

"He does when they are Israeli mobiles."

Mbali frowned. "Okay. So lay it out."

"This Efrim Brodksy works for Olympus Security in their Tel Aviv office. Danny thinks he probably killed Dawid Steyn in August. Then he shows up in South Africa in mid-October. He is near Pretoria on twenty-five October. The tritium heist occurs. Then Brodsky shows up in the Comoros the next day. Then he disappears and is still gone. I say he was part of the tritium heist and then he flies out with it to the Comoros, which just happens to be real close to where the nuclear bombs were stored on Madagascar."

Mbali went to the whiteboard and sketched in blue a map of South Africa and the Indian Ocean to the east. Then she drew lines in red. "What do we know for sure? So, they moved the bombs from South

Africa to Madagascar years ago. We know that is true. Solid line. Then a probable nuclear explosion takes place August ninth in the ocean near here. We know that." She drew a mushroom cloud at sea. "Then they move the bombs from Madagascar August tenth. We know that, too, but we don't know where. Let's take your theory and say they move them to Comoros. Theory, therefore, dotted line. Then they steal the tritium October twenty-fifth from outside Pretoria. Known fact. You say they fly it to Comoros, where this Efrim shows up from Pretoria on October twenty-six. Another dotted line."

"Keep going. This is getting good," Dugout told her.

"It gets good, huh?" she said to him. "Now it is over to you and your big data mumbo jumbo. Check again, what flights left from Pretoria that could have gone to Comoros. Rule out commercial passenger flights that we know went elsewhere. Can you do that with your machine?"

"Sure."

"Good, then look at all the charter flights that left Comoros in the last two weeks and all the ships. Look for something odd about them. Where they went. Who owned them or chartered them. Can you do that, too?"

"Yes, ma'am. On it."

"You are awfully quiet there, Mr. Bow Man," she said.

Ray guided Mbali into the lounge, the break room, next door. "Let's let Dugout do his thing. You gave him enough that he will find something."

"Meanwhile, the big computer is still chugging away on trying to open the Potgeiters' laptops?" she asked.

"It is, but that could take forever. But we may not need it. We have lots of threads now. I tracked down Sergey Rogozin through NSA. He's in London. Turns out he goes there often from Olympus's headquarters in Cyprus. We told the Brits overnight. MI5, the BSS, is putting a very good team on him and NSA and GCHQ will team up to keep a close eye on his mobiles and all the comms associated with anybody from Olympus Security."

"What more do we know about Rogozin? What would he do with nuclear bombs?" Mbali asked.

"He's likely working for somebody. He's got a lot of A-list, heavy-hitter clients, according to CIA. Started out with Russian oligarchs, but then went global and has corporations and billionaires from all over. We've just got to figure out which one of them ordered up some nukes."

"And why," she added.

"There has to be a why," Ray agreed. "What have you heard back from Cape Town?"

"Well, unlike you and the Israelis, we don't track all of our citizens all the time by following all of their mobiles."

"Only because you don't have the technology," Ray laughed.

"Not yet. We have higher priorities, like building houses for our people who still live in shacks and shipping crates. We have many years of Apartheid to make up for. It will take a while."

"Okay, you're right. But what did you find out?"

"Sorry, I'm still sensitive to some issues. What did my people find back home? Well, they confirmed Olympus has an office and a team in Pretoria. Someone broke into their offices last night, these things happen, but we didn't find anything interesting yet. We imaged their computers and are still going through the files. I have guys tailing all of them. And Marcus Stroh is on his way to the Comoros with a small team, and radiation detectors, but there are lots of little islands there. It's not just one."

Bowman shook his head and looked at his shoes. "What's the problem?" she asked.

"We don't know how long we've got. When we thought they were trying to disrupt the election, we had a deadline, we knew how fast we had to run. Until we know why they are doing this, we don't know when it's going to happen. You still think they're going to blow up the black townships, create a white South African breakaway state?"

"No," she said. "I never did. It wouldn't work. Their white Bantustan would be radioactive, too. And besides, those of us who were left wouldn't stop 'til we killed them all."

Ray looked into her brown eyes and knew she meant every word of it, knew she could be a killer. "Did you ever kill anyone? I mean, personally, not just ordering it?"

She nodded and bit her lip. "You?"

"Only the ordering part. Never the trigger, not with my own hands."

"Could you?" she asked.

"I guess you never know until you have to, but, yes, to stop the kind of thing that I think they are trying to do, yes."

"I just hope we get the chance, in time," she said.

38

SATURDAY, NOVEMBER 12
DZAOUDZI, PETITE-TERRE
MAYOTTE, INDIAN OCEAN

Tall, broad, and with a thick head of white hair that seemed to stand straight up, Marcus Stroh did not blend in well for an agent of a secret service. That was true in his native South Africa and seemed even more the case in the airport baggage claim in Dzaoudzi. Pierre Marcoux of France's overseas intelligence service, the DGSE had no difficulty spotting him. The Frenchman, short and wearing a wicker hat and baggy shirt, could have been a pensioner looking for his daughter on the 777 from Paris that had just arrived. He was, instead, the only representative of the French intelligence service in this prefecture of over two hundred thousand people.

"Bienvenue, Monsieur Stroh, à l'Union Européenne," Marcoux said after standing next

to Stroh for half a minute scanning the crowd as Stroh was.

"Pierre?" Stroh asked, slightly surprised. "I meant to ask you when we talked yesterday how I would recognize you. So good of you to come out to the airport to get me."

"Marcus, this is a tiny island. It was not far to come to get you. How was Nairobi?"

"I just switched flights there, never went in to the town. We really have to start direct flights here from South Africa."

The two men began walking toward the line of taxis. "No, don't do that. Then I would have to monitor all of the people who would come from there. Too much work," Marcoux joked. "I don't like work. That is why I chose to be stationed here, the farthest part of the European Union from Paris." Marcoux directed Stroh toward a waiting Renault taxi.

"Boulevard des Crabes, *s'il vous plaît,* Etienne," Marcoux told the driver.

"Lapouz Noz Brochetti?" the driver asked.

"Oui, oui." Marcoux then explained to Stroh, "I assumed you would be famished, so I have reserved a table. I hope you like seafood."

"I would eat giraffe at the moment, but, yes, I do."

"It will also give me a chance to tell you what I have found out about the goings on across the way in the independent part of Comoros. We have been hard at work since you called, checking flights and shipping records over there. And asking about strange comings and goings."

Stroh pointed at the driver and gave Marcoux a questioning look. "Oh, Etienne works for me. Has for years. One of my most loyal employees, aren't you, *mon ami*?" Marcoux laughed, tapping the African driver's shoulder. "In fact, he was one of my men who went over to the Comoros. Just got back late this afternoon. Very productive trip, eh, Etienne? Our man here found out exactly what you wanted to know."

"Well, then, I hope I can offer you a small reward, Etienne," Marcus said, reaching for his wallet. Marcoux placed his hand on top of Marcus Stroh's.

"No need for that. Etienne is a contract employee of mine. Well taken care of, aren't you?"

Marcus Stroh took a card from inside his jacket. "Well, at least we can offer our hospitality. If you are ever in South Africa, or in trouble for that matter, ring us up on that line and tell them to get in touch with me. They always answer at that number. But call me Mr. Robinson. We'll show you a good time if you do visit us."

Etienne was not used to being treated that nicely by white folks. Most of them saw him as a short, skinny nobody, like a piece of the taxi he drove for cover. The "taxi driver" let his fare off at the restaurant, parked a block away, and then circled back to sit as a watcher at the bar as the two white men dined. His role was to see if anyone took undue notice of the two, to intervene in extremis. But on Mayotte, there was never extremis. The only security problems on the island were related to the heroin that came by boat and ship, smugglers looking for a back door into France and the EU. The Sûreté handled the counternarcotics effort; the intelligence service, Marcoux, only assisted.

"Mainly, my concern here as DGSE is who comes and goes. We are a foreign intelligence service and these islands are domestic France, as much a part of the country as Normandy," Marcoux said, as they settled in at their table. "But I also have a watching brief on the independent country of Comoros. After all, before they became a nation, they and Mayotte were joined together and were one French colony at one point. The wise folk here on Mayotte voted to become part of France. Smart move, for now the French taxpayers provide the funding for a very nice life here. And Comoros? Not so nice."

"You don't have a base in your Moroni embassy there, in Comoros?" Stroh asked.

"We do, but his main job is training the Comoros service, such as it is. So, they all know him. He can't run sources. Our last man tried to do both jobs, training and spying, and, of course, they detected it and asked him to return to Paris. So now I run the sources from here. Do you like the Sancerre tonight?"

"I defer to you."

"I think we get a good one tonight, since La Piscine is paying." Marcoux used the French nickname for the DGSE headquarters, the swimming pool. "Ladoucette Sancerre Lafond," he said to the waiter, smiling at the thought of soon tasting the expensive white. *"Pas trop froid."* Then, looking back at his guest, he continued. "I am very glad to help you, of course, but why come to me. Why not go and ask the Comoros people themselves?"

"Mbali, my boss, she said go straight to you. I think she doubts the Comoros security service's, shall we say,

366

competence?"

Marcoux smiled. "Mbali, she is your boss? I worked with her on a case involving Afrikaner mercenary types. Yes, she doubts the Comoros's competence, or maybe even more their honesty. A hard woman, moving fast is Mbali."

Stroh nodded agreement. "So, you like it here, in Mayotte?" he observed. It seemed like quite a likable place, complete with relaxed establishments such as this French restaurant, where Marcoux appeared to be well known. The restaurant was a darkened room with fans turning slowly, one wall missing, open to the sea, letting in a humid, salty breeze.

"I do. I am my own man here," Marcoux replied, lighting a cigarette. "Paris told me to move my office to Mamoudzou on the big island, since that is the capital now. I didn't. Paris forgot." The wine arrived and Marcoux approved the tasting. "I work here when I want, which is mainly at night. Sources don't talk in the sun."

Marcus Stroh knew not to rush people like the Frenchman, but he also knew that Mbali was waiting for his report. Mbali was always in a rush and did not understand people who were not. "And your sources in Comoros, they were productive you said?"

"They were," Marcoux answered, apparently not bothered by the rudeness of getting down to the business before the main course. "Anjouan, you know it?" Marcus shook his head, no. "It's one of the Comoros Islands, although it tried to break away, or rather one of our protégés there, a Colonel Bacar, tried to break it away. It was *une pagaie,* with the African Union invading to help reunite the islands. Imagine Sudanese, Senegalese, Tanzanian troops trying an amphibious landing. *Très drole.*"

"Oh, yes, I do recall," Stroh offered. "Two thousand eight?"

"*Oui.* Well, we had to find Bacar a safe haven when it was all over. We put him up in Benin. He had been our eyes and ears on Anjouan. After he was ousted, I arrive here and start building my own network of sources. One of them, he runs a satellite dish, television and Internet installation company, he is quite good. You can imagine."

Etienne was sipping his whiskey, but downing Perrier, into which he squeezed juice from a lemon he cut and sliced at the bar. His eyes scanned the diners in the dimly lit room, mainly whites, some with African women. He knew most of the crowd, or at least had seen them before.

There were only twelve thousand people on Petite-Terre, the smaller of the two main islands that made up Mayotte.

"Around the time you mentioned, in August, he noticed an unscheduled flight into Ouani, the little airport on Anjouan, from Madagascar. Air Madagascar flies that route, but this, this was a charter. A C-130, cargo plane." Marcoux clearly relished storytelling. "Then within a week there were three other flights by the same plane. And whites took the cargoes away."

Etienne had rated everyone in the dining room as a known quantity, except one blond man, who was with a woman Etienne did know. He saw her with men, with tourists, from time to time. This man was younger, Etienne thought, but he wore a hearing aid.

"Then the plane came back, three months later, on a flight this time from Moroni on the other side of the Comoros," Marcoux continued, "on the date you mentioned. Twenty-six October."

Marcus Stroh wondered if he had told the Frenchman too much, if the French sources were just inventing stories that matched the dates Stroh had provided Marcoux on the phone. "I suppose it is too much to ask if that satellite television man got the tail number of this mystery plane?"

"Perhaps, come to think of it, you should pay for dinner, or perhaps donate that reward to my office fund," Marcoux replied. He handed Stroh his business card, which alleged he was a professor of anthropology. On the back of the card, Marcoux had handwritten "5B-01739." Marcoux poured them both more of the Sancerre. "5B, oddly, is the aircraft tail code for Cyprus. Never seen that aircraft around here before."

Stroh placed the card in his shirt pocket. "If one had flown cargo into Ouani, how would you get it out of the country? Another flight, bigger plane?"

"No bigger plane could land there," Marcoux replied. "In fact, a C-130 can only land there light, not fully loaded. We know that from the support flights l'Armée de l'Air flew in '08, during the African Union's invasion."

The blond man excused himself from his dinner guest, walked through the bar, past Etienne, and went outside. Etienne saw him through the small window above the bar, talking on his mobile. Why not talk at the table, thought Etienne? Was he answering a call from his wife perhaps?

"How would you get the cargo off island, then?" Stroh asked.

"Containers. They ship from the harbor at

Mutsamudu. And before you ask, they are almost always the same little freighters on runs to Durban or Karachi. At the end of October, two new ships, modern things, had maiden calls at Mutsamudu. I will have their names for you in the morning."

Stroh pulled out his iPhone. "I hate to be rude, but I have an anxious boss. Unlike you, I am not my own man. Please forgive me for tapping out a quick note to her. When I have completed that, no more business tonight. I trust there are good cognacs here."

"There was a bottle of Brugerolle, Vieille Reserve, last time . . ."

Marcoux fell forward, toward Stroh. Blood shot from the side of his head, splattering onto the wall and then gushing onto the tablecloth. Marcus Stroh dropped his iPhone and went for his gun as he looked up at the blond man walking toward him. Stroh recognized the silencer on the pistol, just before the gun erupted again. A *thud,* a flash, and then Stroh fell back, out of his chair, a bullet having transited through his forehead and out the back of his head.

Etienne had come off his barstool as soon as he saw the blond man walking quickly toward Marcoux's table. He kneeled and pulled his Smith & Wesson M&P340

Scandium ankle gun from his leg. By the time he stood up, Marcoux was shot. Etienne aimed the small revolver and fired at the shooter, hitting him in the head with the .357 round just after the man fired at Stroh. The tiny revolver created a powerful sound. Women screamed. The blond man fell to his knees. There was a stampede of diners toward the door. Etienne moved closer and fired again. The blond man fell sideways onto the floor, his gun landing next to Stroh's iPhone in the pool of fresh blood spreading on the tiles.

39

"I can tie the shooter to Olympus Security," Dugout blurted out as Ray and Mbali entered the room. It was almost one in the morning. They had been working flat out since the word reached Mbali that Marcus had been killed in Mayotte, near the Comoros. Mbali had been on the phone to his family, helping them make the arrangements to get the body back, planning for an official funeral, making sure his dependents would get a full pension, talking with the French Sûreté about the investigation into who the shooter was.

"Cell phone?" Ray asked. "What does the shooter's phone tell us?"

"Nothing, I can't associate him with a

mobile device, except the burner he had on him when he died. No, the Bulgarian passport he was carrying was a fake. No such person. Bulgaria doesn't have him or a passport by that number in their database. But the picture from that passport that we got from the French police," Dugout said, tapping keys that put a mug shot on the large video screen, "I ran that picture against a bunch of databases and got a .97 confidence match against this picture of a guy in the Cyprus passport database. Different name. In Cyprus, he was Karl Alfson, born in Stockholm. Except there was no Karl Alfson in the Stockholm birth and death database that matches. He made up a Swedish identity in order to get a Cypriot citizenship and passport."

"Sweden, Cyprus, Bulgaria. So where did Marcus's killer really come from?" Mbali asked. "What was his real name?"

"I don't know. I just know Cyprus granted him citizenship five years ago and that he listed his employer as Olympus Security of Polis, Cyprus."

Mbali sat down. For the first time since he had met her weeks ago, Ray thought she looked not just tired, but dejected. Losing Marcus Stroh had hit her very hard. It had hit Bowman, too, who kept thinking about how Stroh had saved his life in Cape Town.

She looked to Ray, "I say we hit every Olympus Security office in the world, round up every one of them."

Bowman winced. "Not yet. We get all of our friends to tail them, yes. And where we don't have cooperative local services to do it, we do it ourselves. We do surreptitious entry into their offices, we copy all of their comms, e-mails, phone calls. I don't want to spook anybody into going early. We need to know who they are working for."

"Exxon, Alcoa, Microsoft," Dugout read out. "They have a lot of the international Fortune 500 listed as clients somewhere in the world. They also work for NGOs like UNICEF, Doctors Without Borders, the Purpose Fund, providing security. Also BBC, WNN, other television outfits that have reporters in war zones."

"You got that client list from hacking into their headquarters in Cyprus?" Bowman asked.

"No, from their public Web site. There doesn't seem to be anything in their Cyprus office to hack into. I can't find an IP address for it. All I can find is a cloud e-mail service that they use worldwide, it's Rackspace. Their web page is hosted there, too, but connected to nothing. The employees all access the e-mail service from their own devices. Talk about BYOD, I don't think this company has any computers of its own. Nothing to hack."

"Isn't that unusual?" Mbali asked.

"It is, but it's also brilliant," Bowman said. "Do they have any files stored in the cloud, other than e-mail?"

"Not that I can find," Dugout said. "Payroll and accounts payable seem to be done by banks in about twenty countries. The banks get funds transferred in every month. Then an authorized payer logs into the banks accounts, always from a public Internet site, and gives the banks instructions on what payments to make."

Bowman shook his head. "No, they must have another identity somewhere, with its own data storage, files, maybe encrypted e-mails. We just haven't found it."

"If they did, one of the guys we know as Olympus would have to access the other network. And every time one of those guys goes online now, we are watching. So far, nothing," Dugout said.

"We do know one damn thing," Mbali asserted. "This Sergey Rogozin is listed as the Head Man of Olympus. Let's assume that is true, that he's not a false front for the real Head Man. If he's the real deal, he will know it all. He will know who paid him to try to kill us, to kill Marcus, to steal the tritium. He will know where the bombs are. I say bring him in and let me at him. Where is he?"

"He was in London last time I looked," Ray said, looking at Dugout to find out.

"MI5 says he got on a private jet for Teterboro."

"Where's that?" Mbali asked.

"New York," Bowman and Dugout said simultaneously.

Mbali stood up. "Raymond, steal yourself another plane from somebody and let's go to New York."

"This time, I think it might be quicker just to buy a couple of tickets. Dug, can you book two seats on the Virgin America flight first thing in the morning?"

"You drag me out here and now you're going to leave me here?" Dug joked.

"We should leave you here until you crack the code on the Potgeiters' computers," Mbali replied. Dugout could not tell if she was serious.

"We may not need that, since we have other leads now. Can't you just leave it running by itself and go back to DC? Or do we just shut it down?" Ray asked Dug.

"There is no way to know if we are halfway

there or one percent of the way. I think even with the massively parallel structure and the power of this machine, the biggest and fastest in the world, it's still a shot in the dark. I'll give it one more day and then hand it over to NSA and go back to DC. But there's still a lot of leads I can run on my own from Foggy Bottom."

Dugout sensed a feeling of hopelessness in his two colleagues. He tried to rally their spirits. "We are narrowing it down. For the first time since we started, I feel like we are on the trail of the bombs." He was not sure his attempt succeeded with Mbali and Ray. They were so tired, it was hard for them to think beyond Marcus Stroh's death.

Bowman drove Mbali back into San Francisco, over the Bay Bridge, its halogen lights blinking into artistic patterns in the middle of the night. He wondered why they kept those lights on, when so few were awake to see them. They drove in silence, until he dropped her off at the Marriott on Market Street. "I'll see you at the airport in a few hours," she said. "Try to get some sleep."

Bowman then drove up Market a few blocks to his friends' apartment in a new luxury, high-rise. They were out of town and had left the key with the concierge. So far,

Ray had spent little time in the apartment and almost all of that asleep. As he dropped the car with the twenty-four-hour valet, he wished his friends were home, wished somebody friendly, some "civilian" would be there to welcome him, as Emma and Linda did back home. He then realized he had just thought of St. John as "back home."

Throughout his mad dash around the globe, he only once called Emma and Linda. He did not want anybody detecting a connection to them, thereby putting them at risk. In the lobby, he saw the twenty-four-hour concierge at the desk, watching television. "Sorry to bother you, but my phone died and I need to make a call. Can I borrow your mobile for a minute? I'll pay you," he said pulling a crumpled twenty from his pocket.

It would be six in the morning in St. John. They would be awake, but still in bed. They had programmed their old iPad to start playing softly at six every morning, a random shuffle. It was a nice way to wake up and see the sunrise on the water. He dialed the number from memory and heard the connection click through a few switches. It rang, once, twice, three times. Emma answered on the fourth ring. "Is this you?"

"Yes, honey, it is," he said.

"I didn't recognize the number, so I wasn't going to answer, but Lin said it was you. She knew, didn't you? I'm putting you on speaker."

He didn't know what to say. "Are you both okay?"

There was chuckling and then Linda answered for them.

"Not 'both,' remember? All three of us."

"How big are you now Em?" he asked.

"Lin says I waddle like a duck."

"Tell him," Linda said.

"No, you tell him."

"Somebody tell me something," Ray laughed.

"Linda and I went to St. Thomas on the ferry to the clinic for the ultrasound," Emma said.

"Well, Daddy, you're going to have a son," Linda almost yelled across the line.

"Wow," was all that he could think to say.

"That means he has to live in the boys' house with you and the dog, Cody," Emma said.

"I can't breast-feed. He's going to have to stay next door with you for a while," Ray heard himself replying.

"Well, you can change diapers and there will be a lot of that to do and feeding him milk we pump for you to give him at three in the morning," Linda added.

"What's his name?" Ray asked.

"We don't know yet, but we have the last part," Emma answered.

"Middle names Reed, Handley. Last name Bowman."

"I like using your mothers' maiden names for his middle names, even if it does give him four names like some British prince," Ray thought out loud.

"We agreed you get to pick his first name," Linda said.

"So what's it going to be?" Emma asked.

"Marcus, let's call him Marcus."

Emma replied first, "Nice. Family name, or somebody you know?"

"Yeah, I like it. Marcus Bowman. Sounds strong," Linda added.

"I'll explain the connection when I get back home, and before you ask, I still don't know when that will be." He hated saying it.

After the call, as he was riding up in the elevator, he realized he was crying. He wasn't exactly sure what emotion had triggered the tears, but he didn't try to stop them. He realized as the elevator stopped at the thirty-third floor that he knew what one of the emotions whirring through him was. It was fear, fear of failing, fear of a messed-up world Marcus Bowman would be born into.

He didn't even try to sleep. He knew the dream would be back, the drone flying in the window, or if not, then the restaurant in Jaffa flying apart.

40

SUNDAY, NOVEMBER 13
DZAOUDZI, PETIT-TERRE
MAYOTTE, INDIAN OCEAN

It had taken Etienne Kafotamaki quite a while to get the French Sûreté to understand that he was a contract employee of the DGSE, licensed to carry firearms, and that he had shot the man who was attacking the island's DGSE chief. For a long time, the Sûreté could not piece together who had shot whom, although all the witnesses agreed that the blond man had shot the two men at the table and that Etienne had intervened to stop it.

Etienne was slightly sympathetic with the Sûreté. When was the last time they had a triple shooting here? Probably never. It had helped that Etienne knew many of the officers and had worked with them. It was just that with Pierre Marcoux dead, there was no one to officially vouch for him. Finally, the DGSE man from Comoros's capital Moroni had flown over to Mayotte, and the formalities were completed to let Etienne free.

Etienne took his liberator, Marcel Baize, back to the DGSE office, unlocking it for him. Baize had been ordered by La Piscine to investigate what the late Pierre Marcoux had been up to that had resulted in his untimely demise. As far as Paris had known, nothing was going on in Mayotte.

"We were helping the South Africans on an urgent case," Etienne explained to Baize. "The white man who was shot with Pierre, he was a South African special services officer. He had called Pierre three days ago and that had sent us scrambling to find out about flights into Comoros and about ships."

"Odd," said Baize. "Why didn't he just call me to find out about Comoros. There I was sitting in Moroni, capital of the Comoros, with nothing to do but try to teach these local fellows tradecraft. Hopeless. I could have done the legwork for Pierre. Who did?"

"I did," Etienne admitted. "And a few other guys he uses."

"Totally out of line, against the rules," Baize said aloud to himself. "I should have been informed."

"Here it is," Etienne said, rummaging through the debris on Pierre Marcoux's desk.

"What?"

"What he was going to give the South African," Etienne replied. He held up a small blue file card.

Baize grabbed it from his hand and read it aloud.

" '5B-01739, MV *Rothera*, MV *Nunatak*.' Pierre died for this? What is it?"

"I don't know, but I think we should tell the South Africans," Etienne insisted.

"We shall do no such thing," Baize replied, tucking the card in his coat pocket. "It will be in my report to Paris, when that is completed. Along with the fact that you were operating in my territory without my permission. We shall see whether you are to be kept on."

Etienne looked at him as he would a drunken tourist getting behind the wheel, with a combination of horror, disdain, and pity. "If you will not be needing me further now, I shall go to my wife, who will have been wondering where I was."

Etienne, who was not married, walked down the street, turned the corner, and took a card out of his wallet. Then he took out his mobile and called the number in South Africa that Marcus Stroh had given him. Stroh may be dead, but someone would answer.

Pierre had told Etienne that he paid him more than the others because Etienne had a photographic memory, he could remember names and numbers after just seeing them for a few seconds. Etienne thought everyone could do that, until Pierre Marcoux had told him it was a special gift. He would miss Pierre, he did already.

He heard the phone ring through. It was picked up on the third ring. "Legal offices," a female voice answered. "Do you need bail money?"

"I need an airline ticket," Etienne responded. "The late Mr. Robinson said you would buy it for me, so I could be there for the reading of his last will and testament."

There was a pause. He thought he could hear her hitting a keyboard. "And who is this calling?"

"I was the man at Mr. Robinson's funeral."

Another, longer pause. Then a man spoke. "Yes, will it be in your name?"

"My name is Charles Dupré," Etienne said. He spelled it out.

"Yes, of course. The ticket will be at the Thomas Cook desk at the airport where you are. We look forward to seeing you. For the reading of the will. Good-bye."

41

"I think we just turned back north. Why would we do that?" Jonathan Kinder asked Sergey Rogozin. They were flying in from London aboard one of Kinder Industries' corporate jets. This one was an aircraft that could carry 189 people in coach, or 12 in this Boeing Business Jet configuration. On this flight the passenger total was 3.

"I'll find out what's going on," Rogozin said, unbuckling his seat belt and walking forward to the flight deck.

"What time is your speech?" Kinder asked his daughter, Victoria. "Not that things at the UN are ever on time."

"It's in the afternoon. I'll be fine, besides it's just to an IPCC Working Group," she replied.

"I don't know all the UN jargon, Vicki, but I know it's important that they hear from you the results of your work," he insisted. "And when you are done, we'll blast it out to all the media, all the blogs, e-mail it to everyone on our lists. I have paid for full-page ads about it in *The New York Times, The Wall Street Journal, Financial Times.* We have to insure that when they think of you, of us, that they think of the good work we did. We will be the last people they think of as the culprits."

"Air Traffic Control is keeping us circling for the next twenty minutes. Morning density over New York, normal," Rogozin explained as he walked back from the cockpit.

"Teterboro is always crowded now. They park the Gulfstreams, BBJs, and Falcons three and four deep. Billionaires' row. You have to wait for them to rearrange all the planes to get yours out. It's like some damn valeted parking garage," Kinder complained.

"It's a nice problem to have, yes?" Rogozin asked. "To be a billionaire?"

Kinder muttered something unintelligible. Rogozin leaned toward him. "Have you thought anymore about what I said? Montana will not be the safest place for you after it happens."

"Sergey, we are going to Montana. I have three hundred and fifty thousand acres, that's almost five hundred square miles. Boston is less than fifty square miles. I have enough room for ten cities that size. I have enough former Special Forces and Delta guys to secure it, my own sources of electricity, water, food."

"And stockpiles of everything in warehouses and storage tanks," Victoria added. "Sergey, he's thought of everything out there."

"With respect," Rogozin pushed back, "I am not sure you have thought of what will happen if they do figure out you are among the, what did you call them, 'the culprits'? Everybody knows it's you that owns that ranch. You may need to be somewhere where no one knows you are there. We have places like that. Very nice places."

Kinder shifted in his seat. "You said no one will ever know who did it. Or if they do, it will be a false trail, what did you call it, ah, a legend."

"That American, Bowman, and the black woman from South Africa are getting closer to us. Somehow they found the Potgeiters. Then the woman sent someone to the Comoros," Rogozin said softly.

"The Comoros? We have to stop her,"

Kinder insisted.

"Don't worry. We got the guy she sent to Comoros before he learned anything. We got there in time."

"I told you to kill Bowman a long time ago," Victoria Kinder interjected. "Why is he still alive?"

"We've tried to kill him twice. We'll get him. In any event, it's almost impossible to connect you two to the bombs," Rogozin replied.

"I don't like the word 'almost,' Sergey," Kinder said slowly. "I do not like it at all."

A bell rang. The voice from the speakers said, "We are cleared for landing. Coming in to New York."

MONDAY, 13 NOVEMBER
YAKUTSK, SAKHA REPUBLIC
RUSSIAN FEDERATION

"The Luna isn't frozen yet," Konstantin Kuznetzov said to his sons, looking down on the river from his estate on the hill ridge outside of Yakutsk. "It's later every year." Behind him one of the world's largest forests spread out to the west. He owned most of it and enormous deposits of natural gas under it, as well as the Sakha Arctic Shipping Company, which kept Yakutsk and other remote cities in the northeast supplied, even when it meant having to break the ice. Just within the Sakha Republic and neighboring Krasnoyarsk Krai, Kuznetzov's land holdings were bigger than dozens of countries, including good-sized ones like Argentina.

He was one of seven Russian oligarchs the *Financial Times* had profiled, contending that each of them was worth more than two hundred billion dollars. Together their corporations controlled three-quarters of Russia's gross domestic product.

Of course, they did not own 100 percent of their corporations. Some of them were traded on the Moscow stock market, but few shares ever moved. There were also the silent partners, those in the government, including the Czar who made this all possible.

Sitting in front of him were his two children, young men now, boys aged eighteen and twenty. He had flown them back from universities in Paris and Oxford, had them tell their friends that their mother was ill. He had told them not to worry, she was fine, but he needed to see them both quickly. "It is an emergency," were his words. He had preceded them to the Sakha Luna Dashas by forty-eight hours. They had landed, each in his own plane, at the family's airstrip and had each been helicoptered to the compound.

After they had briefly recovered from their flights, their father asked them to join him in his library, a room with a wall of glass looking east, across a cleared field, to the river below. Konstantin Kuznetzov withdrew a squat, clear-glass bottle from a mound of ice. In the center of the bottle was a metal rod. The bottle cap was a strange perforated metal plug. "It's Heavy Water," he announced proudly.

"Like what they use in nukes?" his older son asked. "That rod in there, that bottle looks like part of a miniature reactor."

"Don't worry, it's just the name the Norwegians gave it. It's a historical pun, yes? Not radioactive. Is vodka, better even than the Kauffman. Made with water they found under the ice in Sweden, from the last ice age. Very pure."

The young men looked at the strange bottle and then joined in with their father, all three simultaneously taking down a full shot in one gulp. *"Za tvoyo zdorovie!"* they all said and clinked their shot glasses.

"Now, my sons, let me tell you about real nuclear bombs and what is going to happen soon, why we are here in Yakutsk." They were stunned, silent. They could not look at one another. They stared instead at their father.

Finally Yuri, the younger boy, spoke. "This sounds like a line out of Tolstoy, Father, but does the Czar know?"

Kuznetzov walked away, toward the window. With his back to the boys he said, "This is not an act being carried out by any government. The Czar will condemn it. He will call for an investigation. Russian security services will help uncover perpetrators. It will be a difficult two or three years before things begin to settle down, before, what did the old man Bush call it, the New World Order takes hold."

"But, Father, millions will die," Yuri replied.

"Yuri, there are almost seven billion people on this planet. Too many for the systems to sustain. Too many who are just a drag on the systems. Even when we are done there will be over six billion people, Yuri, think of the size of those masses," Kuznetzov said, walking back toward his sons.

"Will you be safe, Father?" Vladimir, the older boy, asked.

"We will all be safe, Vlady," he said, putting his hand on the boy's shoulder. "Here, in our forest kingdom, we will all be safe.

Well supplied and comfortable. That is why I sent for you, so you will be safe, here with me."

For the first time, the boys looked at each other, the horror showing in their expressions. "But, Father, I have to go back to Oxford in two days. I have a very important meeting with my tutor."

"I am afraid that won't be possible, Vladimir," Kuznetzov said.

"How long do we have to stay out here?" Yuri asked, with panic in his voice.

"As I said, it should all settle down in two or three years, maybe sooner, maybe," Kuznetzov said, pulling the bottle out of the ice surrounding it, pouring another round of shots.

The boys looked at each other again, as their father had his back to them. "He's crazy," Yuri mouthed.

Kuznetzov turned and walked toward his sons, carrying three shots of the Heavy Water Vodka. He handed one to each boy. "To the New World Order. It will all be yours."

42

"I'm with the FBI. Please come with me," the Special Agent said to Ray Bowman as he stepped from the Virgin America aircraft on to the jetway. Bowman's Sunday call to Winston Burrell and the National Security Advisor's subsequent call to the FBI Director had set the wheels in motion. The Bureau had put two hundred agents onto the task of tailing and listening to Sergey Rogozin and the Kinders from the time their jet had landed at Teterboro four hours ago. Rogozin's New York office of Olympus Security was being penetrated electronically on its telephone lines and acoustically through the walls and windows.

Ray guided Mbali down the stairs on to the runway, where Bill McKenna, Special Agent in Charge of National Security for the New York office of the FBI sat waiting for them in a Chevrolet Suburban. Mc-Kenna looked young for the job and his accent sounded more Texas than Brooklyn. "I've been told from the top to give you any and all assistance on this case, so you got it," he said. Ray introduced Mbali Hlanganani as his "colead on the case." She didn't blink, but she made a mental note to ask exactly when she had become that.

"Where did they go from Teterboro?" Ray asked.

"Rogozin went straight for his office. It's two brownstones on East seventy-fourth. Very pricey real estate. Looks like he has an apartment in one of them," McKenna explained. "Rogozin came in on an airplane with just two other passengers, Jonathan Kinder, the CEO of Kinder Industries, and his daughter, Victoria, a professor at NYU. The Kinders went to their penthouse on Central Park South, but now the daughter is at the UN. She's speaking at some meeting there."

"Can you get me into the UN meeting? I might want to just confront her and ask her what she knows about Rogozin. See what reactions that brings."

"Already thought of that, Mr. Bowman, set up a top-secret level workspace for you in the U.S. Mission across the street from the UN and got you two passes to the UN meeting through an ex-Bureau guy who now runs security in New York for the UN."

"Thanks, but I'll skip that," Mbali said. "I need to get to the South African Mission and grab a secure phone to call into my office. Among other things, I want to see what we've learned about Marcus's death."

"The South Africans are on Thirty-eighth Street, between First and Second. We can drop you there on our way," McKenna said as the Suburban pulled through the airport gate.

"Did you sweep their plane at Teterboro? Any signs of radiation?" Ray pressed.

"We did, along with Customs, searched every plane that came in or went out of Teterboro so it didn't look like we were after Rogozin. Came up cold, except for some medical equipment on a flight going out to Minnesota. We've been running the rad/nuc detection guys ragged the last two weeks, but even so they are really scrupulous. If there was a trace, they woulda found it."

Bowman was not surprised. It made no sense for Rogozin to personally escort a weapon into New York. The fact that he was in the city suggested that it might not be the target, or at least that nothing would detonate while he was still there.

They were at the end of the morning traffic, approaching noon, but the highway was still jammed and moving slowly. After Ray looked at his watch the third time, Mc-Kenna asked the agent driving the truck to turn on the blue lights and use the breakdown lane to get them into town a little faster. Mbali looked more nervous than Ray had ever seen her be. He wondered if it was the scary driving or her sense that they were getting close to knowing what they were after.

SPECIAL SECURITY SERVICES
CAPE TOWN, SOUTH AFRICA

"I'm sorry you have been waiting so long Mr. Dupré," the tall, young man said to Etienne. "I am Nelson Hutamro, in charge of investigating what happened to Mr. Robinson. They just told me you were here and had been waiting for hours. I apologize. We've been a little crazy here today. Please, come upstairs to my office."

Etienne wondered how old the Zulu was, was he really old enough to be the lead investigator on Stroh's murder? And, if he was, why was he still in Cape Town? Hutamro's office, however, was large and in a suite that said DIRECTOR MBALI HLANGANANI over the outer door. Hutamro's office was only three doors down, inside the suite.

"You said you were there when Mr. Robinson was shot and you knew his Service name when you called. And you knew his special call-in number, you phoned in on it. Can I ask how you learned these things, Mr. Dupré?" Hutamro asked when they were seated on an old leather couch and chair.

"Might I have some tea?" Etienne began. "It was very dry and dusty in the lobby all these hours." Etienne wondered if he could trust this young man with what he assumed from Stroh's comments was a very important case, important enough to have gotten him killed. "Mr. Stroh, his real name, Marcus Stroh, said that he worked for the top person in your Service, a Ms. Mbali."

Hutamro called out for teas, then checked to make sure the recording light was on next to the telephone. "He did. So do I. This is her office suite."

"And you work directly for her?"

"I do. I am one of three Special Assistants to the Director."

"And what I tell you will get to her and no one else?"

Hutamro crossed his long legs and thought a moment. "If you want that, I can report it only to her. What the Director decides after that, who she will share it with, I cannot say. It is up to her."

Etienne was exhausted from the overnight flights and he felt he needed a shower, but he was kept awake by the adrenaline, the realization that by coming to South Africa without the permission of DGSE, he would undoubtedly be fired from his contract job and likely worse. He was throwing his life into a blender, but he felt a compulsion. He kept seeing Pierre and Marcus, bleeding onto the linen tablecloth.

"I am a contract officer of the DGSE, acting without permission. My true name is Etienne Kafotamaki. Mr. Stroh made a request of my boss Pierre Marcoux. To answer his questions, I was sent across from Mayotte to Comoros.

"Mr. Stroh wanted information about aircraft and ships that had moved on certain days that acted unusually. I found that information."

Hutamro sat up in his chair and reached for a notepad and pen. Etienne took a sip of the tea that had now shown up, his hand unsteady with the cup. "Pierre, my boss, was giving that information to Marcus Stroh when he was shot. When they were both shot, I was a few feet away. I should have seen the danger and warned them, but I did not see it until it was too late. I killed the shooter. But it was too late." Etienne stopped and looked down. He rubbed his eyes.

"It is very difficult to act in time in these situations," Hutamro said softly. "I am sure you did all that you could."

"I did not, but now I am finishing my mission. I was to find the information that Mr. Stroh wanted so that it could get to Ms. Mbali. When they know in Mayotte, in Comoros, that I have come here, they will fire me, arrest me. They wanted to take their time and let Paris decide when and if to give this information to Ms. Mbali. I give it to her now." He handed Hutmaro the card that Pierre had been handing over when he was killed, the card with the aircraft tail number. On it, Etienne had added the names of two ships.

"I can tell you when the plane took off and landed, several times, and when the ships departed and from where. I have memorized it all."

Nelson Hutamro took the card. He noted a small stain on the upper-left corner. He was sure that it was dried blood. "May I call you Etienne?"

"But of course, yes."

"Etienne, if all of this proves out, as I am

sure it will, we would like to offer you employment with us, perhaps in Mayotte or Comoros, or perhaps Madagascar or Seychelles. Maybe the DGSE will not know that you came here, as Monsieur Dupré. I am sure Marcus Stroh would have wanted us to do that."

Etienne's eyes moistened, but he did not shed a tear. He again sipped the tea. "Let me tell you the dates and places."

Nelson Hutamro copied down the information carefully, verified it again with Etienne, and then excused himself from his own office and walked down a row of desks to Mbali's secretary. "I need to talk with the Director now, wherever she is."

43

He saw the man coming toward him. "Don't start with me again," Dugout said to the short, balding man in the lab coat. "You can have it back. I just need to terminate some searches and transfer some data to Fort Meade on the trunk line. Give me two hours and it's all yours to do whatever terribly important thing it is you do."

"Professor Michael McFarland," the man said offering his hand. "I model complex interactions with numerous permutations and high quantities of variables. I am overdue to get results to the White House Science Advisor on a climate change excursion. No other computing center can model this set of data in the time we have to finish. No other computing center can display the results with such high-definition graphics. They need visuals to understand things at the White House level, or so I'm told."

"I'll have to remember that," Dugout said, smiling. "Two hours."

Professor McFarland nodded, turned around quickly, and hurried out of the Control Room. There was no thank-you. Dugout sat down and began closing out his programs, transferring data to NSA, whose computers would pick up the attempt to decrypt the documents on the Potgeiters' laptops. As he did, he noticed that one document had begun to open. It was an attachment on an e-mail and it was apparently sent using a different encryption algorithm than the Potgeiters had used on the documents on their hard drives.

The decryption program had actually cracked the header on the four pages of the document and it had made clear the word in the first column in what looked like a chart. The header bore only the word USKO-RITEL. Dugout assumed it was a Pentagon acronym, U.S. Korean Intelligence? But why would the letter N be missing? U.S. Korean International Telephony?

The first rows, were a series of numbers. The first was 9816. What followed were a few more entries with 8 as the recurring third number. 10816. 11816. Then there were other numbers beginning with 9s and 1s, and 6s in common. Then numbers with 1s, 0s, 1s and 6s. Across from each number was text that the decryption program had yet to break.

"Of course!" Dugout yelled out across the vacant room. "It's a fucking schedule." Each number ended with 16, the year. It was the date in European format, with the day and then the month. "Shit," he whispered. So the first number was really meant to be 08.09.16, August 9. "Damn, that was the day the nuclear detonation was detected in the Indian Ocean." This had to be the schedule for whatever they were doing with the bombs. Whatever, maybe the Koreans, maybe the crazy North Koreans, were doing with the bombs? USKORITEL?

He quickly leafed through the four-page document to the end. The last number was 181116, or November 18. That was four days from now. There were no dates after that. He felt his stomach roll and his pulse race. Where the hell was Bowman?

UNITED NATIONS HEADQUARTERS
NEW YORK CITY
Bowman found a seat in the side gallery

where he could look across at the witness table. At the table, Professor Victoria Kinder was reading from a prepared text while charts, graphs, and maps flashed on two large screens that Bowman could not see from where he sat. The screen facing his section was turned off.

Professor Kinder was very pleasant to look at, but very dull to listen to. She was going on in a monotone, her presentation filled with acronyms. The UN panel she was presenting to was, nonetheless, riveted by whatever it was she was saying.

"The Purpose Fund study on subglacial pooling cost fifty-five million dollars and received no outside or government funds. We used our own staff, ships, satellites, and aircraft. We submit the technical documentation here today, along with our Economic Effects Model documentation.

"The EEM program was the result of a six million dollar grant from the Purpose Fund two years ago. It allows for the econometric modeling of changed patterns of agronomy, riverine transportation, access to critical minerals and energy sources, and urban habitat under a variety of assumptions about what the next fifty years will look like.

"The EEM team was drawn from the

faculties of the Wharton School, the Sloan School, Moscow State, Oxford, Zhejiang, and Wuhan universities. They are among the world's leading econometrics experts. What their work shows may be summarized in these few charts, although the extensive detail is being made available online now."

Suddenly, the large flat screen facing Bowman's seating area came to life. The large font words on the screen insisted on their being read. "Global Flooding Creates Economic Collapse."

Victoria Kinder continued reading her statement. "The resources that will likely be used on massive seawall projects and those needed to handle relocation of refugees will cause spending to slowly dry up in other areas such as those shown on the slide. In the United States, for example, countering sea level rise by walling off cities and relocating populations will cost more on an annual basis for decades than the total cost of all governmental activities does now, including state and local administration. The need for this expenditure will come as the tax base is shrinking rapidly. Already preliminary work is underway on new seawalls for New York, London, Petersburg, and Tokyo. The costs are enormous."

The next slide was titled LIKELY DE-

FUNDED PROGRAMS and it listed: "Space Programs, Biomedical Research, Information Technology and Robotics, Defense Research and Major Weapons Systems Procurement, Arts and Humanities, Social Welfare Programs."

"While our model does show some short-term winners, such as the construction industry and related activities, even these cease as financial markets and the tax base take major impacts and eventually collapse in some countries and globally."

The screen now showed three curves, covering the period 2015–2100. All went down, but the one that went down fastest showed signs of upward movement at the end. "We ran six hundred and twenty-three scenarios and excursions, but the results in terms of global GDP clustered around three curves depending upon the rate of the flooding. The fastest and highest flooding models used the IPCC's new Worst Case Scenario. They show global economic depression by 2050. The other two show economic collapse in 2072 and 2086."

There was a gasp in the hall, followed by murmuring as the audience reacted and spoke to those sitting with them. Almost everyone had a mobile device out and was sending off messages, texts, or tweets.

"Of note is that the Fast Case, collapse by 2050, begins to show some signs of recovery by 2075, although the growth is modest and does not end the depression in this century. The other two models show no significant recovery within the timeframe examined.

"The reason for the recovery in the Fast Case we believe is that the diversion of resources occurs over a shorter period of time prior to collapse. In this slide you see the diversion of resources in all three scenarios. In the other two scenarios, the diversion goes on over many decades, growing over time as the water levels rise. In the Fast Case, sea level rise happens so quickly that there is not the slow destruction of industries and institutions as funds dry up."

The chairman of the panel interrupted with a question, in French. Throughout the hall people searched for their translation headsets and began switching the dials next to their seats, through Russian, Chinese, Spanish, to French. Bowman understood enough French that he left his headset alone. "Are you telling us that there is a silver lining to our Worst Case Scenario, that it means the global economic depression you predict will only last three decades? The Great Depression of the 1930s lasted less than one decade, correct?"

Victoria Kinder did not skip a beat. Indeed, she responded immediately and in French. "Yes, Mr. Chairman, you are correct on both counts. One reason is that the Fast Case causes a significant lowering of global population due to flood casualties and a subsequent general reduction in the birth rate, of the type that occurs in recessions and in a depression. Normally a population decline hurts the economy, but in this case it will reduce the burden on government services, allowing some money eventually to be spent on things other than disaster recovery."

As the discussion went on, Bowman was planning his approach to Professor Kinder when the meeting was over. She did not look as he thought an economist should. Tall and well tailored, she appeared more like the chairman of the board of a major corporation or perhaps an executive editor of a fashion magazine. Confronting her was going to be interesting.

He read her biography on the New York University Web site: full professor of Economics at age thirty-eight, specialist in econometric modeling. Her doctorate was from MIT, her undergraduate degree from Penn. Another entry on Google noted that since her appointment, Kinder Industries had endowed five chairs at NYU and built a new building for the business school. No one, however, had suggested that the Kinder money had bought Victoria her appointment. The general impression was that she had earned it and it was Victoria herself who had obtained the grants from her father to help out her new academic home.

Then, a text message from Mbali interrupted his planning.

MUST MEET NOW. MOST URGENT. She had been intending on using the secure telephone at the South African Mission to call her boss, the President of South Africa. Bowman wondered what he could have said on that call that made a meeting now most urgent.

Reluctantly, he texted back. IN TEN MINUTES AT USUN.

Bowman stood and moved to the exit while the professor was continuing to answer questions from the panel. As he made his way through the vast lobby of the UN building, his iPhone vibrated again. He stopped as he moved out on to First Avenue and looked down to what he supposed was a follow-up message from Mbali. Instead, he found one from Dugout. HOW FAST CAN YOU GET TO A SECURE FACILITY FOR A VIDEOCONFERENCE?

He texted back, FIVE MINUTES. GOING TO USUN and then he ran across the avenue before the traffic light changed.

USUN was the U.S. Mission to the United Nations, an ugly high-rise directly across the street from UN headquarters. It housed the State Department officers who represented the United States at the world body. It also had facilities for "Other Government Agencies."

Using the pass Special Agent McKenna had given him, Bowman went to the twelfth floor and was directed to a secure conference room that had been set aside for his use.

Dugout was already up on screen. "I guess you were in the neighborhood. How was your flight to New York?"

"What's so urgent?" Ray replied. "I thought you were wrapping things up there."

"I was, but then one of the documents we were crunching on started to yield up some text. You won't like it."

Mbali entered the room, escorted by a security guard from the lobby. She was almost out of breath as she sat down next to Bowman, looking at the video screen. "Got here as fast as I could. I just got the intel dump from Marcus Stroh's trip to Comoros and Mayotte."

413

"How?" Ray asked.

"Long story for later," she said. "Point is he got what we sent him there for. A mystery plane whose comings and goings into Comoros match up for when the bombs would have been moved there from Madagascar and then, two months later, when the tritium would have moved from Pretoria."

"I didn't find any record like that when I checked flights into Comoros," Dugout interjected.

"Well, Marcus did. Did you just look at Moroni airport? He found these flights into another island in the Comoros, Anjouan. And there is more, the names of two ships that left Comoros a few days after the tritium heist, probably with the mated bombs." She then read out the tail number of the aircraft, the dates of the flights, and the names of the ships, MV *Rothera* and MV *Nunatak.*

"Dug, are you still online out there? Can you check the aviation databases first for that aircraft?" Ray asked.

"Right. I haven't given the computer center back yet. Let me run the aircraft. It's a C-130J, new model, registered in Cyprus to Archimedes Airlift, a cargo firm. Now, checking on ownership of the firm, various front companies in offshore islands. Run-

414

ning link analysis with other front companies. Bingo."

"Don't tell me, it's owned by Polis Holdings," Ray guessed.

"Correct and you get five hundred points and take the lead," Dugout replied.

"Polis Holdings of Cyprus, which also owns Olympus Security of Mr. Rogozin," Mbali added. "Now, how about the ships, Dugout?"

"Hang on a minute," Dugout shot back, his voice rising. "This is all good and all that your guy found the flights I couldn't find because you told me the wrong airport, but I have something you have to hear right now."

Ray Bowman knew that when Dugout said something was more important, it always was and it was also usually something that was not good news. "Okay, Duggie, okay. What did you decrypt?"

"On One document where they used an encryption that was easier to break. It's entitled something like U.S. Korea Itel and it lists dates for things. Still working on the things, but I got the dates. They begin with August ninth and have entries for the days you just gave for the C-130 flights. I think it's the timetable for the operation."

"Nice work," Ray said. "Does it tell us

anything else?"

"Yeah. The last entry on the timetable is for November eighteenth. This Thursday."

"Three days from now," Mbali whispered.

The three sat silently, looking at each other. Finally, Ray Bowman broke the quiet. "You said something about U.S., Korea, something? You think the Koreans are involved now?"

"Yeah, it's an acronym like a header on all four pages. Here it is U-S-K-O-R-I-T-E-L."

"That's not an acronym, it's a word. That means 'accelerator,'" Mbali said.

Bowman looked at her. "It does? In what language? Zulu?"

"Russian," she said. "I took two years of it at Oxford."

"Of course, you did. Why wouldn't you, woman of many talents?" Dugout said from California.

Bowman was quiet. Something was coming into view for him. "The ships, Duggie, the ships. Pull their ownership. Probably also a Polis Holdings front company."

They could see Dugout hitting his keyboard. While they waited, Ray looked at Mbali. "Russian?"

"Seemed like a good idea at the time. They were against Apartheid from the beginning."

416

Dugout was double-checking his results against a series of databases. "No, you would be wrong about Polis this time. Those two ships, or at least ships with the same names, are registered in Iceland to the IGRI, the Ice Cap and Glacier Research Institute, which it seems is an entity entirely paid for by the Purpose Fund. They're polar research vessels. Must be the wrong names or there are other ships by those names that I can't find. Maybe they just painted those names on some tramp freighters that are actually registered in Panama or Liberia in other names."

Bowman closed his eyes. "No, it's them. It's the research ships. And I bet they were in the Comoros."

"There aren't any glaciers there," Mbali noted.

Bowman stood up. "Purpose Fund is one of the clients of Olympus Security, remember, it's listed on their Web site. And who is a big donor to Purpose, but Kinder Industries. And how did Rogozin fly into New York? On a Kinder Industries plane with none other than its CEO, Jonathan Kinder, and his brilliant daughter the econometrics professor, whose expertise is econometric modeling of climate change effects."

"So you're saying that Kinder is in on it? That the Kinders let their ships be used by Rogozin to collect nuclear weapons off the Comoros?" Dugout asked.

"No, I see where he's going," Mbali replied for Ray. "Ray you're thinking that Rogozin's Olympus Security is actually the muscle that Kinder is using to pull off this operation. That they're in on it together or maybe Rogozin is actually a client of Kinder?"

"Or they're in something bigger," Ray thought out loud. "Duggie, who else are the big donors to Purpose? Who is on the board?"

Dugout accessed the Purpose Fund Web page and threw it up on the video screen. "Board of Directors: Jonathan Kinder, U.S., Chair. Konstantin Kuznetzov, Russia; Sir Clive Harcourt, UK; Sheikh Ibrahim bin Mohammad al Dursi, Qatar; and Zhang Wei, China."

Bowman sketched a diagram on his notepad. "Dug, do a link analysis between Kuznetzov and Rogozin."

"Those five guys are all billionaires, you know," Mbali said while they waited.

"Good guess," Dugout said as he threw the link chart up on the screen. "They were both in St. Petersburg, then Leningrad in the eighties. Both appear to have been in the KGB, probably together."

"Right, and we all know who else was in the Leningrad KGB in the eighties," Ray said looking down at Mbali. "I have a sinking feeling that I know what the accelerator is designed to speed up. Dug, can you see what investments those five guys from the Purpose Fund have made individually and collectively in the last, say, three years?"

"That will be difficult. I'm sure they hide some of their activity under fronts and brokers. Can I hack accounts?" Dugout asked.

"Do what you need to do, but do it fast."

Mbali hit the MUTE button on the video link. "He just told you that this thing with the bombs probably happens on Thursday and you are asking him to figure out what investments these guys have made? Shouldn't you be calling the White House?"

Bowman sat back down next to her. "I am about to, but I want to be sure about my theory before I get Winston Burrell running down the hall to the Oval Office."

Mbali looked at him, a man about to jump out of his skin, filled with tension and anxiety, waiting to spring into action, waiting for confirmation. "So what is your theory, Raymond? What are they trying to

419

accelerate?"

"Sea level rise."

"Sweet Jesus, why on earth?" she asked. "What do they use the nukes on?"

"Probably Greenland. To get it over with quickly. To profit. To be in the best shape when it's happened. They intend to use the massive heat of nuclear explosion to melt a glacier, causing a sudden surge of fresh water into the ocean. Before we could react, islands will disappear, cities will flood permanently, the weather patterns will completely alter."

"No way. No way anyone would do that," she asserted. "Thousands of people will die if there is a big sea level rise, especially if it's fast."

"No," Bowman said. "Millions will die. And millions more will wish they had."

44

"We are essentially a light- to medium-sized ice breaker, research station, and heliport. Only one of two in the world that aren't owned by a government," Captain Andrey Sobko explained to his American guest. "And the other one is our sister ship, the *Rothera.*"

"Well. It's great to see the work that the Purpose Fund is doing down here, tracking the glacial melt is extraordinarily important," Glenn Rollins said. He was a geologist from the University of Colorado, working at McMurdo Station on a National Science Foundation grant. "And the work you are doing with the drilling stations, getting down to the bottom of the ice and seeing what the surface is like after five hundred centuries of being covered up."

"Well, the European Union began the drilling work down here, but we have taken it much further with five drill sites now operating," Sobko said in fluent English. "Now that spring has arrived and things are warming up down here, we are bringing in new equipment to each of the five sites. The helo you flew in on will be leaving shortly for the Wilkes Basin glacier."

The American looked puzzled. "Really? But the Wilkes glacier is not deep. It doesn't need deep drilling."

"You are right. What we are doing there is examining the subglacial ponding effects. When the ice melts in the summer and runs down through the troughs, it creates ponds below the glacier. If they get big enough and touch, creating lakes, there is the possibility that the glacier will float off into the sea faster," Sobko said.

"Don't I know it. There's only about eighty millimeters of ice creating a wall, a plug, holding back the Wilkes Basin glacier. If that were to melt, we think you'd get three to four meters of sea rise in a few years," Rollins replied. "That's why I'm here. I'm looking at the entire East Antarctica glacier. My calculation is that the East Antarctic glaciers alone hold enough water to create eighteen to twenty meters of sea rise. Thank god that could only happen over a couple of centuries, long after I'm gone. And my kids."

"Yes, but we have to worry about what will happen after even our children. Imagine what a terrible place it will be for our grandchildren if we do not plan now for the world changing," Captain Sobko replied. "I hope you enjoyed your day and your sleepover with us. Our scientists enjoyed having you visit, I know."

"It was a great experience. I am so jealous of the equipment you have. How long will you be down here this time?"

"We leave today for New Zealand. Between us and the *Rothera,* we have flown in all the new equipments to the five Purpose Fund drill sites in East Antarctica. We will come back at the end of the summer to swap out crews and the like," Sobko explained. "Now, I see your little helicopter coming for you. Let me go see that its landing is all set. Excuse me."

The captain left the deck and went inside to the control room, leaving Glenn Rollins to wonder why these two great research ships would leave Antarctica just as the spring was here, just as researchers from all the other Antarctic countries were arriving. But then, he thought, there were so many strange things about MV *Nunatak* and indeed about the Purpose Fund's polar and glacial research. The scientists he had spoken with over dinner on board last night said they weren't even sure what was in the big equipment pods that were being flown out to the five Purpose Fund bases. One thing was sure, they were pretty heavy to need such a big Russian helicopter to haul them out there.

If only the National Science Foundation had the kind of money for glacier research that the Purpose Fund had. At least somebody understands how important the East Antarctic glaciers are for potential sea level rise, but try to tell that to the Congress, he thought, as he watched the little American helicopter, a Dauphin, circling the ship's helipad.

OLYMPUS SECURITY OFFICES
36 EAST 74TH STREET
NEW YORK CITY

Sergey Rogozin loved the tree-lined blocks of the Upper East Side. He had insisted that their New York offices be in twin town houses on a leafy street. Also, he did not trust high-rise buildings, too many other tenants, too much shared telecommunications equipment.

With his own building, he could install the satellite dish that would connect directly with the Express-AM7 satellite of the Russian Satellite Company. His encrypted link to that bird would be safe, as would the satellite itself. There was no other way he would connect, certainly not over the Internet. This gave him a dedicated link to his Moscow office and from there he had a virtual private network to Kuznetzov in Yakutsk.

The data rate was slow, but he could still do voice and exchange short documents. Today he began by downloading the daily briefing his team had been sending out to him and the board members throughout the operation, beginning in August. As it slowly opened on his laptop, he could see the map of Antarctica. Each of the five research stations was shown, along with the position of the two ships, *Rothera* and *Nunatak*. Four of the five sites indicated red, armed. The fifth, Wilkes Basin, would be armed today.

The ships' captains were told to take up positions at a safe distance and monitor the explosions and the aftermath, to see how fast the ice melt happened, to measure the sea level rise. Only the captains and a handful of the Olympus men on each ship were read into the operation and knew what would happen. Or thought they did. What none of them knew was that the ships would explode at the same time that the bombs did, from hidden conventional explosives on board.

Sergey did not like loose ends. That's why he had killed all the Trustees after they sold the bombs. Everyone, except Potgeiter, of course. He had been useful. It was he whom Rogozin had originally contacted with the proposal to buy the bombs, he who had persuaded the others that it was all right to sell them to Taiwan. Of course, Taiwan had been a false flag for the Trustees to see, just as al Qaeda and Hezbollah had been false flags raised once the Americans and Israelis learned about the bomb theft. Sergey liked false flags.

Ray Bowman was a loose end, Sergey thought, he and his South African friend. They had been getting too close. They had somehow managed to trace the bombs to Madagascar and then to Comoros. But they had been stopped there, he was sure. There was no way that they would figure out that the bombs were bought by the Purpose Fund, no way that they could learn that the Purpose Fund owned Polis Holdings and Olympus Security, no way that they would ever connect anything back to the Czar. In

426

any event, Bowman would be eliminated, this time successfully, as would the South African woman.

When the detonations take place, Sergey knew, there would be a major investigation. Time for more false flags, but soon enough every nation would be diverted to dealing with the effects of the bombs. If not, if they did somehow find a trail, it would maybe mean that Kinder or Sir Clive were at risk. If that happened, they would disappear before the authorities could arrest them. No one would ever get near Kuznetzov and himself, not in the middle of Russia.

COMPUTER CONTROL CENTER
LAWRENCE LIVERMORE NATIONAL
  LABORATORY
LIVERMORE, CALIFORNIA

"You said you would be gone by now," Professor McFarland said, as his normally pallid face turned red. "I am taking it back. The computer center is mine now. I have an important project for the President's Science Advisor."

"Yes, you do," Dugout replied. "In fact, I have the Science Advisor waiting by the secure telephone to personally tell you all about it. Seems the National Security Advisor asked him to get you to run your model on a specific scenario, one in which there is rapid and significant sea level rise. We want to see what the climatic effects are.

"We also want to see how that theoretical possibility would effect certain real estate and other investments. It's all set up on the network for you."

McFarland looked confused, but then Dugout handed him the phone. "Yes, this is Professor McFarland," the professor said into the phone. "Yes, sir, I can run that model right away. Oh, probably no more than a few hours now that I have the world's fastest processor back under my control. No, sir, thank you."

The professor was smiling as he handed the phone back to Dugout. He then wandered off to begin applying his model to the data set Dugout had set up for him.

Dugout reconnected the videoconference with USUN, where Ray and Mbali had been poring over the partial list of Purpose Fund holdings that Dugout had found.

"Between the Fund itself and the five board members, they have almost six hundred billion dollars in assets," Mbali observed. "And these boys have been busy lately buying up land in strange places."

"Well, I don't need the professor's model to tell me that when that much fresh water hits the ocean, the climate patterns will change. Dry places may become wet and vice versa. Frozen places may become warm. Certainly some inland places will become coastal. A lot of cities will be abandoned and inland cities or cities on higher elevations will grow," Dugout said.

"So they used Victoria's model to figure out all of that and buy up what will become important," Ray Bowman added. "And now they are going to create the biggest flood since Noah, using nuclear bombs to melt the glaciers, playing God on a global scale."

"And the bombs are already in place," Dugout said.

"How do you know that?" Ray asked.

"I tracked down the two ships, *Rothera* and *Nunatak*. They both arrived in Port-aux-Français in the French Southern and Antarctic Lands a week ago. That would have been en route from Comoros to where they are now, off Ross Island in East Antarctica."

"But how do you know they have put the bombs ashore?" Mbali asked.

"Because I just read Sergey Rogozin's mail. I knew he had to connect to a real network at some point so I hacked into the satellite dish on the roof of his office in New York and then down the wire to his laptop,

429

where the traffic is decrypted. I know where all five bombs are, all on glaciers."

"Maybe sixty hours until they go off?" Bowman asked Dugout.

"If that timeline is right, yeah, but maybe less."

On the small television screen on the side wall of the conference room, the news channel was showing the President-elect meeting with the President in the Oval Office before having a one-on-one lunch together in the Private Dining Room off the Oval.

"I think Winston Burrell has a lunch he has to crash," Ray said as he picked up the secure phone.

45

WEDNESDAY, NOVEMBER 16
FORT BRAGG, NORTH CAROLINA

Despite what armchair generals on Capitol Hill might think, even the U.S. military cannot appear magically anywhere in the world at any time. Indeed, no U.S. military unit wants to conduct an operation without weeks of preparation and rehearsal, but there are a handful of units on alert for immediate mobilization. Most of them are Army, and most of them are in the sprawling campus that is Fort Bragg, North Carolina.

In the hour after midnight, those units were alerted. The 82nd Airborne Division always has one brigade assigned to an unspecified global mission. This time it was the 3rd Brigade. Its ready battalion was the 505th. They had equipment and uniforms for almost every climate, but that did not include the white overalls used by the units designated to fight in the snow.

Across the base, in the fenced-in command run by Special Operations Command, the 1st Special Force Group's Operational Detachment Delta had a ready group that included operators who had been trained on nuclear weapons seizure and disablement. They were activated just after midnight.

At Hunter Airfield, outside of Savannah, Georgia, a ready company of the 1st Battalion of the Army's Ranger Regiment was called up, at 0200.

Throughout the country at Air Force bases, C-17 pilots and crews were also getting calls. So were the KC-10 and KC-135 aerial refueling tanker crews, many of them members of the Air National Guard.

At Dam Neck in Virginia, a SEAL unit trained in ship seizure was notified to be ready to fly. It would be a long flight.

There were no aircraft carriers, no submarines, no drones, or bombers anywhere near Antarctica, but off the coast of the southern continent was a ship of the U.S. Coast Guard. The captain of the U.S. Coast Guard Cutter *Healy,* the largest U.S. ice breaker, was woken to receive a highly unusual message for that ship. It was top secret and flash precedence. The thrust of the message from the Commandant of the Coast Guard was that there would be a U.S. Navy SEAL unit coming on board and then *Healy* would be ordered to intercept two nearby research ships flying the flag of Iceland. He was instructed to tell no one on board until further authorized, which he thought was a good thing, since no one on board would believe him if he had told them.

Antarctica did not fall into the Area of Operations of any of the U.S. Combatant commanders, who divided up the world into exclusive zones for their forces. So the Joint Chiefs of Staff Organization in the Pentagon took control, supported by Special Operations Command at MacDill Air Force Base in Tampa. Every operation needed a name and there was a list available to choose from, meaningless code words. This one was designated Operation Ready Anvil. Ignoring that, the team in the Pentagon started calling it Ice Station Zebra.

The President signed the "execute" order for the operation at 0500 Washington time. The Global Hawk surveillance aircraft were the first to take off from California and head south. They would soon be followed by a wave of other southbound aircraft.

Ray and Mbali left USUN a little after midnight. They had spent the night sharing a pizza and fielding questions over the secure video from a variety of agencies in Washington. It had taken a while to convince the bureaucracy that they were not mad, but had actually succeeded in finding the missing South African bombs in the most unlikely place on earth.

Dugout had continued working all day documenting the leads, the evidence, the connections, the timeline. And working with the now-cooperative and friendly Professor McFarland, he had demonstrated to the Washington team that the effects of the almost immeasurable heat of tritium boosted nuclear explosions would melt vast amounts of centuries' old ice, sending a sea of fresh water into the world's oceans. In the Atlantic, the Gulf Stream would cease its circulation and the climate everywhere would change, some places becoming arid, others frozen, some very, very wet.

There was no disputing that if all five bombs detonated, the likely global sea rise would be nineteen meters from the East Antarctic ice alone. The only differences the experts had was over how quickly the flood would occur. The longest period anyone projected was thirty months.

Some island nations like the Maldives and others in the Pacific and Caribbean would cease to exist. Others, like Bangladesh, would see land now occupied by eighty million people washed away. In the United States, fourteen major metropolitan areas would see their urban centers destroyed in ways worse than Hurricane Katrina had done in New Orleans, and that was just on the East and Gulf Coasts. Florida would disappear as far north as Jacksonville.

Some nations might be better off comparatively to the rest of the world when it was all over, among them perhaps Canada and Russia, both of whom would have new, year-round ports and vast stretches of newly arable land, but the world's economy would be devastated.

At the end of a long day filled with such depressing images, Mbali and Ray walked out of the U.S. Mission on to First Avenue. She had booked them rooms at the Harvard Club on West 44th Street, using some reciprocal privilege. The FBI office had left a team of two agents and a Suburban waiting for them. They hopped in.

Traffic was light for Manhattan. Even the city that never sleeps thins out in the early morning hours on a weekday. As they passed Grand Central Terminal and pulled into 44th Street, a motorbike passed them, almost brushing up against the Suburban. The agent riding in the front passenger seat saw the sticky bomb being attached to his door and yelled the warning, "Get out — bomb!" The agent also opened the door, so the blast went down to the side of the vehicle, rather than directly into it. Nonetheless, the agent died seconds later.

Those seconds seemed like minutes to Ray, who was seated behind the agent on the right of the vehicle. In those long seconds, he leaped across the vehicle, opened the driver's side passenger door, and pushed himself and Mbali out of the moving vehicle onto the street. He was halfway out when the sticky bomb went off.

He later learned that it was what the bomb technicians considered a small charge. It had been lethal to both the driver and to the other agent. Had the agent on the right not opened his door in time, it would have been lethal to Ray and likely to Mbali.

Afterward, Ray did not remember how he got out of the vehicle. His first memory was of the fire to his left. He was laying on the street and there were flames and an intense overpowering heat to his left. He forced himself to crawl away from it. That's when he realized he was bleeding, blood running from his scalp down the back of his neck. He could not hear and he was having trouble focusing his eyes. Mbali was dragging him farther away from the fire in the street. There were people around. And then there was a paramedic. He remembered being in an ambulance and he could recall the doctor and the nurses in the ER. He woke in a private hospital room. He had bandages on his left arm and leg. There was a large bandage on the back of his head and it felt like he had been given a haircut back there. His whole body ached and his ears were ringing. He saw his suit and shirt on a hanger. He found the bathroom, looked in the mirror at the back of his head, and washed up. Then he got dressed and walked out of the room to find Mbali. The FBI agents on the door went with him.

EAST 34TH STREET
NEW YORK CITY

McKenna was a professional in Ray's mind. The FBI man had come to the hospital in the middle of the night to check up on Bowman and bumped into him, sneaking out through the Emergency Room. Rather than telling Ray to go back upstairs and recover in a bed from the sticky bomb attack on the car, McKenna had taken him to an all-night diner and briefed him on the latest intelligence they had learned from monitoring Olympus Security. One team of Olympus men would be escorting Vicki Kinder in midmorning from the UN to a nearby heliport. From there, they would chopper her to Teterboro airfield where a second team would be taking her father, then the Kinders would get out of New York for points west.

Bowman did not want to see the Kinders leave town quite yet and McKenna had agreed, then made a few calls. Then they both had the fried eggs and grits, which were not bad for a greasy spoon in a northern city at three in the morning.

At ten thirty, a Chevrolet Suburban had turned into 34th Street, sped under the Roosevelt Highway, and pulled up to the heliport dock on the East River. Vicky Kinder jumped down from the Suburban, stylish in a mauve business suit, and moved quickly across the dock to the Kinder Industries helicopter. Her two Olympus bodyguards scurried to catch up with her, while a third went for her bags in the back of the vehicle. She did not notice behind her as the Olympus men were quietly and quickly detained by armed men, McKenna's

438

men, who had been posing as the heliport crew.

Bowman slid open the passenger door to the helicopter from inside and hopped out onto the dock. In his right hand was a Glock that he had insisted McKenna provide him, just in case. The look on Victoria Kinder's face said she knew who he was. She looked behind her and saw her men being hauled off. Rather than running, she simply stopped and smiled. "I see you're not dead yet, Mr. Bowman. Do you plan on using that thing on me?"

"I always liked that Monty Python routine. 'I'm not dead yet.' But a lot of people are, Professor Kinder, and a hell of a lot more will be if your plans go ahead," Ray replied. "How do you live with that?"

"I don't know what you're referring to, of course, but after all, death is a part of the cycle of life," she said. "The question is not if we will die. We will. The question is what one will do while alive that will make a difference, changes the future."

"And you think the future will be better if this city and a lot like it are under water?" Ray asked as two FBI agents moved in on either side of her. "You had better tell me now how to stop it."

"That is the future. I can't stop it. Neither

can anyone else. It's just a question of when it happens and how fast. If it takes a long time, if it is a slow death, then those death throes will take civilization down, too. By trying in vain to hold back the waters we will deplete the treasury, destroy government, wreck the economy, everything will collapse into a new Dark Age. If it happens quickly, we can adjust, survive, some of us will even flourish. Trust me, I know. I have run all the models."

"Maybe you will get to watch the waters rise from your prison window," Bill McKenna said as he signaled for his men to take her. He turned to Bowman. "Are you sure you are in shape for a helicopter ride with an FBI pilot?"

TETERBORO EXECUTIVE JET AIRPORT TETERBORO, NEW JERSEY

"I may not see you for a long time. At least, not in person," Jonathan Kinder said, as he stood with Sergey Rogozin in front of the Russian's Boeing Business Jet. "I can't tell you how much I am in your debt, how we all are, the entire board. From the day Konny proposed this idea right up to this week, we could not have done it without you. You know that."

"It was, it is, a bold idea. Historic. It will

change history, change the world," Rogozin said. "It has been my honor to be part of it, to watch you and the others decide on where to move billions of dollars to be ready for the new world. Amazing. We, I, would never have figured it out."

"Well, most of that work was Vicki," he said like any proud father. "She's the one who is amazing. Her models about what land would be newly valuable, what industries would survive and be needed afterward, buying the foodstuffs, the gold, the diamonds, the other commodities and storing them in safe places.

"She should be here in a few minutes," Kinder added. "She had more meetings this morning at the UN. She is flying in by helicopter from the landing area on the East River near the UN. Otherwise, the traffic here, it's becoming like São Paulo, where you have to own a helicopter to get anywhere."

"Are you sure you still want to go to Montana? My professional advice is that you would be safer with us, with Kuznetzov and me," Rogozin urged. "I am sure they will never connect you to the explosions, especially after the last problem for us was eliminated last night, but, it's always safer to be in a country where the security services are friends."

Kinder shook his head. "No, you get on your flight and head to wherever the hell Kuznetzov is in the middle of frozen nowhere Russia and I will get on mine and head for the middle of God's country in Montana. There the security guys for miles in all directions are my guys."

They both looked up at the S-76 helicopter that was flaring up for a landing between their two jets. Rogozin could see the logo of Olympus Security on the side of the aircraft. "Well, here is Vicki now. I guess we have a daring pilot this morning."

The door to the Sikorsky slid open even before the helicopter had touched down. Ray Bowman and Special Agent Bill Mc-Kenna jumped out, followed by two other FBI agents in black tactical gear. Simultaneously, sirens began to wail and black vehicles began speeding down the tarmac toward them. McKenna yelled, "FBI, hands behind your heads, you're under . . ."

Rogozin had pulled his gun and fired, striking McKenna in the torso, knocking him down. Bowman was glad he had insisted on being issued a weapon. He aimed the Glock at Rogozin's head and fired twice, before the volley that the two agents let loose from their M4s, ripping up

Rogozin and bouncing his body in the air before it fell onto the pavement. Kinder dropped to his knees with his hands over his head. The agents cuffed him and then, joined by the team arriving in the vehicles, moved on to the two awaiting aircraft as FBI Suburbans blocked both from moving. Ray turned to help Bill McKenna up. The new model bullet-resistant vest had done its job. "I'm gonna have one hell of a black and blue from that impact," McKenna said, rubbing his chest. Mbali had arrived in the cars with the other agents and she joined Bowman and McKenna. Bowman was still holding the Glock.

"Did you use that thing?" she asked.

"He did, thank god," McKenna answered for him.

Together the three of them walked over to where the agents were holding Jonathan Kinder.

"You need to tell us how to stop the bombs from going off and you need to tell us now," Bowman said to him.

Kinder's mouth had gone dry and he struggled to get out his reply. "I don't know anything about any bombs. That man you killed, maybe he did, but you killed him, you idiot." McKenna signaled for the agents to take Kinder away.

"So that will be his defense? I knew nothing about bombs, I was just doing hedged investments against global warming," Mbali asked.

"That won't fly," Ray answered. "We can tie him to the whole thing, but he may be right that he doesn't know how to stop the bombs. Maybe Rogozin did, but we didn't have much of a choice after he opened up."

"Are you afraid that whoever has their finger on the trigger will set it off now?" Bill McKenna asked.

"They might. Can we keep this incident here under wraps for a few hours?" Ray asked, although he knew better.

"We're telling the Jersey State Police it was a drug bust. Cocaine coming in on an executive jet. That won't stand up for long, but it may buy you some time," the FBI agent replied. "Now that we have this helicopter, can I offer you a ride somewhere. Where do you go next?"

Ray Bowman stood on the tarmac in New Jersey, surrounded by private jets and federal agents. His hand went to the bandage on the back of his head, where the nurses had shaved his hair off in the ER. He looked confused, almost lost. "I don't really know."

"Seriously?" Bill McKenna asked.

"Well, maybe to the shuttle at LaGuardia. I guess I should go to DC and wait to see what happens down south." He looked at Mbali. "Have you ever been to Washington?"

46

THURSDAY, NOVEMBER 17
OFF MCMURDO SOUND, ANTARCTICA
The SEAL team had dropped out of the
sky at night and landed one by one on the
Coast Guard cutter *Healy.* Most had managed to hit the big helipad deck. No one
wanted to land in the icy water, and none
of them did. Then the *Healy* set a course
for the last known location of the MV *Rothera* and MV *Nunatak,* which had
rendezvoused and were at anchor together a
few hours away. *Healy* would get there a
few hours after dawn and then the SEALs
would board them.

At dawn the C-17s came out of the rising
sun. They were less than five hundred feet
above the ice. Fifty men jumped into each
of the five drilling sites on the East Antarctic
glaciers. They had been in the aircraft a long
time, as they flew through multiple in-flight
refuelings. Hitting the ground, they

unbuckled their chutes and then began running across the ice toward the round white igloo-like buildings on stilts above the snow. Most of the staff at each base were still waking up when they looked up to see armed American soldiers in their rooms.

The gunfire was limited and brief. At two sites there was no resistance at all. Olympus had few shooters at the sites, hoping to obtain security by maintaining the image of scientific research facilities. No one knew anything about nuclear weapons and some of the research staff joked nervously that maybe the American troops got the wrong continent. The researchers were predominantly Russian, but there were also Americans, Brits, Canadians, Japanese.

The nuclear bomb specialists from Delta began spreading out and at each of the five Purpose Fund research sites quickly located the radioactive signatures. All five weapons were located in drill houses, the little super structures above what were to become drill holes into the ice. Quickly they looked for radio or Internet connections to the cases in which they knew there were nuclear bombs. There were no signs of connectivity to the outside world. The Delta nuclear explosive ordnance disposal teams set up electronics to image inside the containers.

They popped up their own satellite dishes and began streaming images and readings back to nuclear bomb specialist teams standing by in Washington. This was going to be like remote surgery carried out by an EMT with a doctor watching on video giving directions from a hospital hundreds of miles away. In this case, it was nuclear physics PhDs who were thousands of miles away at the Department of Energy facilities in Maryland. They had been flown in the day before from three nuclear labs across the country. Handpicked, these scientists had worked for years with the Delta team in exercises and drills. This was the first time it was for real.

Together, they went by the book that, together, they had written. First, look for booby traps, hidden triggers that will set off the bomb or some explosive package protecting it. Even a small explosion designed to protect the package might ignite the weapon by mistake. It would certainly spread radioactive material and, of course, it would kill the Delta nuclear explosive ordnance disposal team.

In each of the five sites, the Delta operators were working with a separate group of advisors back in Maryland. No one was making assumptions that all five devices were identical. A supervisory team in Maryland listened to all five conversations and tried to make sure data from one team was shared with the others, but all five teams went ahead at the same time. No one knew when the bombs were programmed to detonate, if indeed they were, but not knowing meant that there might be no time to waste. For most steps, they would not do one weapon at a time, but proceed in parallel.

While they were in the air flying to Antarctica, the Delta teams had received crude diagrams of what the original South African weapons looked like inside. Mbali had her people extract that information from Roosmeer. She had also asked Danny Avidar for help from Avraham Reuven. From what the teams could see, there were tritium gas bottles in all five weapons. That meant that the blasts would be high yield.

After they determined that the travel case in which each weapon sat appeared to be safe, with no booby traps, the teams opened the outer packaging. This they did in sequence, with Able team calling out that it was complete, before Baker team began. Finally, Easy team had opened its package. Now all five teams were looking at nuclear bombs. They began to try to unscrew the fasteners on the metal casing of the bombs themselves. The screws were hard to turn. Small drills were carefully used to remove the screws.

The external acoustic and electronic sensors had detected some electrical activity inside the bombs. In other words, something was alive and running on battery power. It wasn't clear what the battery was running. Very carefully, the outer casings were removed on each weapon. The experts in Maryland debated what the next step should be and agreed that the tritium gas bottles should gently be removed. One by one, they were, and the containers taken from the rooms.

In the movies, there was always a clock with numbers visibly running down to zero. But here, there was no clock visible. There were, however, at least two battery packs, of different designs and in locations well separated from each other, in each bomb. The experts wondered whether disconnecting one battery would cause a detonation. They advised the Delta teams to simultaneously pull out both battery packs.

They agreed to do the extractions in sequence, beginning with Able Team. The two operators counted down and on zero, they each both pulled out a battery pack.

Nothing happened.

As they were exhaling and about to announce that they had extracted the batteries, they heard the rumble, then felt the ground shake, the ice move. They knew one of the devices had detonated. There had been a clock.

Outside the Delta operators turned away from the flash to prevent damage to their eyes. Behind them, the column of churning gases shot up, up into the bright blue Antarctic sky. One of them ran into the room to tell the bomb team that they had seen the mushroom cloud to the west, where Easy team was working, about 120 miles away. In the heavens above the Vela package registered a Pinnacle Event and notified operations centers on the Earth below.

The explosion had fried their electronics by sending out a wave of electromagnetic pulses. They were cut off from communicating with the experts in Maryland, and from the other teams. Able Team waited, wondering what the other teams would do, knowing that they should pull the batteries.

At the other sites, Baker, Charlie, and Dog, the bomb technicians had waited after the explosion to determine where it had happened. If it happened at Able team, they knew to not pull the batteries. When they determined that Able team had not detonated, each of the remaining teams extracted the battery packs. Then, without communicating with each other or their rear area experts, each of the remaining four teams extracted the high-energy explosive initiators and removed them from the buildings. They then removed the enriched uranium cores and placed them in protective cases for safe transport out.

At each of the four remaining sites, the Delta nuclear explosive ordnance disposal team members stepped outside into the cold. Some prayed. Some lit cigarettes. Some downed shots of whiskey or vodka. A few just wandered off alone into the ice for a time. They all looked up at the mushroom cloud that was still swirling in the distance. Eventually, they knew, somehow there would be helicopters, helicopters to get them and the Rangers and the Airborne guys, to take them home.

The crew of the *Healy* saw the mushroom cloud in the distance before they saw the research ships. When they heard another explosion and then another, they at first thought there were more nuclear detonations. It was only when they saw the fires on the horizon that they realized that the second and third blasts were ships blowing up, the ships that they were going to board and seize. As the *Healy* approached the two burning hulks, the Coast Guardsmen leaped into action to do what they are trained to do, rescue mariners in distress. They were able to save thirty-four. The others, estimated at almost 150 scientists and crew, died in the explosions and subsequent fires and sinkings.

At Easy site, the Rangers, Delta special forces team, and the Purpose Fund researchers were all incinerated before they knew what had happened. The resulting hole in the ice, almost a mile across, went through to the rock core below and after the steam cloud dispatched, a circular waterfall sent melted ice plummeting down into the hole, pooling below the glacier, creating a subterranean lake of hot water spreading out under the ice.

47

"Don't get in the TOLL LANES, take the airport only road," Ray yelled at Dugout. "You don't drive much do you?"

Dugout let his sunglasses slip down his nose and looked at Bowman. "I bike to work. I care about the environment, unlike some people whose jet-setting around the world creates a huge personal carbon footprint."

"Really, Duggie? You don't think what I just did for the environment has given me some sort of exemption?"

"We don't know yet. There's a hell of a lot of radioactive fresh water pouring out of where the Wilkes glacier had been. The computer models differ on what the effect will be, but none of them are good. There will definitely be some sea level rise in the

454

next year. Would have been better if we had stopped all five bombs from going off."

"Well, maybe next time you and Winston Burrell can get somebody better to do your dirty work," Ray replied.

Dugout pulled the car over on to the shoulder and stopped. He took off the sunglasses and looked at Ray Bowman. "I'm just pissed off that you're going back to that island. So is Winston. So are the Presidents. This one and the new one." He reached into the backseat and grabbed a package. "I was going to give you the Cohibas to celebrate your getting a new job with the new Administration, but I guess you did earn them and a lot more by what you did on this assignment. Nobody else could have done what you did and certainly not in the time you did it. It's just, I enjoy working for you, with you, and now you're going away again."

"You can work with me anytime, Duggie. I can always use a barback, maybe even teach you how to mix drinks." Ray took the box of cigars. "I just can't keep working at jobs where people try to kill me, where I have to shoot, where people die all around me. You'll forgive me, but the next life I save is going to be mine."

Dugout started the car back up and pulled

into the traffic to the airport. "I googled that guy you mentioned who had the New Year's party, Jost Van Dyke. All right, so it's an island. How was I supposed to know? Anyway, if Brian, he's the new guy in my life, if he and I come down for the holidays, can you find a place for us to stay?"

"With us. You two can stay with us, anytime. You'll fit right in."

They pulled up to the long, iconic terminal. "Mbali's flight leaves an hour before yours, from B-34, South African Airways nonstop. Seventeen hours to Joburg. Yours is at B-21," Dugout said.

"See you next month."

He found her at a table near the Starbucks by her gate.

"Is it true that the new President offered you the head Intelligence job?" Mbali asked.

"No, it's not true, and I declined."

"Did you hear that the British found Sir Clive finally, hunkering in some drafty old castle of his in Scotland? What do you think will ever happen to the others?" she asked.

"The Kinders will be convicted, both of them. We'll get the guy from Qatar soon enough. The Chinese will probably deal with their guy. Kuznetzov will be okay as long as his boss is running the show, but even that can't go on forever, especially after this."

"You really should have taken the intelligence job. You're not half bad at this stuff," Mbali laughed.

"I have a job and my boss has been getting testy about my absence. Our Thanksgiving holiday is next week and that is a big-time weekend at the bar. She needs me there," Ray replied as the two sat at the food court in the middle of the terminal awaiting his flight to St. Thomas and hers to Johannesburg.

"And I have to get back to my son, before he thinks his auntie is really his mother." She smiled, thinking of Nelson. "Tell me now, Mr. Bowman, what do your big American scientists say will happen to us all now that the ice has begun melting so fast in East Antarctica? Is there going to be a good world for Nelson to grow up in?"

"Let's hope that explosion was the wake-up call everyone needed," he replied. "It will raise the sea level faster, but by how much it's too early to tell. The fact that the tritium gas bottle had been removed meant that the explosion was much smaller than it could have been." Ray Bowman shook his head in amazement of what might have been. "If all five had gone off, with the

457

tritium, we would not have had a chance to react to it. The flood would have happened. Now we do, we have some time, not much, but some. If we act now, in a big way, we may be able to deal with what is coming, may be able to slow it down, to contain it, maybe prevent the century-long global economic depression that the sea level rise would cause. Let's hope it was the accelerator, the accelerator for acting on climate change."

"I pray to God that this incident will wake people up," she said.

"Don't just pray. Tell your boss, the President. Tell him what he has to do. Everyone has to do their part."

"Easy, preacher man. What will you be doing now? What is your part?"

"My part is to live a simple life, with a tiny carbon footprint and hope the sea doesn't flood my bar. You need to come and visit us. Bring Nelson. Come for New Year's, we have a big beach party."

"Maybe next year, if the bar is still there," she said. "This year I am taking Nelson to Jerusalem for Christmas. Danny Avidar is hosting us. For now, I have to get back for Marcus Stroh's memorial service in Cape Town."

"I wish I could be there for that, but there

is another Marcus I need to go see about, Marcus Bowman, who is soon to come into this wicked world."

"Thank you for naming him that," she said. Ray thought he saw a tear forming, but she quickly put on her sunglasses. "It's because of your Marcus that we need you, because of all the Marcuses about to join us on this crazy planet. We need you to make this place safer. We can't be wasting you pouring beers onto that tender bar." She bent forward and kissed his cheek. He held her hand.

"Perhaps someday again, I'll go back, if Marcus and his mothers let me."

She stood and gathered her bags. *"Ube no-hambo oluhle,"* she said wishing him a good trip.

"Sala kahle, Mbali," he said. *"Ukuthula,* peace."

AUTHOR'S NOTE

This is, of course, a work of fiction. However, there really was a secret South African nuclear bomb program. The Apartheid regime wanted the bomb to deter invasion by black African nations, led by the Cuban Army. Castro had stationed thousands of his troops in neighboring Angola and Mozambique.

The rumors at the time were that South Africa had help in its bomb program from Israel, although the Israelis denied it. In 1979, the American Vela satellite detected a possible nuclear explosion in the ocean near South Africa. The media were filled with stories that the flash seen by the satellite was an Israeli nuclear test, or a South African nuclear test, or some sort of joint test involving them both. President Carter asked a group of experts to study the incident. They reported that it could have been a malfunction of the satellite. Most of us in national security agencies at the time saw the report as a cover-up.

President Reagan appointed me to be Deputy Assistant Secretary of State for Intelligence in 1985 and in that capacity I became one of the few in government entitled to see all that we knew about the South African nuclear program. My boss at the time, Ambassador Morton Abramowitz, sent me to South Africa for an extended "look around" and I became convinced that the Apartheid regime would soon perish, raising the question in my mind of what would happen with the nuclear program in the chaos of a transition.

In 1986, the U.S. Congress passed the Comprehensive Anti-Apartheid Act, making clear our opposition to the South African regime. One provision in the law required the State Department to report on what nations supplied South Africa with arms. It instructed the Administration to propose steps to be taken against countries which were in violation of the UN Arms Embargo. No one in the Department wanted personally to write that report because it was widely known that the chief arms supplying nation to South Africa was our ally, Israel. Thus, I was assigned the task.

While it did not discuss any nuclear

program, the draft report documented a substantial conventional arms cooperation program between South Africa and Israel. It was damning. With the permission of my State Department superiors, I went to Israel with the draft, unclassified report. I told my Israeli friends that we were not seeking their confirmation or denial of the facts in the report; we were hoping that they would consider what they might do before the report was finished and published. The Israeli government in 1986 announced that it would not enter into any new contracts to sell defense materials to South Africa. Existing contracts would be completed.

In 1989, with six nuclear weapons completed, South Africa decided to stop production. By 1991, it had signed the Nuclear Non-Proliferation Treaty and told the world that it had destroyed six nuclear weapons. Then the International Atomic Energy Agency was invited in to look around. Some inspectors were reported to have thought there were "anomalies" between, on the one hand, the records of production and destruction that they were given and, on the other hand, the capacity of the facilities they observed. Nonetheless, South Africa was given a clean bill of health by the IAEA.

What remained were the missiles. South Africa had made long-range ballistic missiles to deliver nuclear weapons. The RSA-3 missile was based on the Israeli's Jericho missile system. It could not have carried the large bombs that South Africa said it had built and destroyed, but seemed designed for a more advanced and smaller weapon. By 1990, President Bush (41) had appointed me Assistant Secretary of State for Politico-Military Affairs. In that capacity, I went back to South Africa (a lot like the "young hotshot from the State Department" in chapter 10) to persuade the government to stop the missile program, including any use of it for space exploration or satellite launching. The missiles and their related facilities were then destroyed under American supervision.

In the 1990s, serving as President Clinton's Special Assistant, I was concerned with our abilities to prevent, detect, and respond to nuclear weapons smuggled into our cities. With the President's support, we assembled key cabinet members in the Blair House, opposite the White House, and ran them through an exercise of what it would be like for them to handle reports of a nuclear weapon in Washington, followed by its detonation. The Clinton Administration increased funding, training, and capabilities to prevent, detect, and dismantle a nuclear weapon in the hands of terrorists.

In 2009, a week before the Inauguration, we ran a similar exercise for the new Obama security cabinet officials, at President-elect Obama's request. These exercises always had the same effect on the participants: they realized the detonation of a nuclear weapon in New York or Washington would be the worst catastrophe in American history, one in which our disaster response capabilities would be largely useless. American cities would empty out. The economy would collapse. The Obama Administration has since organized three global summits on the security of nuclear weapons and material. According to the State Department, those summits have resulted in:

- Removal and/or disposition of over 2.8 metric tons of vulnerable HEU and plutonium material.
- Completely removing HEU from 11 countries — Austria, Chile, the Czech Republic, Libya, Mexico, Romania, Serbia, Turkey, Ukraine, Vietnam, and Hungary.
- Verified shutdown or successful conversion to low-enriched uranium

(LEU) fuel use of 24 HEU research reactors and isotope production facilities in 15 countries — Bulgaria, Canada, Chile, China, the Czech Republic, Hungary, India, Indonesia, Japan, Kazakhstan, the Netherlands, Poland, Russia, the United Kingdom, and the United States.

- Completion of physical security upgrades at 32 buildings storing weapons-usable fissile materials.
- Installation of radiation-detection equipment at 250 international border crossings, airports, and seaports to combat illicit trafficking in nuclear materials.

There is some debate among the world's experts on how fast the Earth will experience sea level rise and how high the seas will go, but not on the fact that there will be significant ocean rising. The melting of the ice in Greenland and Antarctica will not only flood coastal cities, it will alter weather patterns, changing the value of vast regions. The rate at which the flooding occurs will, of course, determine how and whether we respond to it, by building dams around some cities, by having controlled mass migration from other, doomed cities. The cost of both saving some cities and losing others and building new ones to replace them will stress economies to the breaking point, however slowly or quickly it occurs. Nothing like it has ever taken place on this scale in human history. Some observers wonder whether human civilization can actually sustain itself through the transition, or whether there will be a new Dark Age in which the global economy and many nation states will collapse, along with scientific progress. Such considerations raise the issue of whether, rather than just debating about the veracity of climate change or measures to mitigate it, perhaps we should also start doing the modeling and planning for what happens if sea level rise occurs faster than we now assume it will. The UN's Intergovernmental Panel on Climate Change (IPCC) recently admitted that its previous Worst Case Scenario of the rate of climate change was inaccurate; the Worst Case had understated how rapidly glaciers were actually already melting and how quickly climate change was occurring.

ABOUT THE AUTHOR

Richard A. Clarke served for thirty years in the United States Government, including an unprecedented ten continuous years as a White House official, serving three consecutive Presidents. In the White House he was Special Assistant to the President for Global Affairs, Special Advisor to the President for Cyberspace, and National Coordinator for Security and Counter-terrorism.

Prior to his White House years, he served as a diplomat, including as Assistant Secretary of State and held other positions in the State Department and the Pentagon.

Since leaving government in 2003, Mr. Clarke has served as an on-air consultant for ABC News for ten years, taught at Harvard's Kennedy School of Government for five years, managed a consulting firm, chaired the Board of Governors of the Middle East Institute, and written six books, both fiction and non-fiction, including the national number one bestseller *Against All Enemies* and *Cyber War: The Next Threat to National Security and What to Do About It.*

Jonathan Davis has narrated numerous audiobooks, receiving widespread critical acclaim for his performances in a variety of genres including an Audie Award nomination in the Thriller/Suspense category for his narration of Michael Gruber's *Night of the Jaguar.* His work includes *The Stranger, The Brief and Wondrous Life of Oscar Wao, Battlestar Galactica, Halo: Ghosts of Onyx,* and *Atherton.* His performance in *Naked Statistics* by Charles Wheelan won an Audie nomination in 2014. He has also narrated over thirty *Star Wars* titles, including *Attack of the Clones, Revenge of the Sith* and *Dark Lord.* Davis gave voice to Vladimir Lem, one of the central figures in the video game "Max Payne 2: The Fall of Max Payne", which won several Editors' Choice Awards.